WINNING
PASSION

WINNING PASSION

LAURANCE L. PRIDDY

SUNSTONE
PRESS

SANTA FE
NEW MEXICO

Library of Congress Cataloging in Publication Data

Priddy, Laurance L., 1941-
    Winning passion / Laurance L. Priddy. -- 1st ed.
        p. cm.
    ISBN 0-86534-200-8
    1. Football--Texas--Coaches--Fiction.   I. Title.
PS3566.R559W56   1994
813' .54--dc20

                                                    93-13982
                                                    CIP

Published by Sunstone Press
            Post Office Box 2321
            Santa Fe, New Mexico 87504-2321 / USA
            (505) 988-4418 / FAX: (505) 988-1025
            orders only (800) 243-5644

Winning
Passion

ONE

Bobby Thompson turned the pickup off the highway onto a sideroad leading to a scenic overlook. He drove around several curves to the top of a hill, parked next to a Texas historical marker telling of some long-ago Indian battle, and turned toward his wife, Paula.

"You can see the town good from here. Let's take a look."

She looked at Bobby with resentful green eyes and shook her head of wavy, red-blonde hair in protest. "It's too hot to get out of the car."

"Come on, it'll just take a minute."

He opened his door, and a blast of August heat overwhelmed the airconditioned cool of the truck interior. He stood and flexed his shoulders to relieve the tightness in his tall, sinewy body.

With a weary look, Paula opened the door on the passenger side and got out. She stretched her arms above her head, accentuating the contours of her full figure.

She curled her lips sarcastically. "Where's this wonderful view?"

"It's over this way."

Together, they walked past the marker to a barbed-wire fence marking the edge of the highway department right-of-way. Before them, the hillside, covered with yucca, prickly pear and mesquite, fell away toward the valley below.

The highway descended down the slope through scrubby under-growth toward a town shimmering in the heat haze. The dark green foliage of large trees marked its outlines. Highways ran into it from four directions out of the surrounding scrubby ranch country. Church steeples and the white dome of a courthouse poked through the trees. On the outskirts, dark pumpjacks and silver storage tanks marked the sites of the oil wells that had given the town its sustenance for so long.

"Kinda pretty, isn't it?" Bobby wanted Paula to like this town.

She screwed her face up in a sour grimace. "Looks like shit to me."

He boiled with quick anger. "What in hell's wrong with you today?"

She turned furiously toward him. "You know damn good and well. I didn't want this move in the first place."

"Did you want to stay in Lamesa?"

She shook her head in bitter amusement. "One of these days, the wind's gonna roll Lamesa up and blow it away like a tumbleweed, and no one'll ever find it again. I'm not sorry to leave, but not to move to another town just like it."

Paula had always said she didn't like the small, windy high-plains town where Bobby had held his first high school coaching job, but the place seemed to have some hold on her.

He remembered the times he had been away at coaches' meetings when no one had answered the phone at home when he called late at night. Had she been with Sam Phillips, the hardware store owner she was always joking with at the country club? Or with Walter O'Dell, the philandering owner of the radio station? Or was he wrong in his suspicions; had there really been no one else?

He looked at her with skeptical eyes. "You oughta like Comanche Springs. It's twice the size of Lamesa."

"That makes it a real metropolis, doesn't it?" She waved her hand toward the distant town. "I don't see any law school down there."

"Don't start that crap again."

"I can't help it."

Tears shone in her eyes and Bobby felt sudden tenderness for her. He understood her volatile temper. Her anger would soon pass, like a summer thunderstorm.

He took her hands in his. "We've been through all this before. Sooner or later, we'll move back to Lubbock, or to Houston or Austin. Maybe even Dallas. To some place with a law school."

She smiled acridly. "Some day when I'm old and grey."

She had grown tired of teaching high school history in Lamesa. They had planned for their next move to be to a large city with a law school, where Paula could fulfill her dream of becoming a lawyer, like her father in Dallas.

Bobby tried to placate her. "I really appreciate the sacrifice you're making."

"It's not of my choosing. Why should your life take precedence over mine?"

"It doesn't."

"Why are we here then?"

"I couldn't pass up this chance."

"And my career can wait?"

"Just for a few years"

"Whatever you say, honey." She put her hand to her forehead and wiped the sweat away. "Let's get out of this heat and go down and look over this miserable little burg."

They walked back to the pickup and drove down the hill toward the town.

Comanche Springs lay more than 150 miles east of Lamesa, in the rolling plains and flat-topped hills between the eastern edge of the high plains of the caprock and Fort Worth. Its school board had been forced by the sudden resignation of their old coach to hire a new one.

At thirty, Bobby was young to be head coach in a West Texas town with a rabid interest in high school football. He knew the strong recommendation of Burly Phillips, the head coach at Lamesa, had gotten him the job. Coach Phillips had said he hated to lose Bobby, but that Bobby deserved the opportunity at Comanche Springs.

Bobby drove past the forlorn, nearly abandoned yards of the oilfield drilling and service companies on the edge of town. Like other West Texas towns, Comanche Springs had fallen on hard times. For fifty years, it had been affluent, its economy fueled by the oil industry. Now, with oil prices depressed by the world oil glut and all the easily recoverable oil already pumped, exploration and recovery of new oil was too expensive to be profitable. Many businesses had failed; many people had left town.

Bobby looked toward Paula, studying her face for her feelings. She was looking straight ahead through the front windshield with a bored frown.

"What do you think?" he asked.

"Not much to look at."

"It looks better when you get in toward the center."

They drove past a small shopping strip with a supermarket and a drug store, past a line of fast-food places, into a residential area where the branches of large trees met overhead and well-kept older houses lined the road.

Paula looked out the window, an approving look on her face for the first time. "This looks pretty nice."

The passing of her anger relieved Bobby. "It's a lot better than Lamesa."

"At least it's bigger." She leaned back in the seat, stretching her full lips in a yawn.

The road led into the central business district, past rows of old, single- and double-story stores, to the courthouse square, where Bobby made a right turn to go around the white-domed courthouse.

"I hope I can remember how to get to the house."

"I still can't believe you rented a house I haven't even seen."

"I can get out of the deal if you don't like the place."

When the job offer had come, Paula had been vacationing in Europe with her father and mother. Bobby had stayed behind. He had not wanted to impose on Paula's parents. He had reached her by telephone to get her grudging approval for the move, then had gone house-hunting without her.

He made several turns and drove down a two-lane highway that ran straight out to the north part of the town, where he turned onto a street of small, brick-veneer houses standing unsheltered from the sun in a former cow pasture. He pulled up to one of them and stopped at the curb.

"This is it," he said, cutting the engine and opening the door. As they walked together up the sidewalk, he fished around in his pocket for the house key.

Paula looked dubiously around the neighborhood.

"Wasn't there any place available with some shade?"

"There were a couple of older places with some trees, but they didn't have central air."

He unlocked the front door and held it open for her. She walked into the baking heat of the unairconditioned living room and looked around. A few children's crayon marks marred the off-white walls and stains stood out on the ragged shag carpet. They walked together through the house. In the kitchen, Paula wrinkled her nose with disgust as she kicked a dead roach into a corner.

"Can you live with it?" Bobby asked.

"How long did you lease it for?"

"Six months."

"I can stand it for that long. Maybe by the time the lease runs out, we can find a better place."

"That's what I want to do."

She walked back into the living room, where she turned the airconditioning on and set the thermostat.

"How long will it be before the moving van gets here?" she asked.

"Sometime this afternoon."

"Let's get to cleaning, then." She started toward the front door.

They went back to the truck and brought in the vacuum cleaner, the mop and bucket, and the other cleaning things they had brought with them.

After they had worked for several hours, the van arrived, with Paula's dented old Chevrolet, driven by one of the movers, behind it. The moving men parked the car in the driveway and brought in the meager furnishings Bobby and Paula had accumulated in Lamesa.

By the time they had finished arranging the furniture and unpacking most of their things, the hot, late-summer dusk of West Texas had fallen, and the laboring central air had finally reduced the temperature to a tolerable level. They sat on the newly-placed sofa, fatigued by the day's work.

"You hungry?" Bobby asked.

Paula nodded.

"Let's go get some chicken," he said.

"I'm tired of that stuff."

"Do you want to cook something?"

She pushed herself up from the sofa. "Let's go."

They ordered two dinners at a Kentucky Fried Chicken on the highway, and sat under harsh bright lights at a pastel-painted table, eating fried chicken and reconstituted mashed potatoes.

As they walked together back to the truck, Bobby put his arm around Paula's waist, resting his hand on the firm curve of her hip. She relaxed her body against his. The stifling heat of the day had abated, and the night breeze pleasantly teased the little hairs on Bobby's arms. Overhead, a bright full moon shone from a clear sky.

"Is the house really okay?" Bobby asked.

She turned to him, smiling indulgently. "The air seems to work. It'll be fine."

"I want to show you the high school."

Bobby drove back out the highway they had come in on earlier, almost to the edge of town, where he turned and drove on an intersecting street to the far west side. Between the last row of houses and the beginnings of the brushy ranch land stood a two-story, yellow-brick school building bathed in floodlights, with the bulk of a gymnasium rising from one end.

"Nice looking school," Paula said.

"It's only about ten years old. The stadium's on the other side."

They drove around the block to the other side of the school, where darkened twin concrete bleachers rose above the football field.

"It's really a good stadium," Bobby said. "The school district still had some money when they built it, and they did it right. It's got concrete bleachers and one of the best lighting systems I've ever seen for a high school stadium. I checked the grass when I was here last week. They've got a groundskeeper who's been watering every day. It's good and thick and green, even with the dry summer we've had."

"It's good to see you so excited about this job," Paula said wistfully.

Bobby's conscience pricked him. Comanche Springs held little to excite Paula.

"I had to take this chance, Paula. I know I can do good here. In a couple of years, we'll move to a town with a law school."

She shook her head sadly. "That's what you said last time."

"Next time, it'll be for sure."

Later, while she slept next to him, he studied her handsome, full face. She lay on her back with her lips parted, her breasts rising and falling with her placid breathing. Her strawberry-blonde hair billowed over the pillow.

He loved her with painful intensity, and wanted to believe she was true to him, but he sensed something deceitful about her that gave him doubts.

◆

Can I hold her here in Comanche Springs? Bobby asked himself. Or am I gonna lose her whatever happens? I wonder who it was back in Lamesa. That bastard Sam Phillips, or O'Dell, with all his stories about the women he's screwed? Did Paula add her name to his list? Knowing for sure would be better than these suspicions. How can I ever trust her, or feel secure about her?

Bobby lay awake in spite of the fatigue of the move, troubled by his doubts of Paula, then thinking of the path that had brought him to this point in his life.

He came from an oilfield trash family. His father Bill had been a roughneck, following the oil booms all over Texas and Oklahoma in the heyday of the oil industry. They finally settled in Borger, on the flat plains north of Amarillo, where Bill got a job in the big refinery in nearby Phillips.

Bobby grew to be a tall, dark-complexioned boy with a head of curly brown hair. In the rough-and-tumble West Texas oil town, he became a tough kid, quick to answer an insult with a fight. In his first year of high school, he spent a lot of time in the principal's office, getting licks and lectures for first one thing, then another. One day, in the spring of the year, Bill Mattingly, the football coach, took him aside and told him any kid that wanted to fight so much ought to be playing football.

At first, Bobby scoffed at the idea, but it grew on him over the summer, and the next fall, he went out for the team. Soon, playing football became the dominent interest in his life. He still had fights off the field, but his grades improved and he made fewer trips to the office for licks. Coach Mattingly became his hero.

The coach lectured the boys frequently on the religion of football. A boy who could hit hard and fair on the field, Mattingly said, would hit hard and fair in life. A boy could not be a successful football player without a burning desire to play and win. If he had that burning desire, it would carry him beyond his football playing days and prepare him for success in the world beyond boyhood.

Bobby became a convert to the coach's religion, making all-district end twice at Borger and then going on to play for Texas Tech at Lubbock, where he made all-conference his senior year. He decided he would become a coach, leading young men in the path of football like Coach Mattingly.

At Lamesa, he became Burly Phillip's able and well-liked assistant. Now, thanks to Phillip's recommendation, at the age of thirty, he had the job he wanted most in all the world, as head coach at a prominent West Texas high school.

As Bobby lay next to his wife in the still-strange bedroom of his new home, he thought of his mentor, Bill Mattingly, with his zealot's

face, large balding head and compelling blue eyes. Coach Mattingly
had died in a car wreck two years earlier, so now Bobby could not call
him on the telephone and talk about strategies for his new team, as
he had done in his first years at Lamesa.

"I know you'll be with me, coach," Bobby whispered aloud.

He could almost hear Coach Mattingly lecturing him even now:
Forget the past, make the best of the future. Be the best husband you
can to Paula and things will work out okay. Give this new job all
you've got. Reach down inside yourself for that burning desire to
succeed and no one can stop you.

I'll do it, coach, Bobby thought. I'll find that burning desire and
put together a winning team. And somehow, I'll hold onto my marriage, too.

◆

The next morning, Bobby and Paula drove over to the high
school, where they had an appointment with the principal, Leon
Purvis. Bobby had met Purvis several weeks earlier. He was a
Sunday school teacher sort of man, who wore plain frame glasses and
conservative, baggy-seated suits. He had thinning black hair running to grey at the sideburns.

Bobby and Paula walked down the hall of the school to the
administrative offices, their footsteps echoing hollowly through the
empty building. A wall with glass windows separated the administrative offices from the hall. Overhead fluorescent lights illuminated the
office, but no one sat at the desks. Bobby opened the office door and
he and Paula walked in. A chair scraped on the floor in an inner
office, and Purvis came out to greet them.

"Come in, come in," he said, his high-pitched voice cheery and
solicitous.

He motioned them into the inner office, following them into the
room. "Did you have a good trip over?"

"Real good," Bobby said.

"Get moved in okay?"

Bobby nodded. "Got it all done yesterday."

Purvis smiled patronizingly at Paula. "You must be Mrs. Thompson."

Paula put out her hand and Purvis shook just the fingers.

"Nice to meet you," Paula said.

"Sit down, sit down." Purvis motioned them into chairs in front of his desk.

He sat down and looked at them across the neatly aranged papers on the desk top.

"I'm here by myself today," he explained. "Our secretaries don't start working full time until next week, and the week after that's registration."

Bobby leaned forward in his chair. "We're going to start our two-a-day workouts tomorrow. I'm anxious to see what kind of shape the boys are in."

Purvis beamed at Bobby. "Coach Winslow was a tough taskmaster. He worked them pretty hard last year. They know they've got to be in shape to play football. I've seen a bunch of them working out on their own on the practice field the last several weeks."

"It's too bad Coach Winslow won't be here this year," Bobby said. "The game videos from last fall show that the team has a lot of promise, and most of the boys are back."

Purvis turned his head away to look out the window, furtive confusion in his eyes.

"He told me he was going to miss coaching, but his wife's father wanted to make him a partner in his carpet business. He said he just couldn't pass the deal up."

Purvis spoke uncertainly, as though he didn't believe his own words. Bobby wondered if there was some hidden reason for Winslow's sudden departure.

"They were moving to Dallas, weren't they?" Paula asked.

"Yes, she was from there originally. I don't think she ever got used to West Texas."

"I'm from Dallas."

Bobby heard a note of envy in Paula's voice for the coach's wife who had just been privileged to move back to God's country.

"We were wondering if any sort of teaching job had come up for Paula," Bobby said. "We talked about it when I was here two weeks ago, and you said there might be something."

Purvis shook his head. "Nothing full time has opened up, but Mrs. Thompson can certainly work a good bit as a substitute until we find a full time place. You don't have any children, do you?"

Bobby shook his head, thinking how hard they had tried. In the early years of their marriage, they had avoided having children, but they had wanted a baby the past several years. The doctors had no good explanation for their failure. Bobby lay awake at night sometimes, thinking it resulted from his own inadequacy. It seemed impossible the fault could lie in Paula's lush body.

Purvis smiled a sugary smile at Paula. "Without children, there's no reason you can't work full time. I'm sure we can find something pretty soon. We usually lose some teachers in the elementary schools every semester. I'll give you a call when a position opens up."

Bobby and Purvis discussed some details of the preseason workouts, then Purvis took them on a tour of the building, showing them the room where Bobby would teach mathematics to eleventh and twelfth graders, the auditorium, the cafeteria, the gymnasium and the teachers' lounge. Finally, they walked with Purvis to the front of the building.

"I'll look forward to working with both of you this year," he said. "We consider ourselves very lucky to get someone of your caliber on such short notice."

Bobby shook Purvis's hand. "I'm lucky, too, to get such a good chance so early in my career. I'm looking forward to the season."

Purvis held the front door open for them, then pulled it closed and locked it. He smiled earnestly at them through the glass, then turned to walk back to the school office.

"What do you think of him?" Bobby asked, as he and Paula walked toward the car.

"I always mistrust these ultra-cheery types. I can't say I look forward to waiting around the house for him to call."

"I'd like to know the real reason Winslow left like he did."

"What makes you think it's different from what Purvis said?"

"It's just a feeling I have."

◆

The following day, Bobby got up at first light, shaved and showered, and dressed in T-shirt, knee-length football pants, and cleated, low-top football shoes. He found his whistle among the still-unarranged things in the top dresser drawer and fished around in the chaos of the closet until he found his sweat-stained baseball cap. He put a change of clothes into a paper sack.

He bent over the bed and gently shook Paula's shoulder. She

mumbled in her sleep, then opened her eyes.

"I'll see you in a couple of hours," Bobby said. "We'll go get some breakfast."

She nodded and rolled over on her stomach. Bobby put on the baseball cap and walked out the front door, carrying the paper bag with the change of clothes. Outside, he locked the door behind him and walked to the truck. It was 7:30.

The morning sunlight slanted brightly in the window as he drove toward the stadium. He rolled down the front windows, leaving the airconditioning off. The dry, warm air blowing through the window suggested the hot, blue-skied day to come.

At the stadium, he parked under the bleachers in a row of other vehicles. He followed a group of several young men into the fieldhouse built under the bleachers. One of the boys turned toward Bobby as they walked through the door.

"Morning, coach."

Bobby assumed the boy knew him from the picture the local paper had run when the school board had hired him. The boy had a round build and a round face covered with stubble. He looked more like an Irish prize fighter than a high school student.

"Good morning," Bobby said. "You ready to play football?"

"Yessir, coach."

"What's your name?"

"Ned Chambers."

"You're a center, aren't you?"

"Yessir."

"What kind of shape are you in?"

"I'm in good shape, coach."

"We'll see about that."

Ned Chambers turned and followed the rest of the group who had come in with Bobby into the locker area, where more than forty boys in various stages of dress and undress were changing from street clothes to football practice uniforms.

Bobby had already formed a good impression of Chambers from watching the videos from the last year. He centered the ball quickly and smoothly. When he centered to the kicker in fourth down situations, the ball spiraled back directly into the kicker's hands. He got off the line quickly, and blocked with low, ferocious precision.

Bobby doubted if he was in very good shape. He had too much of a spare tire. The summer living had probably been easy. The two weeks of two-a-day workouts would take care of that problem.

Bobby saw Coach Melvin Morris standing at the far side of the dressing room near the entrance to the showers, talking to several boys who had already suited out. He had a short, thick build and looked like a plug of dark brown chewing tocacco.

He had deep wrinkles around his eyes from squinting against the West Texas sun on practice fields. Bobby judged him to be about forty. He wore his wispy strands of thinning hair combed over the top of his sun-darkened head and punctuated his speech with frequent profanity.

Morris had been Coach Winslow's defensive coach. He had applied for the head coaching job, but the school board had hired Bobby instead. Bobby expected him to be resentful at taking orders from a younger man who had gotten a job he had wanted. Bobby put his change of clothes into a spare locker and walked over to the group.

"Morning, Coach Morris."

Morris turned toward him. "Morning, Coach Thompson."

Bobby seemed to hear a barely suppressed note of insolence in Morris's voice. Bobby turned to the group of players.

"You men ready to hit?"

"Yessir, coach," answered a medium-sized boy with curly red hair. He held his helmet in his hands.

"Let's head on out to the field, then." The red-haired boy trotted toward the door with the others following, their cleats clattering on the cement floor.

"What's that one's name?" Bobby asked Morris.

"Bill Foster. He's a guard."

"Oh yeah. He looks good pulling and blocking on trap plays."

Morris nodded. "He's the best man on the team blocking on traps."

"Looks a little small for a lineman."

"Last year, he was around 180. He's got a lot of power for a guy his size."

Coach Art Bennett walked over from across the room. He wore a snow-white T-shirt and white shorts. About twenty-six or twenty-seven, he had sun-bleached blonde hair, and curly little blonde hairs accented the golden brown skin of his legs and arms.

He looked like a lifeguard at a country club swimming pool. The year before, he had coached the offense. Bobby planned to keep Morris coaching the defense and Bennett the offense, but Bobby planned to do more of the coaching himself than Coach Winslow had.

Bennett stuck out his hand with a little superior grin. "You ready to go, coach?"

Bobby shook the offered hand. He didn't like Bennett's patronizing tone.

"Absolutely. I want us to hit the ground running on this season."

Bobby asked if all the players had checked in. Morris said all but two or three had. As they talked, the outside door opened and several boys burst into the room.

"You pissants are late," Morris yelled across the room. "Get your asses in gear and get suited up."

The players hustled into the locker area and started undressing. Bobby looked at his watch. It was almost eight o'clock.

"I want to go ahead and get started. Let's get them on the field."

Morris nodded. "Let's go, men," he bawled at the boys still in the field house, "hit the pavement, and I don't want to see any of you walking."

All the boys still in the dressing room except the three new arrivals crowded together toward the door. Bobby, Coach Bennett and Coach Morris followed them. At the door, Morris turned toward the latecomers.

"You guys will run an extra windsprint for every minute past eight o'clock that you're late getting on the field. See me after practice, and don't forget it."

The coaches walked out the door and trotted after the group of players moving toward the practice field on the other side of the stadium. It had a track around it, but no bleachers or sideline benches. A barbed-wire fence ran parallel to the field about thirty yards from its edge on the side away from the stadium. Beyond the fence, Hereford cattle grazed among the mesquite and cactus.

Bobby walked onto the surface of the field, kicking at the sod with the toe of his shoe. He thought the Bermuda grass was in good enough shape for a practice field, although a few goathead sticker plants thrust up from the grass, and the bare ground showed through in places.

"Passing drill, men," Coach Bennett yelled.

The boys ran to him, and he arranged them in several groups to run out for passes. On the snap, the men took off from the line, ran down about ten yards, and cut across. The passer took the ball from center and drilled it at the runners. The backs and ends usually caught the ball, while the slower linemen frequently dropped it.

Bobby frowned at the number of times he saw the ball being dropped. Even a lineman ought to be able to catch the ball.

"Follow the ball with your eyes," he yelled to one big boy, probably a tackle, judging from his size. "You're taking your eyes off it. You'll never catch it if you do that."

The boy trotted ponderously after the ball he had dropped, threw it awkwardly back to the center, and returned to the end of the line of players going out for passes.

After the passng drill, Coach Morris lined the men up in four lines in front of four blocking dummies mounted on a frame on slides. Morris parked himself on the slide behind the dummies and barked out commands for the men to come off the line in groups of four and hit the dummies with their shoulders.

The first four groups of four hit the machine evenly and drove it straight back several yards, but one of the men on the end in the fifth group did not fire out with enough force. The slide turned on its axis and had to be squared away before the next group could hit.

"What's the matter," Coach Morris shouted at the offending player, "tripping over your third leg? See me after practice. Two extra wind sprints."

After the coaches had run drills with the boys for almost two hours, Bobby blew his whistle.

"Line up for wind sprints, men," he yelled, "linemen with linemen and backs with backs."

The players ran to the end of the practice field where the backs lined up on one goal line, facing toward the other goal. The linemen formed another line behind the backs.

"All right, men, get down," Bobby called, and the men dropped to three-point stances.

Bobby raised his arm, then blew his whistle, dropping his arm at the same time, and the backs sprinted at full speed toward the opposite goal. The linemen moved up to the goal and took their stance. When the slowest of the backs reached midfield, Bobby set the linemen off. After the first fifteen or twenty yards, the faster of the ends were well ahead of the slower tackles and guards.

"Hustle, men!" Bobby called after them.

At the other end of the field, as soon as the linemen had cleared the full hundred yards, Coach Morris set the backs off again back toward Bobby, followed by the linemen.

Bobby had both groups of players run five one-hundred yard dashes. After the last one, many of the players stopped just across the goal, their hands on their knees, gasping for breath with their mouths wide open.

One of the players started puking. Bobby recognized Ned Chambers. Sweat streamed down his red face as he vomited his breakfast onto the playing field.

"I thought you were in shape, Chambers," Bobby gibed sarcastically.

The boy looked up with an angry fire in his eye that Bobby liked. He wiped the sleeve of his jersey across his mouth to clear off the vomit.

"I ain't bitching, coach."

"Can you run another one?"

"Damn straight."

"Okay, men," Bobby called, "one more and this'll be the last. Run hard to the other end, and keep running back to the showers, except those of you who owe Coach Morris extra windsprints see him at the far end."

Bobby set the boys off. When the linemen reached the fifty-yard mark, Bobby noted with satisfaction that Ned Chambers was running well ahead of most of the linemen.

Suddenly, he stumbled and fell to the ground where he lay motionless. Bobby sprinted to his side, arriving along with the other coaches and several players. Chambers lay on his side, eyes closed, his breath coming in heavy gasps. The sweat on Bobby's skin felt cold in spite of the intense heat. Something might be terribly wrong with Chambers. He turned the boy on his back.

"Manager!" Bobby yelled, and the little, dark-faced team manager came running from the sideline, carrying a carton of water bottles.

Bobby raised Chamber's head.

"Drink some water, son."

Chambers opened his eyes and shook his head, then drank some of the water.

"What happened, coach?"

"You passed out. Are you okay?"

Chambers sat up, shook his head several more times, then got to his feet.

"I'm okay, coach. Should I finish the sprint?"

"Go on to the showers."

Slowly, Chambers trotted toward the dressing room. Bobby stood and spat to clear his mouth of dry, cottony spittle, then turned and followed Chambers to the showers, while Coach Morris organized the hapless players who had incurred his displeasure for more windsprints at the far end of the field.

In the dressing room, Bobby showered and changed to his fresh clothes, putting his practice outfit into the locker. He looked around the dressing room at the boys changing back into their street clothes.

The little sad-eyed, unsmiling team manager was gathering up dirty towels from the benches. Bobby walked over to him.

"What's your name, son?"

The boy looked at Bobby with the suspicious, wise dignity of a donkey.

"Tom O'Leery, coach, but they call me Cheery O'Leery."

"Where'd you pick up a name like that?"

O'Leery shrugged, his mouth a thin, noncommittal line. His look told Bobby the ironic origin of his nickname.

"You have the keys to the place?"

O'Leery nodded.

"Stick around until all the boys have gone, then lock up."

"Right, coach."

"I want you all on the field at 3:30," Bobby yelled to the players in the room. "Anyone late will see Coach Morris again for extra windsprints."

A few of the players vented good-natured groans. Bobby told Coach Morris and Coach Bennett to be back at 3:00 to talk about the afternoon practice, then left the fieldhouse. As he walked to his truck, cicadas hummed their heat song in the trees around the parking lot. The announcer on the truck radio said the temperature already stood at ninety-two degrees. Bobby knew it would be well over one hundred during the afternoon practice.

At home, he parked in the unshaded drive and went into the house. Paula sat at the formica-covered table in the dining nook. She wore an old housecoat. Disheveled strands of hair fell across her face. She was drinking a cup of coffee.

"You just get up?" Bobby walked behind her and put his hands on her shoulders. He loved the feel of her firm body under his fingers.

She nodded. "How did it go?"

"Pretty good. One of the boys passed out during windsprints, but he's okay. Most of them need a lot of conditioning, but that's normal."

Paula dressed, and they ate breakfast together at a restaurant on the highway. Back at the house, Bobby lay on the bed, enjoying the cool of the airconditioning after the heat of the morning practice. He slept for an hour and a half, then got up and studied his play books. At 2:30, he drove back to the fieldhouse and changed to his practice clothes.

While the players suited up, Bobby had a conference with Coach Morris and Coach Bennett in the coaches' office. He told them they would concentrate on conditioning for the next two days while he sized up the players. Then, they would start running plays and deciding who would play on the first and second strings.

"Here are some new plays I want to use this fall," Bobby said, handing Bennett and Morris copies of plays he had devised and used at Lamesa. "I'd like your ideas on how they'd work."

Art Bennett put on a disapproving frown as he looked over Bobby's diagrams.

"Coach Winslow pretty well left the offense to me, Coach Thompson," he said, giving Bobby's name and title an almost contemptuous emphasis.

Bobby felt blood rush to his face.

"I've got to run the team my way instead of Coach Winslow's, and I'm gonna call the shots myself. But I do want your input, and I'd appreciate it if you'd give me your ideas on how these plays will work."

Angry red showed through the bronze of Bennett's face. "You're the coach. I'll look 'em over tonight."

A few minutes later, the coaches followed the players onto the field, where the blazing sun beat down with stifling intensity. Halfway through the practice, Bobby had the players take a break, and Cheery O'Leery passed around the water bottles.

During the second half of the session, the coaches ran more blocking drills, then tackling drills, and then had the players run short dashes. Coach Bennett took the backs and Coach Morris took the linemen.

They would set off a group, let them run a few seconds, then yell "down!', and the players would go down into starting stance. Then the coaches would set them off again. Through this drill, the boys would improve their quickness and short-distance speed, and develop stamina.

After the cycle had been repeated many times, Bobby saw the lethargy of fatigue setting in. He looked at his watch. It was almost 5:30.

"Circle 'round, men," he yelled, holding up his hand.

The players broke from their drills and trotted slowly toward Bobby.

"Hustle, men! You're running like you're dead."

He had them all group around him and rest with one knee on the ground. Many of the boys breathed heavily. Sweat gleamed on their dust-caked skin. Bobby looked at the earnest upturned faces around him with a feeling of pride. These boys would be his first team as a head coach, and he meant for them to be excellent.

"We've worked hard today, men. I understand some of you have been working out on your own to get ready for this. I think you all know you should have been." Bobby looked at Ned Chambers's grimy upturned face. "Isn't that right, Chambers?"

Chambers smiled ruefully. "That's right, coach."

"To tell the truth, most of you are in pretty pitiful shape, but I guarantee you that will change. Now we're gonna run some more windsprints, and I don't want to see anyone loafing. Hustle off the field after the windsprints, hustle on into the dressing room, go home and get a good night's rest, then be on the field at 8:00 sharp. I don't want to see any one late like they were this morning. Coach Morris, let's see how they run."

"Hustle up, pissants," Morris yelled.

The boys had caught their wind while Bobby talked. With calls of mutual support, they trotted toward the goal line and the torture of the windsprints. Bobby stood at midfield and watched them run, looking for signs of shirking.

When the last player had finished the windsprints, he followed the team into the dressing room. He had a tired, happy, excited feeling. He felt satisfied with the first day of pratice. He had a growing conviction that this team had more potential than any of the teams he had helped coach at Lamesa.

TWO

That night, Bobby sat at his desk in the bedroom sizing up the players, using Coach Winslow's notes from the last season and his own impressions from the practice that day. The first game of the season lay less than three weeks ahead. In that time, he would have to decide who would start and who would sit on the bench.

In each case where one of last year's starters had graduated, the second-string player had returned. The team should be much better than last year's, because of the depth in each position and the extra strength and experience that came of the boys being a year older.

Winslow's notes said many laudatory things about the scrappy, bulldog-like Ned Chambers. He had proven he was not in good condition by passing out during the windsprints, but Bobby felt sure the plucky center would lose the weight he needed to lose and get in shape in time to win a starting slot.

Winslow had also made approving comments about the little, red-haired guard, Bill Foster. Even though he was really too small to be a lineman, Bobby thought that Foster would be the starting right guard, because of his speed and skill in executing blocks on trap and pullout plays.

On the line, the guards, the tackles and the center needed to be big, strong and quick for five or ten yards. The center also had to snap the ball between his legs to one of the backs. The ends needed to be faster than the other linemen, so they could block downfield and catch passes.

The team had some huge, strong boys, but some of them seemed far too slow, and Bobby still knew little of their mettle. He would have a much better idea who to start after another week of blocking and tackling drills, and after the players learned their plays and started scrimmaging.

The backs carried the ball and passed. They and the ends made most of the touchdowns and got most of the glory. Bobby had already

decided that a boy named Rutherford McAlpin would be the starting
fullback. He had been all-district last year as a junior, and seemed to
be in good condition.

The largest of the backs at 210 pounds, he had finished first in
the windsprints almost every time that day. He had the build of a
prize animal, sleek and well-toned, with muscles waving under his
skin. He had pale-blue eyes, incongruous with his dark complexion
and curly black hair.

Coach Winslow had made a number of critical comments about
McAlpin. "Attitude stinks," Winslow had noted at one point. "Thinks
the rules are for someone else," he had written in another place. "May
have to suspend him," ran Winslow's final comment on McAlpin,
written late in the last season.

Bobby understood Winslow's dislike for McAlpin. Bobby didn't
like the way Rutherford looked around at the other players and the
coaches as though they were beings of inferior stripe. Bobby would be
careful that McAlpin showed proper respect and got no special treat-
ment, but he would be the starter if he played up to his potential.

Bobby finished reviewing Winslow's notes. The enigmatic final
entry had been written just six weeks earlier. "Can't take this
bullshit--I'm giving it back to the bastards." What bullshit did he
mean? Was he talking about the day-to-day frustration of being a
coach, or something else?

◆

Late in the afternoon practice the next day, Bobby stood next to
Coach Bennett with his hands on his hips, his eyes shaded from the
sun by his baseball cap, watching the contenders for the quarterback
position throwing passes. The quarterback did most of the ball handling and called the plays. A good quarterback had to be quick, smart
and something of a magician in the way he handled the ball. He also
had to command the respect of the other players, since he was the
leader of the offensive team.

The starting quarterback from the last year had graduated. He
had been good on running plays, but weak on passes. Bobby had
decided while watching the game videos that the team needed a
stronger quarterback. Rusty Stedman, the second-string quarterback from last year, did not look good in the videos. Coach Winslow's
notes expressed strong reservations about his ability.

He looked clean-cut and attractive with his wide shoulders and narrow hips, but he tended to give away the direction of the play in the way he positioned himself behind the center, and he frequently drilled passes into the ground yards from the intended receiver. Bobby watched as Rusty threw practice passes, looking for signs of improvement.

Rusty alternated in throwing passes with several other players who had come out for quarterback. Bobby watched closely as a young black man named Terrance Brown took his position behind the center. A sophomore, Terrance had just moved to town a few months earlier. He had told Bobby that morning that he wanted to go out for quarterback.

He had a tall, straight build and a lean, firm-lipped face. He wore his hair in a Frankenstein-like style, flat on top, shaved close on the sides. He father had come to Comanche Springs to be the preacher of the True Word Baptist Church. Terrance and his family had lived in Fort Worth the year before, where, as a freshman, he had played second-string at one of the big inner-city high schools.

Bobby watched Terrance take the ball from the center. In one fluid motion, he spun and faded back to pass. He threw the ball straight and true, and it spiraled with no wobble to the target, a big, clumsy tackle who dropped the perfectly thrown ball.

Bobby nodded approvingly. "That black boy's got good moves."

Coach Bennett set his movie actor's mouth in a tight line of supercilious contempt. "His passes look good, but I bet he can't run plays."

"Just 'cause he's black doesn't mean he can't run plays."

"I've never seen a black player yet that could. Lots of them are great at other things, but I've never seen one yet that could move a team down the field."

Quick with anger at Bennett's prejudice, Bobby started to make a heated reply, but rapid movement across the field caught his eye. Over where Coach Morris had been running tackling drills, two players had squared off against each other. Behind the flying fists, Bobby recognized Ned Chambers and Rutherford McAlpin. Morris circled the two, looking for a chance to get between them. Bobby and Coach Bennett ran to the scene just as Morris finally separated the boys.

"Extra windsprints for both of you," Bobby told them. "If you can't control your tempers better than that, you'll be getting us penalized all during the season."

Chambers looked toward Bobby, outrage on his face. "I couldn't help it, coach. He kneed me in the groin."

"Liar!" McAlpin snarled, his conceited eyes narrowed in contempt.

Chambers lunged toward McAlpin, lashing out with clenched fists, but Coach Morris held him back.

"Take two laps, Chambers," Bobby commanded. "Coach Morris, when he finishes, McAlpin can run his two."

Morris nodded. Chambers trotted toward the edge of the field to start his two runs around the track. The extra exercise would cool the boys' tempers and help prevent further trouble.

◆

Bobby got home from practice around 6:30. The scorching sun still beat down with unabated intensity. Dusk would not come for more than two hours. In the welcome cold of the airconditioned house, he smelled the good smell of meat cooking, and walked into the kitchen. Paula bent over the open broiler under the oven, turning a couple of steaks.

Bobby put his arms around her waist from behind. "Boy, that steak smells good."

Pressing himself into her buttocks, he reached under her arms and cupped her breasts in his hands.

"Cut that out!" The timbre of her voice encouraged him.

"I was thinking about it all during the afternoon practice."

"Thinking about what?"

"You know. I could hardly keep my mind on the practice."

"Don't give me that bull. You'd rather practice football than make love any day."

"But it's so distracting to be thinking of sex all the time."

"Well, we'll see if we can't relieve your tension later this evening. In the meanwhile, supper's almost ready."

Bobby went back to their bedroom and changed to a pair of old blue jeans and a T-shirt he wore around the house. When he came back to the kitchen, Paula had the steaks on the table, with hot rolls, mixed salad, and baked potatoes.

"What's the occasion?"

"No occasion. I just thought we both deserved a break from all that fast food while we were getting moved in."

As they ate, Bobby told her about the fight between Chambers and McAlpin, and how the players were shaping up.

"I'm worried about the quarterback slot. Rusty Stedman, the second-string quarterback from last year, doesn't look too good. There's a black kid who just moved to town who looks a lot smoother."

Paula raised her eyebrows. "You think you can get away with a black quarterback in this town?"

"I don't know. There'd be sure to be some resentment, and the other players might not follow him."

"If you start him, you'll just be asking for trouble."

"I know that. Maybe Rusty Stedman will look better to me once we start running plays."

"I hope so."

That night, after the late news on television, Paula got up from the sofa and went back to the bedroom. In a few minutes, Bobby heard the sound of the shower running. He went back to the bedroom and changed to his pajamas, then lay on the bed, waiting.

Paula came out of the bathroom in a cloud of steam, with a bathrobe loosely wrapped around herself. She came to the foot of the bed, took the lapels of the robe in her hands and suddenly stretched them wide apart, revealing her thrusting, wide-nippled breasts, her taut stomach with its appendectomy scar, and her triangular mound of red-brown pubic hair.

"I'm the flasher!" she announced in triumphant tone, letting the robe fall off her shoulders onto the floor behind her.

Bobby sat up and grabbed her around the waist, pulling her onto the bed beside him. He kissed her, running his tongue around the inner recesses of her mouth. She unbuttoned his pajamas and he took them off and cast them onto the floor next to her robe.

He lay on his back and she moved over him, reaching down to put his penis into her. She thrust an engorged nipple forward and he took it in his mouth, running his tongue around its contours. They rolled over as one unit so that Bobby lay on top of her. He thrust himself rythmically into her.

Faster and faster, they moved together in physical union. Finally, Paula moaned and her whole body shuddered as her release

came in a long spasm. Bobby found his own trigger and shot his hot
sperm deep into her. They held each other close for several minutes,
then moved apart and lay on their backs, with the cool air from the
airconditioner playing over their bodies.

"The way we make love, we ought to be able to make a baby,"
Bobby said softly.

Paula pushed her cheek against his bare shoulder. "Quit worrying about it so much. We'll get into Dallas to the doctors in a couple
of months and see if they can figure out the problem."

Soon Paula slept. Her breath came slowly and evenly through
partly-open lips. Bobby raised himself on his elbows and looked
tenderly at her untroubled face.

He remembered her on their first date at Texas Tech. They had
gone to a Double T Association beer bust celebrating the end of spring
training at a lake in a canyon that cut deep into the caprock near the
city. Bobby had been supposed to go with a girl who his teammates
assured him would screw like a snake, but the girl had broken the
date, and Paula Malone had been a last-minute substitute arranged
by one of her sorority sisters.

Bobby got drunk and tried to seduce Paula back in the bushes
away from the campfire, but she kept pushing him away with firm
amusement until he passed out. Someone else took her home, and
Bobby couldn't remember how he got back to the dorm.

He called and apologized the next day. They started dating and
eventually began having sex together. Her father, Walter Malone,
worked in Dallas as the legal director for a big electronics firm. Bobby
remembered the intimidation he had felt when they had driven to
Dallas to tell Paula's father and mother they were engaged.

Walter and Mamie Malone lived in a big Greek-revival house
with Doric columns two stories high in Highland Park, an exclusive
enclave surrounded by north Dallas. The house had manicured, park-
like grounds surrounded by a wrought-iron fence.

"Is this really your house?" Bobby asked Paula as they drove up
the noble driveway.

Walter and Mamie hadn't liked the idea of Paula's engagement
to Bobby. Walter had shaken his head of carefully groomed, red hair
disapprovingly and Mamie, a large, windblown-rose of a woman, had
retired to her bedroom in tears. They had both envisioned an advan-
tageous society wedding for their only child.

Bobby and Paula persisted, and eventually won grudging approval from Paula's parents, but it seemed to Bobby they had never really accepted him. He dreaded the obligatory trips to Dallas several times a year to pay respects to Walter and Mamie. They always made Bobby feel inadequate and unworthy.

In the darkened bedroom of their new home, Bobby leaned over Paula, stroking her sleeping face gently with his fingers. How long could he hold her love? Would he lose it in Comanche Springs, or had he never really had it in the first place?

◆

The season's first meeting of the Warrior Booster Club took place on Thursday evening during the first week of practice. After the season started, there would be a meeting every Monday night, where the boosters could ask questions about the previous Friday's game.

Bobby drove to the McKeever Steak House on the highway leading out of town to the east. He parked in the gravel parking lot at a quarter to seven. The angled rays of the sun burned his neck as he walked into the restaurant, a white building with windows framed by green shutters. It had a big sign out front saying that truckers were welcome.

Bobby stood inside the door for a few seconds, waiting for his eyes to adjust to the inside light. The eating area sprawled over several rooms of formica-topped tables and booths with unpleasant green upholstery.

A waitress approached, smiling. "Can I help you, sir?"

"I'm looking for the booster club meeting."

"It's right back this way." The girl led Bobby through the public dining area to a door opening into a private room.

"Enjoy your dinner, sir." The waitress left Bobby standing at the open door.

Inside the room, two long rows of tables extended out from a head table on a raised platform. Behind the head table, the flags of the Lion's Club and Optimist Club drooped from staffs by the speaker's podium. Men filled most of the seats at the tables. They all looked toward Bobby as he walked into the room. Melvin Morris scraped back his chair from one of the tables and came over to Bobby.

"The video's all set up, Coach Thompson." Morris waved toward a television monitor on a pedestal next to the speaker's table.

"Thanks, Coach Morris. After we eat, I'd appreciate your show-ing the video, and then I'll tell them about this year's plans."

Morris nodded. Bobby thought he caught a little resentful light in Morris's eye, as though he thought Bobby had taken his place in the sun.

"Come on up to the head table," Morris said. "I'll introduce you to the president."

Morris led Bobby up onto the raised platform supporting the speaker's table. The four men sitting at the table got up as Bobby approached. A large man of fifty-five or sixty stepped forward. He had a full head of white hair combed back into a leonine pompadour. He wore lizard-skin cowboy boots, a western-cut sports coat and a belt with a big silver buckle in the shape of the State of Texas.

Morris spoke deferentially. "Mr. Timmons, I'd like you to meet our new head coach, Bobby Thompson."

Bobby put on a smile and stuck out his hand, thinking Timmons looked like the blowhard type.

"Good to meet you, coach." Timmons shook Bobby's hand enthu-siastically. "I'm Joe Timmons. I'd like to introduce you to our vice president, Gerald Stedman, our secretary, Ned Zablonsky, and our treasurer, Willis Fullerton."

Bobby shook hands all around. "Nice to meet y'all."

He took stock of each man in turn. Stedman had straight, rust-colored hair, pale-blue eyes and hornrimmed glasses. He wore a brown business suit of good cut. Zablonsky had a dark, serious face and wore clean khaki work clothes. Fullerton, tall with humorous eyes, wore slacks, loafers, a white shirt with no tie, and a checked sports coat.

"Have a seat, coach." Timmons motioned Bobby into a seat next to the speaker's podium.

While waitresses with the fresh, innocent look of small-town high-school girls started serving the meal, Bobby engaged in small talk with the men seated around him. He learned Timmons owned one of the largest ranches in the county and had an avid interest in the team even though his own children had grown up years before.

Zablonsky and Fullerton both had children in the school system, but none of them played football. Zablonsky owned a couple of gas stations, and Fullerton worked as an engineer for the local office of the Texas Highway Department. Zablonsky, Fullerton and Gerald Stedman all served as members of the Comanche Springs School Board. Bobby had met them when he had interviewed for his job a month earlier.

Stedman had recently been chosen president of one of the two downtown banks and he served as a leader in the town's largest Church of Christ. He asked Bobby how his son, Rusty, looked at quarterback. Bobby lied, saying that Rusty seemed to be coming along fine.

The knowledge that Rusty Stedman's father fell into the prominent citizen category made Bobby uncomfortable. He wondered how he would handle the politics of the situation if he decided to start Terrance Brown instead of Rusty.

As Bobby ate the chickenfried steak and English peas of the booster club dinner, he looked over the men seated at the tables below him. They were like the men he had known in the booster's club in Lamesa: all Anglo, from young to old, some in business suits, others in jeans and cowboy boots, many with skins darkened by the sun.

Bobby judged that, like the fans at Lamesa, they all had the holy fire of football in their hearts. When most of the people in the room were down to the small dishes of peach cobbler that came with the meal, Joe Timmons got up from his chair and moved to the podium.

In a hearty, room-filling voice, he told the assemblage it was good to see so many of them here for this first meeting of the season, and that if they hadn't yet paid their dues, they should see Willis Fullerton after the meeting. Then he launched into a glowing introduction of Bobby.

"I got a sick feeling in my heart when I learned that Coach Winslow was leaving so suddenly just a few weeks before the start of the season. It didn't seem to me we could possibly fill his shoes in the short time we had before the start of the two-a-day workouts. But then I heard about this fine young man at Lamesa, and the wonderful record he had there. I made inquiries of people I know there, and the reports I received told me we had found our man."

Timmons continued in this vein for several minutes, lauding glory on Bobby in a way suggesting that Timmons had personally discovered him. Finally, he concluded.

"It is with great pride, then, along with great expectation, that I introduce to you the new head coach of the Comanche Springs

Warriors, the man who will lead us to the district championship and who knows how much further, Coach Bobby Thompson."

Bobby stood up amid a great swell of applause and approached the podium, gratified in spite of himself by the overblown description of his abilities. He stood at the podium with the most modest look he could muster. When the noise subsided, he addressed the crowd.

"I want to thank Mr. Timmons for that undeserved introduction and to thank y'all for the opportunity to coach here at Comanche Springs. The workouts are going real good so far, and I think we're gonna have a real fine team this year. Coach Morris is gonna show some of the highlights of the last season, and then I'll talk to you about our strengths and weaknesses and kinda give you a blue print of what we plan to do this year."

Someone cut the lights and Coach Morris turned on the monitor and started the video, featuring thirty minutes of highlights from the Warrior's last season, with commentary narrated by a newsman from the local radio station. The video showed the team in its finest moments and glossed over the three lost games that had kept them out of the running for the district championship.

The boosters gave appreciative grunts, whistles and comments with each sack of the opposition quarterback, each touchdown pass, each long run from scrimmage. They hissed and booed as the announcer explained how they had been deprived of victory against arch-rival Breckenridge by the callback of a critical touchdown run because of a clipping penalty. The narrator implied the official had been bought off.

The video concluded with glowing optimism for the coming year's chances. Coach Morris turned the lights back on, and the men blinked as their eyes adjusted to the brightness. They gaped and stretched as the waitresses served coffee. Bobby stood at the podium again.

"Ya'll had a real good team last year and deserved to win the district championship. I think that bad call in the Breckenridge game took a lot of heart out of the team. If you'd won that game, you might have gone all the way. But that was last year, and we got another chance now. Most of the good players are back, and they ought to be twice as good this year."

He outlined his plans for the season, then opened the floor to questions. Several in the audience asked about the schedule, and which of the opposition teams would be toughest.

Bobby answered these easy questions, knowing there would be harder ones to answer once the season started, where there would be miscues for the fans to criticize. When the questions ran out, Bobby turned the meeting back to Joe Timmons, who asked a Baptist preacher to dismiss them with a prayer.

As Bobby walked toward the door with Timmons and Melvin Morris, another man approached with his hand extended. He had wide shoulders, pink cheeks, sun-bleached blonde hair, and a handsome smile.

"You remember me don't you, coach?"

Bobby recognized Mike Proctor, the president of the school board. He took the offered hand.

"Sure do, Mr. Proctor. It's good to see you again."

"I sure enjoyed the meeting, and I'm sure looking forward to the start of the season."

"I don't think you'll be disappointed."

Bobby walked with Proctor and the others through the regular dining area and out into the lighted parking lot. Timmons turned to shake Bobby's hand again.

"It was a good meeting, coach, and I'm sure we're gonna have a real fine team."

"I enjoyed it too, Mr. Timmons. I'll have more to report next time."

Timmons turned and walked to a shiny Chevrolet pickup with wire-spoke wheels. He waved as he drove away. Melvin Morris said he'd be getting on home, and walked toward his car at the far side of the parking lot. Mike Proctor clapped Bobby on the shoulder, with a heartiness that made Bobby uncomfortable.

"I think you went over good, coach," Proctor said, in a patronizing tone.

"I hope so."

"I'm sure of it." Proctor flashed an ingratiating smile with his even white teeth. "I want you and your wife to come out to the house and have dinner with me and meet my wife. Could you come this Saturday?"

Bobby hesitated. He and Paula had no plans, but he had a natural aversion to socializing with people he didn't know well. And he felt he ought to keep some distance from all the school board members and boosters until he understood the political climate of the town.

"I hate to be any trouble."

"It's no trouble, coach. Can you come about seven?"

What harm would come of having dinner with the Proctors? Now that Bobby was a head coach, he would have to do more pressing of the flesh and socializing than before.

"Okay. I'll check with my wife and let you know for sure, but I don't see any reason why we can't come."

Proctor wrote directions to his house and his telephone number on a slip of paper. Bobby said he would call the next day to confirm the engagement. Proctor drove off in a Lincoln Town Car with gold trim and an antenna for a telephone on it.

Fifteen minutes later, when Bobby walked into the living room, Paula looked up from the late news on television. "How'd it go?"

"The meeting went fine. I made a date for us to eat dinner with the president of the school board this Saturday, subject to your approval."

"That'll be great. I'm about to go stir crazy just sitting around the house."

◆

That Saturday, they drove in the bright sunlight of late afternoon on the main highway out the northern end of town. Several miles beyond the city limits, Bobby turned onto a paved ranch road that led past the Comanche Springs Country Club. It had greens of well-tended emerald separated by long stretches of browning fairway. The modern, native-stone clubhouse with its red-tiled roof perched on the side of a small, flat-topped hill covered with cedar and mesquite.

Beyond the country club, the road wound between more of the flat-topped hills through an area where the large houses of the county's wealthier citizens stood at the ends of long drives. They came to a drive with a sign that said "Proctor Ranch--Registered Angus," and Bobby turned and drove along its smooth pavement to a closed gate with an intercom mounted on a brick wall. Bobby rolled the window down and pressed the button of the intercom. Mike Proctor's voice came from the speaker.

"I'll open the gate. You're about half a mile from the house."

"Thanks," Bobby said, feeling resentful of the affluence that supported a remote-controlled gate to isolate the inhabitants of the place from common humanity like himself.

He contrasted Proctor's lavish holdings with the five-room frame house in Borger where he had grown up. There, the hot panhandle sun scorched the scraggly Bermuda grass a dingy yellow, and long strips of blistered paint peeled from the weatherbeaten eaves.

Proctor's gate swung open and Bobby drove through it, past irrigated green pastures where stolid black Angus cattle grazed. At the far side of one of the pastures stood a tall oil derrick painted bright silver. Beyond the derrick stood the hangars of a small airstrip, with its runway stretching off into a stand of mesquite trees and cactus.

"Pretty impressive spread," Paula said.

"Sure is." Bobby did not like the feeling of hostility that came over him as he drove through the rich man's holdings.

The road started up a little hill and rounded a corner. A few hundred yards before them, half-way up the side of the hill, rose a sprawling house of white brick, with a lawn so green it looked unreal against the straw and brown shades of the surrounding landscape. To one side of the house, the waters of a large swimming pool glistened under a tall diving board. They drove up the wide concrete drive and parked before the closed doors of a triple garage.

As Bobby and Paula got out of the truck, Proctor walked toward them on a winding brick walk leading up to the massive double front doors of the house. He wore jogging shoes, lightweight tan slacks, and a Mexican-style shirt worn outside the pants. His tanned cheeks had highlights of healthy pink and his wide smile looked like it came from a denture ad.

"Good to see you, folks." He put out his hand several feet before he came up to them.

Bobby shook the hand, forcing a smile he knew did not match Proctor's. "Nice place you got here."

"We like it." Proctor turned toward Paula with his effervescent smile. "You must be Paula." He put out his hand and she shook it.

"You really do have a beautiful place here."

"It's nothing compared to some of the places in Highland Park."

"It would be way above average, even there."

"Sure beats my part of Borger," Bobby said laconically.

"Well, it's home," Proctor said in a deprecating tone. "Come on in and meet the wife."

Bobby and Paula followed Proctor up the walk to the double doors, and into a living room with oak beams across a plaster ceiling, wide, panoramic windows shaded from direct sunlight by overhanging eaves, southwestern ranch-style furniture, and Indian blankets and artwork on the walls. A thin blonde woman rose from a chair with a frame of limed oak and rich leather upholstery.

Proctor took her hand and led her forward. "Liz, I'd like you to meet Coach Thompson and Paula."

Mrs. Proctor smiled thinly. "I'm glad to meet you."

She had her short blonde hair arranged in the current style. Her silken slacks and blouse fitted her perfectly. The skin on her thin arms and cheeks seemed almost translucent. Bobby thought she looked like a high-society fashion model.

"Let's have a drink," Proctor said robustly, leading them to a bar against the far wall of the room. "What'll it be?"

"Beer for me," Bobby said.

"How about a screwdriver?" Paula asked.

"You bet," Proctor answered, flashing her an approving smile.

He opened a small refrigerator built into the bar, pulled out a beer and handed it to Bobby. Bobby pulled the tab, and a little mist of beer spewed into the air. Bobby took a long pull from the can. Proctor got out a jug of orange juice and fixed Paula's screwdriver, poured his wife a glass of Chablis, and fixed himself a Scotch and water.

"Manuel's cooking the steaks now," Proctor said, "let's sit out by the pool till they're ready."

They walked out a side door onto a redwood deck next to the pool, where they sat in deck chairs around a metal table under a striped canvas parasol. The red ball of the sun sat on the edge of the western horizon, surrounded by pastel-hued clouds.

Paula sat looking at the scene. "What a beautiful sunset!"

Proctor smiled at her. "Yes, it is. This old West Texas country is harsh and dry and hard to live in, but it is pretty when the sun's going down."

"Have you lived here all your life?" Bobby asked.

"All except for the five years I went to SMU and a hitch in the army. SMU's where I met Liz." Proctor nodded toward his wife, who raised the corners of her mouth in a chilly little smile.

"My daddy was a rancher with a sixth-grade education. They hit oil on his land during the big oil boom of the thirties, so I got to go to college and marry a socialite from Dallas instead of castrating livestock and grubbing mesquite stumps."

"Don't be so crude, Mike." Liz spoke with a cool, measured tone.

"Oh, don't be so stuffy. You can talk natural around a guy from Borger."

She shot him a sharp glance with narrowed eyes. He continued talking.

"Did you see that big, silver-painted oil derrick on the road in?"

Bobby nodded.

"That's one of the derricks from the original field on daddy's ranch south of here. Most of the others are still standing, rusting away a little more every year. I brought that one up here and had it painted to remind me of those days."

"Is there any more new drilling going on around here now?"

Proctor shook his head. "Naw, they tried some secondary and tertiary production a few years ago, but everything shut down when the OPEC price dropped."

"Did that cause you any problems?"

"Not really. Had to draw in my belt a little here and there, that's all. Daddy was plenty smart. He put most of what he made on oil into stocks and bonds. My holdings have lost some value with the decline in stock prices, but not enough to really hurt me. Most of the guys who were trying to make money out of the recent production went broke, but I'm pretty safe unless the whole national economy folds."

Paula sipped her drink, then turned toward Liz. "Do you have any children?"

Liz shook her head.

"Do you want them?"

"I used to think I did."

"We don't have any, either."

Bobby shot a warning look at Paula. He didn't feel like getting into an intimate discussion of their fertility problems. Paula saw the discomfort on his face, and said no more. A middle-aged Mexican man wearing a white apron over his jeans came out the door from the house.

"Everything's ready, Mr. Proctor."

"Okay, Manuel." Proctor rose from his chair. "Let's eat, folks."

They all followed him back into the house, through the living area to a formal dining area where a huge, carved-oak table held a large platter of steaming steaks, with large bowls of green salad at the individual place settings. Other serving dishes held baked potatoes and baked beans. Several bottles of wine in ice-filled coolers stood on the table.

"This looks great," Paula said.

"Manuel does the best steaks of anyone I know. He grills them over mesquite coals." Proctor started pouring glasses of wine.

After the meal, they returned to the living area, where Proctor fixed more drinks. They talked of the Texas economy, of going to school at Texas Tech and SMU, and about the indulgences of Dallas and Houston. Finally, Proctor turned the conversation to the upcoming Warrior season.

"How do you think the team's gonna do this year, coach?"

Bobby had drunk three or four beers and several glasses of wine, and he had found himself liking Proctor more with each drink. He seemed natural and down-to-earth for a man of his means. The alcohol had dulled Bobby's reserve and whetted his enthusiasm.

"They've got the potential to be the best team I've ever coached. They could win district and go a long way toward state."

Proctor leaned forward with an intent look. "But will they realize their potential?"

"You never know. I think there's a good chance they will."

Proctor asked which positions looked the strongest, and Bobby mentioned Rutherford McAlpin at fullback, Ned Chambers at center, and Bill Foster at guard. Proctor nodded approvingly.

"Foster's really too light, but he's sure a fighter. McAlpin's just like a football machine, and Chambers mows 'em down like a bowling ball. There's plenty of talent at most of the other positions, too. But what do you think about quarterback?"

A warning light flashed in Bobby's brain. It would not do to be too critical of the banker's son in any quarter until he understood the town's alliances.

"I'll probably start Rusty Stedman. He still needs a lot of work, but he's improving, and I think he can do the job."

Proctor nodded slowly. "That's what I thought you'd say. But you don't sound too enthusiastic about it. Does anyone else look good?"

Bobby stiffened in his chair, resentful of Proctor's prying. "There's one or two others."

Proctor nodded again. "I don't want to tell you how to do your job, coach, but I'm worried about whether the team can win with Rusty at quarterback. Don't feel like you have to play him just because his dad's a leading citizen."

"I'll play whoever's best for the job."

"I know you will, coach." Proctor sat back in his chair and let his face relax into another condescending smile.

Bobby felt an angry tightness in the pit of his stomach. He didn't mean to let anyone second-guess him on his starting lineup.

"I've still got a few days to decide," he said, keeping his voice cordial. "I'll designate the lineup for the first game a week from Monday."

"I'll be looking forward to seeing what you come up with."

Bobby looked at his watch. It was almost eleven.

"We'd better get going, Paula."

They thanked the Proctors for dinner, took their leave, and drove out the winding drive to the main road.

"Proctor seems to me like a pompous ass," Bobby said, as he pulled back onto the mian highway.

"I thought he was kind of charming."

"He went out of his way to make you think so. I liked him okay myself, until he started trying to tell me how to run the team."

"He didn't go quite that far."

"That's what he was getting at, though."

"You can't blame him for being interested."

"Just as long as he doesn't think his money can tell me what to do."

"If you're going to be a head coach, you're going to have to get used to putting up with Monday morning quarterbacks."

Bobby looked over toward her. By the dim light from the car instrument panel, he saw her eyes laughing at him.

"Oh, just go to hell!" he said in mock anger.

She had made him see he was taking himself too seriously. They drove toward home through the darkened streets of the town, clinging to each other like young lovers.

THREE

The next week, Bobby started making his choices for the rest of the starting lineup. He watched the players at the scrimmages, making mental notes of their strengths and weaknesses. After each practice, he and the other coaches went into the office and talked about who had looked good and bad that day.

Bobby told the others to decide who they would recommend for each first- and second-string position. The coaches would discuss the positions after the Friday practice, then announce the lineup the following Monday, on the first day of school, one week before the kickoff for the first game of the season against Jacksboro. Bobby didn't plan for the decision to be a consensus; he would make the ultimate choices, but he knew Morris and Bennett needed to feel their opinions had been considered.

Melvin Morris seemed to have overcome his initial hostility toward Bobby. Foul-mouthed, sunburned and balding, Morris loved the game and the players but lacked the organizational and political ability to be a good head coach.

Bobby liked Morris, but he did not like Art Bennett. Bennett had an unbecoming arrogant streak and too much consciousness of his own male beauty to be likeable, but he had a good concept of offensive football and how to teach it to high school boys.

The team had been scrimmaging for over a week, and the smarter players had learned their plays. Bobby still worried most about the quarterback position. Three players were trying out for the slot: Rusty Stedman, Terrance Brown and a short, funny, gravel-voiced little junior named Rob Wilson.

Stedman acted as though he had the first-string position sewed up. The players responded quickly when he called them to the huddle, but he performed very inconsistently. Frequently, he tele-graphed the type of play by his first moves with the ball, fumbled, or passed wildly. The players also rallied quickly to Rob Wilson, but he didn't have either the size or ballhandling ability to be the starter.

◆

At first, the other players did not want to follow Terrance Brown. When he called the team to huddle, the boys trotted slowly to him, taking their time in putting their hands on their knees, then cutting up and talking while he tried to call the plays.

When he broke the huddle for the line of scrimmage, the other players moved slowly up to the line, as though they didn't want to take his lead. Bobby began to think that Coach Bennett was right; Terrance had good moves but wouldn't be able to move the team down the field.

But over the week the team had been scrimmaging, the other players had begun to respond to Terrance. They seemed inspired by the speed and precision of his execution, by the beauty of his spiraling bullet passes, by his snappy fakes and cuts, and by the way the corded muscles in his arms and legs moved like precision springs. And by his intriguing, high-jiving way of calling plays, like a rap singer chanting a song.

He would drop to one knee within the circle of the huddle, looking earnestly around at the others.

"Now we're gonna run that ol' number twenty-five," he would say, "and I want you ends to run like there was a piece of ass waiting for you at the goal line. Ya'll got it? Let's go." He would clap his hands and the players would break sharply for the line of scrimmage.

As the week went on, Bobby began to think seriously about starting Terrance instead of Rusty. He hesitated to share his thoughts with the other coaches. He decided to wait until Friday, then raise the proposition for full discussion before he made up the starting lineup for Monday.

Bobby had little doubt about his other starters. A number of players had established clear superiority: Ned Chambers at center, Bill Foster at right guard, and Rutherford McAlpin at fullback. The ends would be Eddie Ritterman, tall with a willow-like build and a facility for snagging passes that seemed uncatchable, and Lee Shaugnessey, a sandy-haired boy who made up his lack of height with a quickness that got him behind the defenders.

Left guard would be Freddie Alhamid, son of a displaced Arab who had come to town as an oilfield worker many years before and stayed to run a small grocery store. Freddie had a deep olive complexion, deep chest and curly black hair.

Juan Guerrero had earned one tackle slot. At 270 pounds, he was the largest man on the team. He had sloping shoulders, a round belly and legs like tree trunks. A little dull, he was having trouble learning the plays, but Bobby thought he would do all right, since most of what a tackle does is to manhandle whatever comes his way.

Albert Walker, the only black on the team besides Terrance Brown, would start at the other tackle. He weighed about 250 and had the build of a weightlifter. He also had an inclination to be mean.

One of the other running backs would be Joe King, a quick 175 pounder who ran with fear in his eyes. He had such an aversion to being tackled that he regularly avoided tacklers for extra yardage. The same aversion to contact kept him from being a good blocker.

Curtis McInnes would start at the other running back slot. He had a wave of blonde hair over light blue eyes, and kept his uniform immaculately clean. He preened himself in the mirror after practice so much the other players had nicknamed him Canary, but he had plenty of guts, and could block much better than Joe King.

All in all, Bobby knew these players, with their defensive counterparts and backups on the second string, would make the finest team he had ever coached.

◆

Toward the end of the week, Joe Timmons, Mike Proctor and several of the other boosters started coming to the afternoon practices and watching the scrimmages. Timmons and Proctor often walked with the coaches back to the dressing room after the practice.

"How do you think they're shaping up, coach?" Timmons asked, as they walked together in the late afternoon heat after the Thursday afternoon practice. He wore old jeans and a western shirt with snaps and a vivid floral pattern. His substantial gut overhung his silver belt buckle.

"They're really looking good. Some of them still need to get their plays down better and improve on execution, but we've got another week to work on those things."

"Who's gonna be the quarterback?"

The question made Bobby uncomfortable. "I'm gonna talk about that with the other coaches tomorrow. The list'll be up Monday."

Art Bennett shot a quick, questioning glance at Bobby. Bobby knew Bennett had assumed Rusty Stedman would start.

"Everybody figures it'll be Rusty," Timmons said. "That black kid looks pretty good, but I bet he'd get flustered under pressure."

"I just don't want to say anything in advance about any of the positions," Bobby said.

Mike Proctor looked toward Bobby with a friendly smile. He hung around the dressing room until the players and the other coaches had left, then walked with Bobby out to the parking lot.

"You know Terrance Brown's ten times the quarterback Stedman is, don't you, coach?" Proctor asked. He wore an open-throated, knit sports shirt and trim-fitting slacks.

"I wouldn't say that." Bobby knew his voice betrayed his resentment at the question.

Proctor nodded, smiling slightly. "But you know it, anyway."

Why does he want me to start a black over a popular white boy? Bobby asked himself.

"I think I'd get a lot of flack if I started Terrance," he said.

"You mean because of prejudice?"

Bobby nodded.

"Times change, coach. This town has to move beyond old attitudes, just like everywhere else. Like I said before, don't be afraid to do what's right. You may take some flack, but some of us will back you up."

"Don't worry, Mr. Proctor," Bobby said cooly, "I'm gonna do what's right."

"I know you will, coach." With a final knowing nod and pearly smile, Proctor walked toward his car.

◆

The next day, at the coaches' meeting after the practice, Bobby came quickly to the point.

"I've got a good feeling about every position except quarterback. I'm not at all sure Rusty Stedman can do the job there, but I'm not sure about Terrance Brown, either. Rob Wilson's out of the question.

He's just too little."

Art Bennett leaned forward on his folding metal chair with his eyes narrowed defensively. "There's no real choice. Stedman may not be as smooth as he ought to be, but at least the other kids respect him. You can't say that about Brown."

"I thought that way too, a week or two ago, but I think things have changed. I think he's gained the respect he needs to run the team."

Bennett gave an angry, contemptuous jerk to his head. "I don't think what you're seeing is respect. They're going along with him for the novelty of it. All that jiving he does tickles them. But he won't be able to keep them together in a crunch. Stedman's the natural leader of the team."

Bobby turned to Melvin Morris. "What do you think, Coach Morris?"

Morris gave a slight shrug of his shoulders. "I like that little fart Wilson the best of the three. But you're right that he's too little. I'll say one thing for Terrance Brown, he's a lot smoother than Rusty is on passing and ballhandling, but I think Art's right that he couldn't run the team."

Bennett looked at Bobby with angry eyes. "There's another problem with Brown. You'll have a citizen's revolt in this town if you start a nigger at quarterback over Rusty Stedman."

The small-minded contempt in Bennett's voice angered Bobby. He felt his own cheeks flaming. "Don't you think we ought to start the best man, regardless of what people think?"

"No, I don't. You can't put together a winning team in a town like Comanche Springs if you ignore the politics of the situation. Besides, Rusty Stedman *is* the best man."

Bobby started to argue, then thought better of it. "I want to think about this over the weekend. We'll have another short meeting before practice Monday before I make up the list."

They discussed the other positions, eventually deciding on the starters Bobby had already picked out. As he drove home, he felt pleased that Bennett and Morris had agreed with his judgment on all the positions except quarterback, but the lack of consensus there gnawed at him.

"Have you decided about quarterback?" Paula asked at supper.

He shook his head. "The other coaches think I ought to start

Rusty Stedman, but Proctor thinks I ought to start Terrance Brown."

"What do you think?"

"I'm having a hard time with it, but I do think Brown's got the best physical ability."

"It's a tough decision. Maybe Proctor's right, especially since you lean that way yourself."

Bobby resented Paula's taking Proctor's side. "You said before I couldn't get away with starting a black quarterback in this town."

"Proctor knows the place. If he thinks you can get away with it, you probably can."

He shot her an angry look. "I'm the coach, not Proctor. Are you gonna start trying to run the team, too?"

"I'm sorry I said anything." She got up and started to clear the table.

For the rest of the evening, she fixed her face in a stoic mask and spoke tersely. Her anger bore heavily on Bobby, but he kept his own mouth grimly set and made no effort to break the tension.

After Paula slept, he lay awake worrying until the early hours of morning. He lay flat on his back with his hands behind his head. His eyes had grown used to the dark, and he could see all the objects in the room by the lights outside. The ordinary furnishings looked sinister and menacing in the dim light. He knew he should sleep, but when he closed his eyes, conflicting thoughts spun in his head.

He felt in his gut that Mike Proctor was right; that Terrance Brown was ten times the quarterback Rusty Stedman would ever be. On the other hand, Brown's superior ability would count for little if the other players would not follow him, or if he could not run plays under pressure, as Art Bennett feared.

A small voice in his heart told him that Bennett was wrong; that Brown would inspire enough respect to lead, but then he had to consider the politics of the situation. Could the team function in the atmosphere of displeasure that was sure to result if he started a black player over the banker's son?

The strong, benevolent face of Coach Bill Mattingly came into his mind. "What would you do, coach?" Bobby whispered, but the vision gave no guidance. Finally, fatigue overcame him, and he slept with the burning issue still undecided. When he woke up, Paula had risen before him. He stumbled into the kitchen, where she sat drinking a cup of coffee.

"I'm sorry I jumped on you last night," he said tentatively.

She looked out the window and didn't answer.

"Don't be mad," he said. "I'm having a real hard time."

She turned toward him with angry green eyes. "Is that a reason to be such a bastard?"

"No. I'm sorry."

"I'm having a hard time, too. I just sit around the house here all day twiddling my thumbs, and you come in with your face like a thundercloud and I can't even express an opinion without getting cut to pieces."

"I said I'm sorry."

"That doesn't take away what you said."

Frustration rose in his throat. "What do you want me to do, grovel on the floor?"

She smiled a wicked little smile. "That might be entertaining."

"Just go to hell!"

"Now who's mad?"

"I am. Are you satisfied?"

"I'll let you know later. Did you decide who you're going to start?"

The stress between them had evaporated.

"I'm still worrying over it."

"I'm not going to say anything else about it. Just let know what you decide."

Bobby walked to the counter and poured himself a cup of coffee, then sat at the table with Paula.

"It's the hardest decision I've had yet as a coach."

"I know. I won't bug you any more about it."

They got up early Sunday and went to church at the First Methodist Church, a venerable building of red brick with a tall white steeple. Bobby's father, Bill, had always said he was a Baptist, though he couldn't prove it by his attendance, but Paula had been raised a Methodist and Bobby found the free-thinking tenets of the Methodists to his liking.

The preceding Sunday, they had met the pastor, Bill Blevins, an earnest-looking man in his mid-thirties with blond, blow-dried hair. Bobby had liked Reverend Blevins's sermon the previous week, but this Sunday, he did not follow the pastor at all. Instead, the pros and cons of Rusty Stedman and Terrance Brown kept his brain boiling.

Paula had to pluck him by the sleeve to get him started toward the door after the benediction.

After lunch, he lay on his back on the bed, trying to decide who would start. As he went over and over the two options, it seemed to become apparent to him that he must start Rusty Stedman.

True, Terrance had more ability, and the school board president, Mike Proctor, would back Bobby in starting Terrance, but Bobby finally concluded he could not expect to field a harmonious team if he overruled the opinions of his two assistants and subjected himself to the disapproval of Banker Gerald Stedman and the boosters and school board members who favored the banker's son.

Bobby told himself that, right or wrong, he had made his decision. He got up from the bed and went out into the living room, where Paula sat reading.

"I'm going to start Stedman," he said defensively.

Paula nodded. "That's probably the safest thing to do."

Bobby didn't like the idea that he was doing the safest thing. "Stedman can run the team better."

Paula nodded again. "It's your decision."

Bobby felt he had lost a moral battle, but when he thought of changing his mind, all the problems involved with starting Terrance Brown seemed to magnify.

◆

The next morning, he told Coach Morris and Coach Bennett that Stedman would start. Bennett's face showed relief and satisfaction.

"I'm sure glad you see it that way, coach. I've worried all weekend about what would happen if we went the other way."

The two-a-day workouts had ended. Students crowded the high school grounds waiting for the building to open for the first day of school. Bobby and the other coaches walked from the fieldhouse under the bleachers to the school building, where they separated to go to their home room classes.

Bobby entered his assigned class room and started arranging the desks into neat rows. When he had finished, he put his briefcase on the desk and opened it, taking out the list of thirty students assigned to him for home room.

Bobby did not enjoy the academic part of his job. He lived and breathed football to the exclusion of most other subjects, and regarded the duties of administering a home room and teaching high school mathematics as necessary evils required by his contract.

He had a stern, no-nonsense attitude about discipline, and didn't tolerate unnecessary talking. He taught math with clean, clear examples and gave short but fairly hard tests. Although he did not shirk his teaching responsibilities, he regarded every minute spent on administrative and academic things as time he would rather spend working on new plays for the team.

The bell rang and the halls outside the room filled with the sound of students moving through the building. The door of the room opened and Ned Chambers came in, followed by Juan Guerrero and Cheery O'Leary.

"Morning, Coach Thompson," Chambers said, standing before Bobby in a slump-shouldered slouch and grinning as though it was a good joke that he had been assigned to Bobby's home room. His summer breadbasket had shrunk during the two-a-days, but he still had the wide-set appearance of a jowly bulldog.

"Did you shave this morning, Chambers?" Bobby asked critically.

Chambers put his fingers to the stubble on his cheeks. "Sure did, coach."

"You need a better razor. And you can stand straight and tall, instead of looking like you don't have a backbone. I expect you guys to set an example for the other students."

"Sorry, coach," Chambers said with a crestfallen look.

Other students started filling the room. Bobby showed them a seating chart he had made, and told them to find their seats. Juan Guerrero eased himself down in a desk that barely held his bulk, while Cheery O'Leary, with his usual morose look, slid into a desk that seemed to swallow him.

The class had sixteen girls and fourteen boys. Bobby looked them over as he checked the seating chart. Some of the boys had the sunburned complexions and blue jeans of farm and ranch boys, while others looked almost collegiate in tailored slacks and button-down collar shirts.

Some girls wore simple print dresses and little makeup, while others looked like models of current teen fashion. Still others wore jeans and cowboy boots. Several of the girls had breasts that thrust hard against the fabric of their clothes, and hips accentuated by their jeans and skirts. Carnal thoughts ran through Bobby's head, although he told himself he would never act on such desires.

The first day of school passed quickly. Bobby introduced himself to each successive class, gave out the homework assignment and the textbooks, and told the students he would brook no nonsense. He ate lunch at the faculty table where Leon Purvis presided. Bobby sat at the end of the table with Coach Bennett and Coach Morris.

In mid-afternoon, his scholastic duties for the day over, he walked to the fieldhouse, where he posted the lineups for the first-, second- and third-strings on the bulletin board in the dressing room.

Immediately, players began to cluster around the board. Bobby went to his locker in the coaches' area and changed into his practice clothes, knowing the joy and despair being generated by the lineups posted on the board.

When he walked back into the players' area, he saw Terrance Brown standing by himself with his helmet in his hand, grim-faced, looking out the window. A wave of guilt started in the pit of Bobby's stomach and moved over his body. He knew what Terrance was thinking. Fixing his mouth in a strong look, Bobby walked over to Terrance.

"You ready to get 'em today, Terrance?"

Terrance turned toward him with angry eyes. "I'm always ready, Coach Thompson. I'm gonna prove it to you, too."

"They'll be plenty of chances for that, Terrance,"

Terrance gave a tight little nod and walked toward the door leading to the outside. On the field, after the warmup exercises, Bobby called the team around him.

"You've all seen the lineups, men. Deciding who would start wasn't easy. We have a lot of good talent on this team, and a lot of the second-string players are just about as good as the first-string guys. I want you to know these lists are not set in concrete.

"We'll be looking at all of you all the time, and you'll all have a chance to move up. For you guys that aren't on either the first- or second-string, I can tell you that you're just as much a part of the team as anyone else.

"We've got to have backups in these positions, and we've got to have someone who will keep the starters on their toes. Even if you never move up to the first- or second-team, you're still an essential part of this team, and don't you ever forget it. Now, let's hustle up and get ready to beat Jacksboro."

Bobby blew his whistle for the first drill, and the players trotted toward their positions, calling encouragement to each other. During the two-a-day workouts, Bobby had moved the players around in different positions, and mixed them up among the different scrimmage teams. Now, with the first- and second-string positions assigned, he started fine-tuning the two teams.

After the blocking, tackling and passing drills, he had them run their plays over and over, so the players would sharpen their execution, and get used to the way they interacted. During the final hour of practice, he scrimmaged the first-string against the second-string.

Rusty Stedman seemed to find inspiration in being chosen for the first-string, and led his team with strong voice and few mistakes. Bobby began to feel he had made the right choice. Stedman stood straight in the huddle, looking like a military recruitment ad with his tall, wide-shouldered build. He called the plays with confidence, threw straight passes and accurate pitchouts, and ran the option plays with the unpredictability required to make them work.

Terrance Brown, by contract, seemed sullen and demoralized. He called the plays in a low voice, without the cocky jive talk he had been using. His team responded to his execution sluggishly. Halfway through the scrimmage, Art Bennett sidled up to Bobby.

"Just like I thought, Brown can't perform when things don't go to suit him," Bennett spoke in a gloating, low voice out of the side of his mouth.

"He'll do better when he gets over his disappointment."

"What good is a quarterback who goes to pieces when he doesn't get his way?"

Bobby thought that Bennett had a good point. He felt vindicated in choosing Stedman. Toward the end of the practice, Bobby noticed Mike Proctor standing down the sideline from him, his face solemn. After the practice, while Bobby followed the players back to the dressing room, Proctor fell in beside him.

"Stedman's not looking too bad today, coach. But I still think in the long run, Brown's your man."

"He'll have another chance. If he looks better later in the season, I'll start him instead of Rusty."

"I wish you'd seen your way clear to starting him for the first."

Bobby turned toward Proctor, his neck swollen in anger. "I've got to be the judge of who starts, Mr. Proctor. That's the job y'all hired me for."

Proctor nodded, a little smirk on his mouth. "You're the judge okay, coach. And like you've told me before, I know you'll do the right thing in the end." He turned and walked away from Bobby without waiting for a reply.

"Bastard," Bobby muttered, keeping his voice low enough so no one would hear. He feared the fallout of his disagreement with Proctor, but he would not brook being patronized. Neither Mike Proctor nor anyone else would tell him what to do. Right or wrong, he would run the team. Anyone who didn't like the way he did it could go to hell.

In the dressing room, a thin young man with red hair and freckles accosted Bobby. He wore ill-fitting slacks and a wrinkled sport shirt, and moved quickly but awkwardly, like an enthusiastic puppy.

"Coach Thompson, I'm Ray Stewart of the *Comanche Springs Courier*. Can I talk to you about the team?"

Bobby shook Stewart's hand. "Sure, Ray. You saw our starting lineup?"

Stewart nodded. "Sure did. I'd like to write a story highlighting the team's strong points before the game Friday."

Bobby told the young reporter that Rutherford McAlpin at fullback had all-district potential, along with Ned Chambers at center. "Actually, we're in pretty good shape at all the starting positions, but those two guys have been the most outstanding so far."

"What about Rusty Stedman?"

Bobby looked into Stewart's guileless face, wondering if he was looking for a controversy.

"Stedman's been looking pretty good. He's got plenty of talent for the job."

"I've been hearing he hasn't been looking too smooth."

"He's got room to grow, all right, but he's been looking a lot better the last several days."

"What about this new black kid, Terrance Brown?"

Had Stewart been talking to Mike Proctor? "Terrance has been looking pretty good. We're fortunate to have him in the number two position."

Stewart nodded. "Thanks coach. I'll see you at the game."

The next day, the paper ran two stories in the sports section under Ray Stewart's byline. The first story highlighted the talents of McAlpin, Chambers and other players, and discussed the strengths and weaknesses of the Jacksboro team.

"Hot Contest at Quarterback," ran the headline of the second story. Bobby read the story closely. Stewart said that Terrance Brown had very nearly beaten out Rusty Stedman for the quarterback position, and that Brown could still be the starter if Stedman didn't perform well in the Jacksboro game.

"Where the hell did Stewart get that information?" Bobby asked the other coaches after practice. Both shrugged their shoulders.

"I haven't told anyone we had any controversy about it," Art Bennett said. Bobby looked at Bennett's bronzed, conceited face, half-believing he had leaked the story.

Melvin Morris screwed up his face belligerently. "I didn't tell that peckerwood anything. I don't know where he got it."

How had Stewart put together enough information to write the story? Bennett and Morris might have leaked the fact the coaches had disagreed, or Stewart might have pieced together enough facts to guess the truth.

Possibly, Mike Proctor had dictated the story to Stewart to set the stage for a change at quarterback after the Jacksboro game. Either Stewart had real talent as a reporter, or he had been influenced by Mike Proctor. Either way, Bobby would need to be wary of him.

◆

That evening, Bobby stared ahead with dogged intensity as he ate his supper, barely talking to Paula.

"Hey," she finally said, "lighten up. We're not expecting Armageddon, you know."

"I feel like Armageddon's just around the corner."

"It's just a game."

"Yeah, but this game will be my first as head coach. I guess I never did appreciate the sweat Coach Phillips went through when I was his assistant."

"The buck stops here."

"Yeah, it does. These people really want to win this one, too, even though it's not a district game. I don't want to disappoint them, right out of the box."

"All you can do is your best, and let things take their course."

"It doesn't help that the paper ran a story about the trouble I had deciding who would start at quarterback. I don't know how that little pecker of a reporter got the information. I sure didn't tell him."

"Those guys can be pretty ingenious."

"Or someone can feed the information."

"No point in being paranoid about it."

"You're right. But I sure don't look forward to the booster club meeting Monday night, if we don't win Friday."

After the practice Wednesday, the players held the election for team captains. Traditionally, the Warriors elected co-captains from among the senior players. Bobby and the other coaches watched from the far end of the dressing room while Rob Wilson, the little, gravel-voiced junior quarterback, presided over the meeting.

The players nominated Rusty Stedman, Ned Chambers and Bill Foster, then voted to cease the nominations. Wilson had the nominees leave the room and passed around slips of paper for the voting. When the votes had been tallied, Rusty Stedman and Ned Chambers had the highest totals. Wilson called the nominees back into the room and announced the result.

Foster shook Stedman's and Chamber's hands, and each of them made a short speech asking for unity among the team members. Bobby thought Stedman's election as captain confirmed his selection as starting quarterback.

◆

Thursday afternoon, just after lunch, the school held a pep rally in the gym. The band, with Ernest Lambert, the prim, bespectacled bandmaster, sat in midsection playing Sousa marches as the students came in.

Bobby, the other coaches, and the team filed in and took seats front and center. The band played the school fight song while the cheerleaders, dressed in the Warrior's colors of red and black, went through their routines. The boy cheerleaders wore black duck pants and short-sleeved red shirts, while the girls wore short black skirts and red blouses.

Bobby admired the girls' strong young legs as they somersaulted in the air. The best of the legs belonged to a Mexican girl named

Angie Zamora, who Bobby recognized from one of his classes. Momentarily, Bobby daydreamed of how she would use those legs in the act of love.

The fight song ended, and the cheerleaders sat down. Principal Leon Purvis went out on the floor of the basketball court to the mike stand and faced the assemblage, favoring them all with his most sincere smile. His wrinkled blue pants sagged in the seat and the overhead lights glinted off his glasses.

"I can feel that Warrior spirit in the air," he said with high-pitched enthusiasm. "It's good to see all of you back from the summer for another football season. It's now my pleasure to introduce the man who will lead the team to victory this year. Many of you have already met him in class this past week, and for the rest of you, I'd like to introduce the new Warrior coach, Coach Bobby Thompson."

Bobby walked out to the mike amid cheers and applause. He turned toward the mass of young faces in the stands, stage fright clutching at his stomach.

"I want first to tell you how proud I am to be here," he said, self-conscious at the loud echo of his voice from the PA system. "And I want to tell you how proud I am of this team of yours that I'm privileged to coach."

He extolled the virtues of the team for several minutes, telling the students how hard the players had worked in the hot sun of late summer to get ready for this first game. As he talked, his confidence increased. He exhorted the students in strong voice for the team spirit that would carry the Warriors to victory.

"I don't have to remind you who won this game last year. I think y'all remember how we went to Jacksboro picked to win, led the game until the last quarter, and then got beat in the final seconds by a questionable touchdown pass. I think y'all remember how the Jacksboro students and fans rubbed it in.

"Coach Morris and Coach Bennett have told me about a yell they used when the game was over. How did it go? 'Eleven little Indians came to town, crawled back home with their britches down!' Are we gonna hear that yell from 'em this year?" Bobby paused, spreading his arms to invite response.

"No!" the students shouted.

"That's right!" Bobby nodded his head for emphasis. "This year's gonna be different. This year, they're coming to our town. We don't have a cruddy yell to yell at 'em. We don't need one. But we're gonna kick their rears so hard they'll put their tails between their legs and sneak back to Jacksboro like beaten dogs."

Bobby introduced Rusty Stedman and Ned Chambers as the team captains, and they both came to the microphone and told the students in embarrassed mumbles that the team needed their support. Then Bobby turned the microphone back to Leon Purvis, who had the assembly rise for the alma mater.

Bobby's eyes glistened as he looked over the fervent faces of the students. They burst into a spontaneous cheer at the end of the song, and Principal Purvis dismissed them. Bobby filed out of the gym behind his players, determined they would win this important first game.

FOUR

Team members in their freshly-laundered game uniforms of black and red clustered around Bobby under the harsh overhead lights of the dressing room. Some of the players already wore their helmets; others held them in their hands. Some sat on the dressing benches, while others looked up toward Bobby from where they sat on the cement floor.

Cheery O'Leery crouched off to the side, loading a wooden carton with bottles of gatorade, his face fixed in a concentrated grimace. Coach Morris and Coach Bennett flanked Bobby, looking at the players with war-like intensity.

Stern-voiced, Bobby began speaking. "Those of you who went to Jacksboro last year remember all the hell they gave us when they stole the game in the last minutes. We've worked hard getting ready for this one, and now it's time for the payoff. I want you to remember what we've learned and put it into practice, but there's more to it than that.

"For us to win this game, you've got to find a burning desire to play football! I can't give you that, and neither can Coach Morris or Coach Bennett, but if you do find it, and if all of you play with that burning desire, we'll win this game tonight, and make Jacksboro sorry for all that crap they gave us last year.

"You'll know when the game's over if you had the right feeling, so reach down deep inside and tell yourself you're going to play the game tonight better than you ever have in your life. If you can all do that, there's no doubt how this game will come out."

Bobby called on the team captains, and Ned Chambers and Rusty Stedman exhorted the other players in emotion-choked voices to play to win for the team, for the school, and for the honor of the town of Comanche Springs.

"That's all there is to say, men," Bobby said when the captains had finished, "let's go out there and get 'em!"

The players jumped to their feet with a collective roar and trotted toward the door of the dressing room, cleats clattering on the concrete floor. Bobby and the other coaches trotted after them. Cheery O'Leary followed, lugging his heavy carton of gatorade bottles.

Outside, the air held the aromatic smell of freshly-cut grass from the newly-mown playing field, and a languid, warm, summer breeze played over Bobby's face in the late summer dusk. He churned inside with the same self-doubt and fear he always felt before games. The air carried waves of sound from the school band playing in the bleachers, and the muted murmur of many voices.

The team had responded strongly to Bobby's pep talk. He remembered the first time he had heard this same speech from Bill Mattingly, just before his first game on the Borger High School team. With Mattingly's inspirational words, the conviction had welled up on Bobby that all life was one big football game, worthy of whatever it took to win. He had played the game in an adrenalin-powered frenzy that extracted power from his body far beyond his strength and ability.

Trotting behind his own team with Art Bennett, Bobby pictured the luminous, fanatical eyes of his mentor. "Wish you could see this one, coach," Bobby said softly.

"What's that?" Coach Bennett asked.

"Just talking to myself."

The fans cheered as the Warriors broke onto the field. Near the far goal posts, the Jacksboro Tigers had already begun warming up. They looked smart in their purple and white uniforms as their arms and legs sliced the air with mechanical precision in the motions of the side straddle hop exercise.

Bobby scanned the stands on the home side, looking for Paula, but from the field, the faces of the fans looked like cranberries bobbing in a bowl of water, and Bobby could not pick her out. The night before, Wanda Morris, Coach Morris's wife, had called and invited Paula to sit with her at the game. This friendly offer seemed to mean the end of any resentment Coach Morris had felt toward Bobby.

The captains formed the boys up at one end of the field for calesthentics. On the sidelines, the cheerleaders jumped and spun and exhorted the fans through their bright red and black megaphones. Angie Zamora's perfect young legs flashed with dark beauty. The band played the Warrior fight song loudly, trying to drown the noise of the Tiger band in the far stands.

While the other coaches supervised the warmup exercises, Bobby walked to the far sideline and shook hands with the officials and with Moose Murphy, the Tiger coach, a big, slope-shouldered man with a smart, smirking mouth.

At eight o'clock, the lead official blew his whistle. The players trotted to the Warrior bench, while the two captains met the Tiger captains and the officials at midfield for the toss. The coin spun in the air and came down; the official who caught it signaled that the Tigers had won the toss and elected to receive. Quickly, the starters clustered around Bobby as the captains trotted over to join them.

"This is it, men," Bobby said. "Put your hands in the circle." The boys put out their right hands, stacking them one on top of another. "Remember what I said in the dressing room, men. All it takes to win is that burning desire! They've won the toss, but that doesn't mean anything. Let's go out there and get the ball back and score!"

With a common yell, the boys separated and ran onto the field, where they lined up for the kickoff. Freddie Alhamid, the muscular, compact left guard, had been working ten or fifteen minutes of every practice on his kickoff routine. Now, he lined up as the point man of the vee of the kickoff formation. Even from the sideline, Bobby saw the stony concentration on his olive-hued face as he looked at the ball on its tee in front of him.

One of the officials blew the whistle signaling the kickoff and Freddie moved forward, first slowly, then with more speed. As he came even with each of the other players, they started toward the kickoff line, running with controlled speed.

In the stands, the drummers in the band beat a drum roll. Freddie got his foot solidly into the ball, and it sailed in a tight parabola toward the Tiger goal line. When Freddie connected with the ball, the drum hit a single solid beat and the Warrior fans cheered.

The ball came down around the goal line and bounced into the air, where a small, slightly-built Tiger player caught it just inside the end zone.

"That's Smithers," Coach Bennett yelled toward the field, cupping his hands over his mouth so the sound would carry. "Get him!"

Bobby knew the statistics on Pete Smithers. He had been all district last year, ran the 100 in 9.6 seconds, and had the elusive swivel-hips of a great broken-field runner.

Smithers got out to the ten before he met the first Warrior defender, Joe King, the quick but fearful back. King spread his arms for the tackle attempt and Smithers gave a little gyration of his hips and cut away. Not fooled, King cut with Smithers and grabbed him with his arms, but Smithers jerked free while King fell to the ground.

"I wish that boy would learn not to arm tackle," Melvin Morris said, shaking his head angrily.

At the twenty, Smithers confronted two other defenders, did a little side-to-side dance, spun around, and left them with empty air in front of them. Dismayed at the yardage Smithers was making, Bobby nonetheless admired the smooth poetry of his motions.

Smithers shook off several more Warriors and broke for the center of the field at the thirty-five yard line. Finally, Curtis McInnes, the gutsy preening canary of the dressing room, slammed into Smithers at the forty, nailing him to the ground. Across the way, the Tiger fans shouted in approval of Smithers's run.

"Way to go, Curtis," Bobby yelled to McInnes. Bobby did not like the good field position the Tigers had gained from the kickoff, but at least they had not crossed the fifty.

The Tigers ran two plain-vanilla fullback slant plays into the line, the first for no gain into the hulking embrace of Juan Guerrero, and the second stopped with short yardage by a crunching tackle from Ned Chambers in his defensive linebacker position, bringing up third and seven. The defense loosened, anticipating a pass, but the Tigers ran an option play to the right.

Lee Shaugnessey, at defensive end, drifted with the play, eluded the blocking back, and forced the quarterback to keep the ball and go inside, where Rutherford McAlpin nailed him just a few yards over the line of scrimmage, three or four yards short of the first. The Tigers punted to Joe King almost at the goal line, who made a choppy, stop-and-go run back to the Warrior forty before he went down under a wave of defenders.

"That boy can run like a scared jackrabbit when he wants to," Coach Morris said approvingly.

Art Bennett nodded his tanned blond head, his mouth twisted disdainfully. "He always wants to run if it'll keep him from getting tackled."

Bobby paced the sideline nervously between plays as the Warriors tried to mount a drive. Hands clasped behind his back, he walked five yards up the field, then five yards back. When the team lined up for each play, he stopped and faced the field, hands on his hips.

The Warriors made one first down on a smoothly executed sideline pass from Rusty Stedman to Lee Shaugnessey, then sputtered on the next series and had to punt. This time, Smithers did not break loose. Curtis McInnes tackled him cleanly at the Tiger five-yard line, putting the Tigers in precarious field position.

"That's two good tackles so far for McInnes," Bobby said.

Melvin Morris nodded. "He may be a pretty boy off the field, but he's the best open-field tackler we've got."

The Tigers ran a couple of inside plays, but only got out to the seven or eight, bringing third down and long yardage.

"Bet they'll try a draw," Art Bennett guessed.

The Tiger play started off like a draw, with the quarterback laying his hand in the gut of the waiting fullback, who started for the line and drew two tacklers, but as the fullback went down, Bobby realized the quarterback still had the ball.

"Pass! pass!" he yelled, marveling that the Tigers would be so foolhardy as to pass so deep in their own territory.

The quarterback cocked his arm and threw, and Bobby saw with a cold feeling in his gut that the intended receiver had several steps on the Warrior defender, but just as the quarterback threw the ball, a long arm shot up from the Warrior line, deflecting the ball from its course and toward Ned Chambers, who threw up his hands and clumsily caught it. For a second, he stood still, so surprised he didn't know what to do.

"Run, dummy!" Bobby yelled.

Chambers finally got under way, just as several Tigers reached him. One hit him high and the other low, but he would not be denied, and stumbled toward the goal line, crossing it just as three or four other defenders hit him.

The Warrior stands broke into a frenzied roar, the cheerleaders did somersaults, and Ernest Lambert, the bespectacled bandmaster, waved his arms wildly leading the band in a song no one could hear through the din.

"I think that's probably the only touchdown Chambers has ever scored," Coach Bennett said, when the noise had subsided.

Coach Morris creased his sun-darkened face in a smile. "These fat-fart linemen don't get the chance very often."

"Who was that that tipped the ball?" Bobby asked.

Bennett shook his head. "I didn't see."

"It was Eddie Ritterman, coach," Cheery O'Leery volunteered in his low voice, looking at Bobby with his patient donkey's look.

Ritterman was just coming off the field, replaced for the extra point play by little Rob Wilson, who doubled as third-string quarterback and extra point holder.

"Way to go, Eddie," Bobby said, slapping Ritterman on the rear. "Chambers got the TD, but he wouldn't have if you hadn't tipped the ball."

"Thanks, coach," Ritterman said humbly. He took off his helmet, accepted a wet towel from Cheery O'Leery, and starting mopping the sweat from his face.

Wilson kicked the extra point, and the Warriors led 7-0 as the quarter changed. The teams switched ends and Alhamid kicked off with a high, sailing kick that went into the end zone, preventing any runback. The Tigers gained a couple of first downs on the ground, bringing them close to the fifty.

On the first play of the new series, the quarterback faked a draw, then fell back to pass. Bobby recognized the same play where Ritterman had deflected the pass to Ned Chambers for the Warrior touchdown. This time, the Tigers had plenty of room and plenty of time, as the offense held their blocks for what seemed forever.

"Rush him! Rush him!" Bobby yelled.

At the far side of the field, he saw Pete Smithers racing down the sideline, three or four steps ahead of Joe King. The quarterback cocked back his arm and heaved the ball in a long spiral pass into Smither's arms.

Smithers caught the ball without breaking stride, and raced for the goal, distancing King with every step. Smithers crossed the goal and threw the ball high into the air amid hysteric applause from the Tiger stands.

"Oh shit!" Melvin Morris groaned.

Jacksboro kicked the point to tie the game. In the seconds before the Tiger kickoff, Bobby called the team to the side of the field.

"All right, men. So they scored. It's early in the game, and we've got the ball. Get back in there and get us another one!"

"Sorry I let him get ahead of me, coach," Joe King said, looking at Bobby over the bars of his helmet with frustrated tears in his eyes.

"He's a fast 'un, Joe. Next time, play a little deeper, hang back and go for the ball." Bobby clapped King on the shoulder pads and the boy turned and ran onto the field for the kickoff.

The Tiger kicker kicked the ball over the goal for the touchback, and the Warriors took over on their own twenty. Stedman ran a dive over tackle to the left. For the first time that night, he lined up leaning in the direction of play.

Bobby shook his head in disgust. "He's giving away the play."

Art Bennett nodded. "He does that sometimes when he gets excited."

Stedman handed off to Rutherford McAlpin. He drove into the waiting arms of two linebackers, who had keyed on Stedman's lineup to slant toward the direction of play. The next time, Stedman ran an option to the right, tipping off the direction by leaning to the right just before the snap.

In spite of the tipoff, Eddie Ritterman turned the outside linebacker in, and Stedman cut up the field for five or six yards. Bobby looked at the clock and saw that only a few minutes of playing time remained before the half. If the team could make it to the half with the score tied, he could settle Stedman down before his miscues did any damage.

On the third down from the Warrior twenty-seven, Stedman pulled back to pass. He had a good pocket, but the Tigers kept the receivers covered. Stedman started to look frantically around for an open receiver. Finally, a couple of big Tiger linemen broke into the pocket and rushed him.

"Keep it! Keep it!" Bobby heard Coach Bennett yell, but Stedman drew his arm back and threw the ball away toward the left sideline, toward an area with no Warrior receiver within range. With dread, Bobby saw Pete Smithers racing toward the descending ball from upfield. He caught it on the run, tucked it under his arm, and covered the thirty yards to the Warrior goal without any tacklers even close to him.

"Why didn't Stedman hold onto it?" Bobby asked, his question lost in the cheers from the Tiger fans.

The Tigers kicked the point after and led 14-7, with less than two minutes remaining in the first half. The kickoff went to Curtis McInnes, who got out to the twenty-five before going down. Bobby sent in a substitute lineman with a word for Stedman.

"Tell him to stay on the ground until he gets past the forty," Bobby said.

The player nodded and trotted toward the huddle. McAlpin made a couple of good runs over right and left guard, and got a first down. Then Stedman ran an option to the left, and made a wobbling, end-over-end pitchout to McInnes, who slowed up to catch the poorly-thrown ball, then turned upfield across the forty before going down.

Mel Morris shook his head. "That play would've been good for five or ten yards if Curtis hadn't had to come back for the ball."

The next play, Stedman fell back again to pass. He had a good pocket, and Eddie Ritterman, the tall end, came loping across the middle in position to make the catch. Stedman made a hard throw toward Ritterman, but he had no control, and the ball drilled into the ground short, out of Ritterman's reach. Sudden anger at Stedman's mistakes blazed in Bobby's brain.

"Christ a'mighty, we're beating ourselves." He turned toward the bench. "Come here, Terrance Brown!"

Brown leapt up from his seat, running toward Bobby as he pulled his helmet on.

"Get us some breathing room, Terrance, and try to hold the ball until the half. Start out with a draw and see what happens."

"Yes sir, coach!"

"Are you sure this is a good idea?" Art Bennett asked as Terrance trotted toward the huddle.

"We're sure gonna find out."

Brown entered the huddle, and Rusty Stedman came off the field and over to the bench, chagrin in his eyes.

"I'm sorry about that pass, coach."

"Just try to settle down, son. We'll see how it goes after the half."

Brown crouched down in the huddle, his knee on the ground. He clapped his hands, and the team moved up to the line. At the snap, Brown turned, holding the ball in his gut, as Rutherford McAlpin started churning toward the line, his cleats digging into the turf.

In an almost imperceptible move, Brown handed off to McAlpin, then put his hand back to his stomach as though he still had the ball, and headed back as if to pass, drawing two Tiger linemen with him. McAlpin hit a wide hole in the line, shook off a linebacker, and ran for almost twenty yards, well into Tiger territory, before going down.

On the next play, McAlpin again churned forward, and Brown again laid the ball in McAlpin's gut, but this time, Brown kept the ball, fading back to pass as the defenders swarmed over the fullback at the line of scrimmage.

Pete Smithers had come up from safety, fooled into thinking the play was a run. Joe King slipped behind Smithers, and Terrance lofted the ball to him in a tight spiral. King caught the ball and headed for the Tiger goal.

Smithers turned and gave chase. He gained on King with every step, and made a flying tackle at the two, but King's momentum carried him into the end zone and the Warrior fans went wild.

Rob Wilson held as Alhamid kicked the extra point, and the score was tied at 14-14. The Tigers took the kickoff with almost no time left. They attempted one long pass to Smithers, but it fell short as the buzzer sounded, ending the half.

Bobby trotted behind the team with the other coaches toward the dressing room as the two school bands filed down from the stands for the half-time show. In the fieldhouse, Cheery O'Leery started daubing cuts with antiseptic and replacing the wrapping he had put on some players before the game to guard against injury.

"Hey, Cheery," Rutherford McAlpin called from across the room, "bring me a bottle of gatorade."

O'Leery looked up with expressionless face. "The bottles are in the carton by the water cooler," he said flatly, raising his voice just enough to carry across the room. He looked down studiously at the bandaging job he had started.

McAlpin got up with an angry look on his calculating, conceited face, stalked over to the carton, and pulled out a bottle. Most of the players, after slaking their thirst with water or gatorade, sat on the dressing room benches. Bobby rolled over a portable blackboard and turned toward his team. The boys looked up at him with grimy faces streaked with dirt and sweat.

"We made some mistakes the first half, men, and they cost us pretty bad. We're lucky to have a tie game at this point."

He started putting plays on the board, showing the boys where things had gone wrong. "Rusty," he said, looking at Stedman, "in the second quarter you were tipping off the direction of play by the way you leaned before the snap."

Stedman looked steadily at Bobby with level blue eyes. "I didn't realize I was doing it, coach."

"We need to work on that. We're gonna start the next half with Terrance Brown at quarterback, since he moved us so good there at the end of the half."

Bobby looked around as he made this announcement. Stedman gave a bitter little nod, and Coach Bennett looked down at the ground with a troubled face. Terrance Brown smiled, leaning forward on the bench and beating a little tattoo on the cement floor with his cleats.

Bobby put another play on the board, showing Joe King and the other defensive backs how to contain Pete Smithers.

"If you can keep that boy bottled up, we've got it made." He called on the other coaches, who told the boys what they thought had been good and bad about the first half.

"You pissants have got to get your shoulders into those tackles," Coach Morris said. "Especially you, Joe King. You had Smithers stopped that one time early in the game and he broke the tackle for good yardage because you just grabbed him with your arms."

"I know it, Coach."

"That's okay, though, you made it up when you got the jump on him on that last touchdown run."

When the time came to go back on the field, Bobby motioned the team to their feet. "We're being critical because we want you to do better, men. There's some things we did right the first half, and if we keep on doing those things and quit making mistakes, we'll come out with the victory."

"Remember what I said about that burning desire. If you can find that inside yourself, there's no doubt who will win this ball game. Now let's go out and get at 'em!" The group broke with a shout and trotted from the dressing room back to the field.

Curtis McInnes took the Tiger kickoff and returned it nearly to mid-field. Brown started the play with a trap over left tackle. Red-haired Bill Foster pulled from right guard, ran behind Chambers at center and picked off the penetrating Tiger lineman. Albert Walker, the big, mean black weightlifter, put an explosive block on his man, and McInnes took the ball through the huge hole for more than ten yards.

Staying mostly on the ground, the Warriors picked up two first downs. Terrance Brown executed the plays with near perfection, making snappy fakes and handoffs, and cutting upfield with smooth power when he kept the ball on option plays. Contrasting Brown's ball handling with what he had seen from Rusty Stedman in the first half, Bobby had no doubt of who looked best.

"We should have started Brown in the first place," he muttered to Coach Bennett.

Bennett frowned angrily. "He looks good right now, but he isn't consistent. You'll see."

The drive ended with an intercepted pass Brown had intended for Shaugnessey, who tipped the ball over his head into the hands of a defender. Shaugnessey partly redeemed himself by tackling the interceptor with no runback.

"Not a very good pass from Brown that time," Bennett remarked.

"Sure it was. Shaugnessey would have had it, if he had been in position."

The Tigers could not get any offense going, and had to kick the ball away on fourth. Starting on the Warrior thirty, Brown marched the team right up the field with one first down after another. The drive culminated with a plunge for the touchdown from the one by Rutherford McAlpin.

On the point-after try, little Rob Wilson bobbled the ball, and could not get it in place in time for Alhamid to make the kick, so the Warriors led 20 to 14.

The quarter changed, and the game went into the final period of play. The Tigers eked out a couple of first downs on the ground, but seemed subdued, dispirited and almost unthreatening.

Then, on third and long yardage around the fifty, the Tiger fullback broke loose up the middle in a frenzied run through a minefield of Warriors. He skirted knots of defenders, broke tackles, and finally bulled his way forward with three Warriors on his back to go down inside the five-yard line.

The run galvanized the lethargic Tiger team. Two plays later, amid thunderous din from the stands, the same fullback powered his way across for the Tiger touchdown. Unlike the Warriors, the Tigers converted the point to lead 21-20. Bobby looked at the clock. The Warriors had less than three minutes of playing time to score and win the game.

Bobby called the team over to the sideline before the kickoff. "Don't let them take it away from you, men. Keep your cool and play tough. We've still got plenty of time."

As the boys ran out onto the field, Coach Bennett took Bobby by the arm. "Let's put Rusty back in, Coach. Terrance won't be able to handle this kind of pressure."

Bobby shook his head. "I'm sticking with Terrance. If he messes up, we'll try Rusty."

Bennett turned and walked away, looking down at the ground and shaking his head. Terrance started with an option to the left, making the cut and keeping the ball for five yards. Then he ran McAlpin up the middle for a first. He moved the team quickly in and out of the huddles and called the plays with sharp, decisive voice.

With a minute and a half to go, he ran another option to the right. Ritterman turned the outside linebacker in, and Brown cut up the field. Albert Walker came downfield from his left tackle position to roll up the only defender between Brown and the open field, and Brown turned on all the speed he had in the race for the goal.

Pete Smithers, playing at safety, got an angle on Terrance. For a time, it appeared he would cut him off, but Curtis McInnes, who had come through the line on a fake and continued downfield to block, bumped Smithers, slowing him just enough to let Brown by. A few seconds later, Brown crossed the goal line, slamming the ball into the ground like a pro.

"You still think Terrance can't keep his cool?" Bobby asked Art Bennett.

"He looked pretty good on that series," Bennett admitted grudgingly.

The Warriors converted the lead 27-21. The Jacksboro team took the kickoff with less than a minute to play. They ran a fullback screen for the first time that night, breaking their big fullback out for twenty yards. Lining up without a huddle, they attempted a pass, but big Juan Guerrero stormed the passer with his arms up like a grizzly bear, forcing a fumble which Albert Walker recovered. Only twenty seconds remained on the clock.

"Stedman!" Bobby called.

"Here, coach!"

Get in there and get us another touchdown."

"Yessir, coach."

Stedman ran onto the field and formed the huddle.

"Shouldn't we be playing it safe and falling on the ball?" Melvin Morris asked.

"We probably should, but I want to send Jacksboro a message for what they did last year. Besides, I want to give Stedman another chance."

Stedman took the snap and drifted back deep to pass as McInnes, Ritterman, and Shaugnessey sprinted for the far end of the field. The Warrior line performed heroics in keeping out the Tiger rushers. Finally, several of them broke through the blockers and rushed Stedman, their arms flailing.

Stedman got off a high, arching pass that came down over the goal line in the vicinity of Eddie Ritterman and several Tiger defenders. All the players went up for the ball, and it seemed impossible that anyone had caught it, but Bobby saw the official signaling a touchdown as Ritterman came off the bottom of the pileup with the ball. The clock showed no more time. The Warriors kicked the point after and the game ended 34-21.

The Warrior band played the fight song, but no one heard it over the roar of the fans. When the noise subsided, a group of Warrior students behind the band started chanting "Poor Tigers! Poor Tigers!" Bobby greeted Rusty Stedman and Eddie Ritterman as they came off the field.

"Great play, men!"

"Thanks coach." They jogged away as the other players mobbed them with congratulations.

Bobby trotted over to the Tiger bench, where Moose Murphy shook his hand, looking glum and sheepish.

"Nice game, coach. That last touchdown looked good, but you wouldn't have beat us without that nigger quarterback."

"There's no law against having a black quarterback."

"There oughta be."

"You gonna propose a change in the league rules?"

"Fuck you, Thompson," Murphy said tolerantly. "We'll get you next year."

Bobby trotted back across the field, past the bench where Cheery O'Leery was gathering up his manager's paraphernalia, and on toward the dressing room. At the end of the stands, he caught up with

Terrance Brown, walking slowly toward the showers by himself.

"You did a great job tonight, Terrance."

Brown looked at Bobby with an unsmiling, resentful face.

"You couldn't tell it by who got the congratulations at the end of the game."

"Don't worry about that. That last touchdown was just the spectacular last event. Everyone knows who pulled the game out."

"Do you know it, coach?"

Bobby nodded. "I know it, Terrance."

"You're the one who counts, coach." Terrance trotted ahead of Bobby toward the dressing room.

A crowd of fans stood around the dressing room door, congratulating the players. Joe Timmons grabbed Bobby's arm as he came by.

"Great game, coach!" Timmons's jowls were flushed with victory. "Wasn't that a great pass by Rusty at the end?"

"Sure was."

"I'm sure looking forward to the booster club meeting Monday night."

Bobby shook Timmons's hand and moved toward the door. He saw Paula standing at the back of the crowd with Wanda Morris, a tall, good-natured looking woman built on a plan of triangular planes and right angles. Bobby waved to the two of them and both waved back, smiling.

"Be home in about an hour," Bobby called to Paula, cupping his hands so his voice would carry over the crowd.

Just inside the dressing room door, the news reporter, Ray Stewart, accosted Bobby. His freckles stood out in strong relief under the bright overhead lights. He gave Bobby a clammy handshake.

"Great game, coach! Can you tell me for my story why you substituted Terrance Brown at quarterback for so much of the game?"

"Sure." Bobby made his voice affable. "Rusty had a little trouble moving the team there in the second quarter, so I put Terrance in to get things going."

"Which of them did you think played best, overall?"

"They both looked pretty good, at times. But both could use improvement."

"Who's gonna start next week?" Stewart watched Bobby's face closely.

"I'll announce that decision at the booster club meeting Monday night."

"You mean you might start Terrance instead of Rusty?"

"Like I say, I'll announce the decision Monday." Bobby turned, coming face to face with Mike Proctor, who smiled knowingly.

"Terrance Brown sure looked good tonight, coach."

"Yes, he did." Bobby kept his voice cool and noncommittal.

"I'm looking forward to the Monday night meeting."

"It'll be interesting," Bobby said cryptically. He nodded politely, turned and walked toward his locker.

An hour later, Bobby walked into the living room at home, where Paula sat waiting for him . She got up as he came in. He moved to her and held her in his arms, feeling the warmth of her body through her clothes.

"Congratulations, coach," she whispered in his ear.

"Thanks," he whispered back.

"You wanta go to a cafe for a late cup of coffee?"

"I'd rather just go to bed with you."

"Let's do it, then."

He locked the front door, turned off the living room light, and picked Paula up in his arms. She nibbled his ear lobe as he carried her to the bedroom.

FIVE

The morning after the Jacksboro game, Bobby sat at the breakfast table drinking coffee with Paula, reading a story by Ray Stewart in the *Comanche Springs Courier* under the headline "Sweet Revenge", giving the high points of the game and contrasting the victory with last year's humiliating loss.

Toward the end, Stewart said that Bobby might start Terrance Brown instead of Rusty Stedman in the game against the Post Antelopes the next Friday. The article said Bobby thought Stedman had not played well and that Brown could do a better job. Bobby swore softly as he read the statements Stewart attributed to him.

"I didn't tell the little fart that."

"What did you tell him?" Paula asked.

"Just that I would make up my mind which one to start and announce it at the booster club meeting Monday."

"That sort of implies what he says."

Bobby shook his head in frustration. "But I didn't say it that way."

"Being misquoted is the price of being famous," Paula said flippantly.

"What I hate is that I've got to defend those statements just like I actually said them, since I am thinking about starting Brown."

"Thinking about it, or are you going to do it?"

"I don't know yet. Brown played better overall in the game, but I really do want to see how they do in the practice before deciding."

Paula smiled. "I think you'll know what to do when the time comes."

That afternoon, as Bobby mowed the yard in the hot afternoon sun, Paula came to the door to call him to the phone. He came in the back door and mopped the sweat from his face with a kitchen towel.

"Who is it?"

"Mr. Stedman," Paula said in an amused, mocking tone.

"Shit! I bet I know what he wants to talk about." Bobby went into the living room and picked up the receiver. "This is Bobby Thompson."

"This is Gerald Stedman, Coach Thompson," came the cool, assured banker's voice, "I wanted to talk to you about the article in the paper."

Bobby pictured Stedman standing with his knuckles tight around the telephone, his brown hair perfectly combed, his superior eyes viewing the world through his horn-rimmed glasses.

"What about it?" Bobby asked.

"It says you're going to start Terrance Brown instead of Rusty because Rusty didn't play well yesterday."

"I didn't tell Ray Stewart that."

"What did you tell him?"

"That I'll announce who'll start at the booster club meeting Monday night."

"You are thinking about starting Brown, then?"

"I haven't decided who will start. I want to watch them both at practice Monday and then decide."

After several seconds of angry silence, Stedman spoke again.

"I don't want to interfere, Coach Thompson, but Rusty has looked forward to being the starting quarterback for the last two years. Since he's a senior, this is his last year to play. If he's going to get a chance to play college football, he has to be the starting quarterback this year. Brown's still got two more years to play."

"I know it's important to Rusty to start, but I've got to do what's best for the team."

"Then you should start Rusty. How could you think Brown is better after that final touchdown pass Rusty threw?"

Bobby wanted to say that Rusty's pass had been a high, wobbling lob, more likely to be an interception than a touchdown. He wanted to remind Stedman of the obvious mistakes Rusty had made toward the end of the first half. He wanted to ask Stedman how he could have failed to notice how much smoother, how much more precise, how much more inspired, Brown's playing had been. Instead, he responded diplomatically.

"They both looked pretty good at times, Mr. Stedman. Like I said, I'm going to look real close at them Monday, and I'll announce my decision at the meeting."

After another angry silence, Stedman spoke again.

"Understand me well, Coach Thompson. I've lived in this town all my life, and I don't expect my son to take a back seat to some upstart nigger who's just moved here, because the new coach thinks he has to show he isn't prejudiced."

Bobby fought for control, telling himself he could not get away with cursing the powerful banker.

"I'll do what I think is right, Mr. Stedman," Bobby said, his voice rough with anger, "but I can't promise you anything. I'll start whichever one of them looks best to me Monday."

"You'd just better make sure you pick the right one."

"I'll do that, Mr. Stedman."

Bobby hung up. "Son of a bitch!" he swore to the air in front of him.

"You have an unhappy daddy on your hands?" Paula asked, from where she stood washing the lunch dishes at the kitchen sink.

"He called Terrance a nigger and said I'd better start his little boy. He'll really be pissed off if I decide to start Terrance. But if I do that, at least I'll make Mike Proctor happy. Instead of Proctor on my ass, I'll have Stedman."

"You can't please everyone, so just do what's right."

"That isn't as easy as it sounds."

"Life isn't supposed to be easy."

"Since when did you get to be such a philosopher?"

"It comes from my unemployed status. I've had lots of time to think about things."

"If you're worried about not having anything to do, you can finish cutting the grass."

"I don't follow that line of work," she said in mock disdain.

"Then I'd better get with it." Bobby walked out the back door into the afternoon heat.

He restarted the lawnmower with a savage jerk of the starting rope. As he cut the grass in neat overlapping strips, his mind churned angrily.

He knew Stedman's type. Stedman didn't drink, didn't curse, probably didn't fornicate, and gave at least a tenth of his substantial income to the Church of Christ. He made a fetish of morality, but had no kindness for those who crossed him. He saw the world with blinders on. Because he was righteous, his son deserved to be starting quarterback. A nigger like Terrance Brown deserved no consideration at all.

"Just go to hell," Bobby snarled aloud, his words lost in the drone of the lawnmower. He didn't care what Stedman thought. The best player would start at quarterback, regardless of the consequences.

◆

At practice on Monday afternoon, Bobby watched Terrance Brown and Rusty Stedman throwing passes during the warmup. Both seemed to put extra show into their moves, snapping out the commands crisply, drilling the ball to the receiver, then hustling into the next sequence. Midway through the drills, Melvin Morris sidled up to Bobby, smiling grimly.

"I haven't seen a pair of quarterbacks working so hard in all the years I've been coaching."

"Damn that reporter, anyway."

"Who you gonna start?"

"I'm still not sure."

Morris nodded. "Whatever you do, you're gonna make someone mad, but I'm with you either way."

"Thanks, Mel."

Bobby looked toward Art Bennett, who stood several yards away with arms folded in classic pose, watching the drill with an intense little frown knotting his suntanned forehead. Bobby knew that starting Terrance Brown would bring severe disapproval from that quarter.

Late in the practice, Bobby scrimmaged the first and second teams against each other, alternating Brown and Stedman between the teams. Both boys played well in the scrimmage, and seemed almost evenly matched. Rusty played better than Bobby ever remembered him playing. Bobby began to think no one could fairly criticize him if he decided to start Stedman again.

Many boosters had turned up to watch the scrimmage, drawn by the showdown promised by Ray Stewart's article. Bobby noticed Stewart talking to Mike Proctor on the far sideline. Bobby wondered again if Proctor pulled Stewart's string. Joe Timmons and several other boosters stood in a little knot around Gerald Stedman, five or ten yards up the sideline from Stewart and Proctor.

Several yards further along the sideline, a middle-aged black man wearing a dark suit and a snappy grey hat with a plaid band stood by himself watching the action. Terrance's father, Bobby thought. The big man stood by himself, isolated from the others by his color like oil from water.

After the final whistle of the scrimmage, Bobby walked along toward the dressing room while Coach Morris and Coach Bennett ran the boys through their windsprints. Ray Stewart caught up with him as he rounded the corner and walked toward the door.

"Who's it gonna be, coach?" Stewart asked, his freckled face inflamed by the heat of the practice field.

Bobby stopped and turned, putting a confident, tolerant smile on his face to conceal his intense irritation.

"Like I said last Friday night, Ray, I'll announce that at the meeting tonight. Come to the meeting and you'll find out."

"I'll be there, coach."

Stewart nodded at Bobby with an almost contemptuous familiarity that made Bobby want to hit him. Bobby showered and changed into his street clothes, then told the other coaches he was going home.

"I've still got some thinking to do about quarterback. It's gonna be a hard decision."

"What's there to decide?" Art Bennett asked. "Rusty's got the problems he had during the Jacksboro game worked out. I've never seen him play better than he did today."

"He looked pretty good, all right, but Brown looked good too."

Bennett shook his head incredulously and walked away. Outside the building, the big black man from the scrimmage field waited for him.

"Coach Thompson, I'm Royal Brown." He put out his hand.

Royal Brown had a strong handshake, almost too confident, too firm, as though he had a point to prove. He had close-cropped greying hair showing under the brim of his hat, and a very proper little grey mustache.

"I'm glad to meet you," Bobby said.

"I've been meaning to get by some of the practices, but being a minister of the Lord keeps me pretty busy."

"I bet it does."

"It's a kind of work that's never finished. You don't quit at five.

Someone's always got something for you to do. But I came by tonight because I've been talking to Terrance, and he's been sounding real frustrated. He doesn't think he's getting a fair chance out here, with only a few other blacks on the team and all the politics of the town working against him."

"He's let me know that, too."

Royal Brown looked intently at Bobby.

"I grew up in the country over in East Texas, but before I got the call to come out here to this congregation, I'd lived in Fort Worth for years. In Fort Worth, most of the kids in Terrance's high school were black. The principal and coaches were black. If Terrance didn't make the grade there, at least I knew it wasn't because he was black."

"It won't be because of that here, either, Reverend Brown."

"Are you sure, Coach Thompson?"

"Yes, I am." Bobby resolved to make his words true.

"My people at the church tell me there's no hope for Terrance to start this year, with banker Stedman's son in the picture. They say this town has never had a starting black quarterback, and I may as well forget about Terrance being the first one."

"There's a first time for everything, Reverend Brown."

"Are you going to start Terrance this next week, then?"

"Both boys looked good in practice today. I'm going home now to make the decision. I'll announce it at the booster club meeting at 7:00. Why don't you come?"

Reverend Brown looked down at the ground briefly then back at Bobby.

"Black people don't usually go to the cafe where they have the meetings."

"But you have a special interest in this situation. You have a son playing on the team. Besides, you have a right to go in there under the law anyway."

"In a town like Comanche Springs, local customs mean more than some law made in Washington, Coach Thompson, and some-times, you ignore them at your peril. But your point is well taken. I do have an interest in what's going on, so I'll be there."

◆

An hour and a half later, just before seven, Bobby parked in the

McKeever Cafe parking lot. He walked toward the door with others who had arrived at the same time. The men just ahead of Bobby bantered with each other.

"We'll never live it down if he decides to start that nigger," one man said. "All the folks in the other towns will be saying we couldn't win without importing a trained ape."

"Next thing you know, he'll be putting chitlings on the training menu," said another.

Bobby felt his face burning with angry fire. Comanche Springs had been playing black players for years. The fact that one of them might beat out the banker's son at quarterback did not call for a resurgence of racial anger.

Bobby hung back from the men in front of him, and they entered the building without noticing he was behind them. He walked through the sparsely-occupied dining room to the meeting room, and took his seat next to Joe Timmons at the head table. Timmons gave a friendly nod of his noble white head.

"How you doing, coach?"

"Pretty good."

"You decided who it will be?" Ned Zablonski asked, his sun-darkened face unsmiling. He had not changed from the khaki work clothes he wore around his filling station.

Bobby looked Zablonski in the eye. "Yep, but I'm not saying just yet."

Willis Fullerton, the highway department engineer, leaned forward in his seat on the other side of Zablonski. "You mean even those of us in the inner sanctum of the head table don't get a preview?" He wore a sports coat with a loud, checked design and smiled with ironic tolerance.

Bobby smiled back at Fullerton. "If I told you guys, everyone would know in thirty seconds. I'll make the announcement after we show the game films."

Bobby looked over the near-capacity crowd of Warrior fans. He did not see Royal Brown. Discretion is the better part of valor, Bobby thought. Brown must have decided not to come. Gerald Stedman sat grim and unsmiling amid a knot of his supporters. Reporter Ray Stewart sat next to Mike Proctor at a middle table.

Bobby spotted Melvin Morris and Art Bennett sitting together at a table to the left of the head table. The Methodist preacher, Bill

Blevins, gave the invocation, and the men fell to eating. The room filled with the din of their conversation.

While the waitresses were serving desert, Bobby saw Royal Brown come hesitantly in. He moved to the back wall and leaned against it, looking very uncomfortable. Bobby stood up at the podium and pulled the mike to his mouth.

"There's still some seats, Reverend Brown. And there's plenty of food left."

All the men seated at the tables followed Bobby's eyes to the lone black man, and Bobby wished he had not spoken.

Brown shook his head. "Thanks, coach. I ate at home. I just came for the meeting."

"Have a seat, anyway," Bobby motioned toward several vacant seats at a rear table.

Brown walked to the table and sat down. A low, angry murmur rose from several parts of the room. Someone gave a low hiss, and others picked it up. The derisive noise seemed to come from everywhere at once. Many of the men stared at Brown, their faces set starkly in shocked hostility. Bobby felt an angry flush rising on his face.

He had been raised around racism, and didn't usually argue with it. His own father spoke contemptuously about the niggers, and blamed them for what was wrong with America. Such talk had never made Bobby wince. But he had asked Brown to come to the meeting and had told him he had a right to be there. The boosters had no reason to treat Bobby's guest this way.

Just as Bobby started to remonstrate with the hecklers, Mike Proctor got up and walked back to Brown, shook his hand, and sat down next to him. Several others leaned across the table to shake the preacher's hand. The angry muttering decreased, and the room filled again with the sound of conversation.

When most of the people had finished their deserts, Bobby motioned to Coach Morris, who dimmed the room lights and started the game video. Bobby talked the boosters through the game. Several times, he had Morris stop the tape and reverse it for replays.

The men cheered at the high points and groaned at the mistakes. As the tape neared the end, Bobby felt a quavering anticipation in his gut. The time had come to announce his decision.

"Well, that's it folks," he said after the tape had played the final seconds of the game, ending with Stedman's dramatic pass to Ritterman for the final touchdown. Coach Bennett turned on the lights, and Bobby looked over the room of expectant faces before him.

"We looked real good at times in that game, and real bad at times. I think ya'll could see that. All in all, the game gave us a good start for the season, and made up for what they did to us over in Jacksboro last year. But I think y'all can see we're gonna have to play a whole lot better if we're gonna win district.

"That brings me to the announcement ya'll have been waiting for--who will start at quarterback next week. Before I make the announcement, I want to tell you that the decision has not been easy. Both Rusty Stedman and Terrance Brown played well at times in the game last week, and both of them made some mistakes.

"Those of you who were with us this afternoon know they both looked pretty good in practice. As your coach, I have had to decide which one of these two quality quarterbacks will start next week, and I want you to know the decision has been mine and mine only.

"Having said all that, I can tell you I have decided to start Terrance Brown this next week in the game against Post." Bobby paused as an angry murmur ran through the room. He held up his hands for attention.

"Of course, who starts this next week is not necessarily who will start the week after that. We are fortunate to have both these young men, and I can assure you both of them will be playing a lot for the rest of the season, but at this time, I believe Terrance Brown can move the team better than Rusty can. Do any of you have any questions?"

Bobby was conscious of his own defiant air as he looked over the crowd. He saw several knots of men muttering together, and several men who seemed on the verge of saying something, but no one took up the challenge. Bobby shot a quick look at Gerald Stedman. The banker sat livid-faced, staring down at the table in front of him.

"If there are no questions," Bobby said. "I thank all of you for coming, and we'll see you at the game this Friday."

The boosters started getting to their feet and moving toward the door. The low din of their conversation sounded like the hum of an angry beehive. Bobby walked with Joe Timmons and Willis Fullerton toward the door.

"Not everybody liked your call, coach," Fullerton said.

"I knew they wouldn't."

"You sure you're doing the right thing?" Timmons asked, his face unsmiling and tense.

"My job's to start the best man. I believe that's what I'm doing."

Ahead of them, Bobby saw Gerald Stedman and Art Bennett walking out the door together. The banker had his face turned toward Bennett, his eyes narrowed in anger. He made rapid little chopping motions with his hands as he talked. Bennett had his lips pressed tightly together. He kept shaking his head as if in disbelief. Neither of them looked back at Bobby.

On the parking lot, Ray Stewart caught up with Bobby as he walked toward his car.

"What made you decide on Brown, coach?"

"He moved the team better, Ray. I'm always gonna start the quarterback that moves the team best. And you can quote me on that."

"Thanks, coach. I'll do that."

Bobby hurried away from Stewart toward his car. Ahead of him, the same three men who had gone into the meeting before him were walking together. They were passing a flask around, each of them taking a long pull.

"Fellas, this day is a real milestone for this town," one of them said, his voice mock-solemn.

"How's that, Jim Ed?" another asked.

"It marks the day our team gave up gatorade for watermelon juice."

Bobby hung back to escape further malicious humor, then moved quickly to his car. As he opened the door, he saw Royal Brown getting into a late model red Buick several cars away. Brown nodded his head and Bobby raised his hand in acknowledgment.

◆

"Was it a pretty rough meeting?" Paula asked as Bobby walked in the front door. She searched his face with her eyes.

"They'll probably vote to fire me next week."

"How did Mr. Stedman take it?"

"Not very well. He walked out of the meeting with Art Bennett, and neither of them seemed to have anything to say to me."

"Next thing you know, they'll be making Bennett head coach." Paula raised one corner of her mouth disdainfully.

"He'd like that."

"What did Mike Proctor say?"

"I didn't talk to him, but he made a big point of being friendly to Terrance Brown's father."

"That's good. It doesn't hurt to have at least one prominent citizen on your side."

Bobby shook his head angrily. "He'd be easier to take if he'd quit acting like he owns both the team and me."

"You ought to be friendly to him. You're going to need all the allies you can get."

He shot a dark look at Paula. Why should she speak so warmly of Proctor and his influence?

"I probably 'oughta' do a lot of things I'm not gonna do."

"Hey, honey, lighten up. I'm on your side."

She came to him and put her arms around him, pressing her face against his chest.

"It's been a rough day," she said softly, "but you did the right thing, and whatever happens, I love you for it."

◆

For the rest of the week after the booster club meeting, Bobby worked under a dark cloud of disapproval. Principal Leon Purvis's overly cheerful face grew sullen and critical when he passed Bobby in the hall. The other teachers congregated in the teacher's lounge fell silent when Bobby came in to get a cup of coffee between classes.

At practice, the morale of the team suffered from the controversy. Rusty Stedman's friends made a big point of hustling out of the huddle and calling encouragement to him between plays, while refusing to show any spirit for Terrance Brown.

Freddie Alhamid, Curtis McInnes and Lee Shaughnessey seemed especially determined to make Brown look bad. They took Terrance's directions with studied lethargy, and executed the plays he called haphazardly. Coach Art Bennett went around the practice field grimfaced and unsmiling, speaking to Bobby only in disapproving monosyllables.

At the end of the Tuesday practice, Melvin Morris trotted to catch up with Bobby as the coaches followed the team toward the dressing room. He turned his creased, sun-darkened face sympathetically toward Bobby.

"Seems like half the team's trying to cockroach things up to make Terrance look bad."

"In spite of that, he still looks better than Rusty."

Morris nodded. "Rusty just doesn't have the coordination and judgment Terrance does. I just wish some of the boys would get over being pissed off and start working with him."

"It's not just the boys." Bobby nodded toward Coach Bennett trotting toward the dressing room ten yards ahead of them.

"You're right. A grown man ought not to be such a goddamn prima donna."

"In spite of the morale problems, I still think Terrance is the best man for the job."

"I'm with you, coach." Morris gave Bobby a thumbs up sign.

With Morris's support, Bobby felt more secure in his decision. If Morris had ever felt resentment because Bobby had the job he wanted, it had long since evaporated.

Not all the boys were trying to make Terrance Brown look bad. Stocky Ned Chambers played his center position with equal enthusiasm under both quarterbacks. The red-haired guard, Bill Foster, obliterated opposing linemen with the same cheerful intensity regardless of who was leading the team.

In spite of the morale problem, Bobby thought the team would pull together for the upcoming game against the Post Antelopes. This game would be the last non-district game before the team started its district schedule. The Antelopes were strongly rated, and a win against them would set the stage for district play.

After lunch on Friday, Bobby supervised the loading of the team and equipment into the two yellow Comanche Springs Independent School District buses that would take them more than one hundred miles west for the game at Post.

While Cheery O'Leery placidly loaded bags of equipment onto the buses, Bobby pulled Rusty to the side.

"I know you've been disappointed at not starting this week, Rusty, but the season's young. You'll have plenty of chances to beat Terrance out."

Stedman looked at Bobby with resentful blue eyes. "I'm better than Terrance and I'm gonna prove it to you."

"You do that. But in the meanwhile, let's all pull together as a team."

"I'm a team player, coach."

"Then prove it. Give Terrance your support this week."

"He's got my starting position."

"That's no excuse to cockroach up the team. Show some leadership. Encourage your buddies to play ball for Terrance."

Stedman looked at the ground with a bitter frown. "That's asking a lot, coach."

"You're a team player, remember?"

Grudgingly, Rusty nodded his head. "Okay, coach. You got it."

The boys laughed and joked with each other as the buses pulled onto the highway toward Post. Mesquite flats hemmed the road on either side. The West Texas landscape held little relief, and the billowing foliage of the mesquites looked like gentle waves in a light green sea.

As the miles passed, the players grew more subdued. Many of them stared pensively out the windows. Bobby felt a growing coldness in his own stomach. He was subject to the pre-game jitters, just like the boys. He would not have it any other way.

Finally, they rolled past the Post city limit sign, and into the outskirts of the town. Just to the west loomed the high escarpment of the caprock, marking the edge of the flat expanses of the high plains. They stopped at a cafe on the courthouse square, where Bobby had made arrangements for supper.

He admonished the boys to mind their manners, and they filed out of the buses and into the cafe, enduring gibes from a few young Antelope fans watching from the sidewalk.

"Take it easy, men," Bobby advised, when Ned Chambers and big Juan Guerrero showed signs of hostility in response to the catcalls.

After supper, they drove to the stadium on the edge of town. The team members carried their own uniforms inside, while Cheery O'Leery made several trips with the team's supplies. After the boys had rested for nearly an hour, they suited up and trotted out to the field.

Dusk had fallen, and the crisp, delicious smell of fall hung in the air. Across the field, the Post Antelopes warmed up, resplendent in their black and gold uniforms. As the coaches lined the players up for their drills, Bobby felt the nervous pull of his stomach muscles trying to knot.

He did calesthentics with the team, knowing he would loosen up once the action started. He paused for a few seconds to scan the stands on the Warrior side. Paula and Wanda Morris had planned to come to the game together, but Bobby could not spot them.

While Coach Morris and Coach Bennett ran the team through the plays, Bobby trotted to the far sideline, where he shook hands with the officials in their zebra-stripe outfits and with Buddy Rourke, the Antelope coach. Rourke had a small man's paunch, skinny shoulders, and a good-humored Irish face. Bobby had met him before when Post had played Lamesa.

"Which one of those quarterbacks you gonna start, Coach Thompson?" Rourke's matter-of-fact tone implied that he knew all there was to know about the Warrior team.

"Well, I dunno, Coach Rourke." Bobby scratched his head as if he were confused. "Looks like your scouts have you pretty well informed. Which one would you start?"

Rourke gave a deep shrug of his shoulders and screwed his face up in a disparaging expression.

"Doesn't make much difference to us, coach. We're ready for either one of them."

The Warriors won the toss, and elected to receive. Because of a light breeze from the north, the Antelopes chose to defend the north goal, so the Warriors would have to run and pass into the wind for the first quarter. The teams would change goal lines they defended at the end of each quarter, so any advantage from the wind would even out in the course of the game.

The Antelope kicker kicked a high, end-over-ender that came down into the arms of Joe King, who made a nice runback to the Warrior forty yard line before going down, leaving the Warriors in possession of the ball sixty yards from a touchdown.

When Terrance Brown raised his hands to form the huddle, a few jeers and catcalls came from the Antelope stands.

"Go back to Africa!"

"No gorillas allowed."

Ignoring the hecklers, Terrance quickly formed a huddle and brought the team to the line of scrimmage for the first play. In quick succession, he ran plays to the left and right sides of the line, giving the ball first to Joe King, then to Curtis McInnes, for good gains. Under Terrance's tutelage, the team marched straight down the field and scored with a dive over the goal line by McAlpin from the two-yard line. Alhamid kicked the extra point and Warriors led, 7-0.

The Antelopes took the kickoff back to midfield, but could not get any offense going, and had to punt on fourth down. McInnes made a good return to near midfield, and Terrance took charge again.

The Warriors made two first downs, then almost fizzled out on the Antelope thirty. A hugh Antelope tackle broke through the line, dumping Terrance for a loss before he could get a play going, bringing up fourth down with long yardage for a first.

On the next play, Terrance took the ball and ran parallel to the right side of the line in an option play that gave him the choice of either keeping the ball, pitching it to another back, or throwing it downfield to one of the ends. Just when it seemed certain he would keep the ball himself and cut upfield, he braced and got off a spiral pass that Joe King caught without breaking stride. King outdistanced the defenders for the touchdown.

Melvin Morris stomped his feet in enthusiasm. He put his fingers in his mouth and blasted out a loud, shrill whistle.

"I didn't know you could do that, Mel," Bobby said, amused at Morris's uncharacteristic enthusiasm.

"I only do it when there's something to be excited about."

The Warriors made the extra point to lead 14-0. The game quickly became a rout. Comanche Springs made another touchdown and extra point before the half, and the team went into the dressing room at midgame confident and exuberant.

With the team so far ahead, Bobby started Rusty Stedman and some other second-string players in the second half. Stedman took the team down the field to score once in the third quarter, and threw a long arching pass to Lee Shaugnessey, the short, sandy-haired left end, for another touchdown in the fourth quarter.

The Antelopes rallied late in the game for two quick touchdowns and extra points, but it was too late to catch up. The game ended with the score 35-14 as the Warrior third-string, quarterbacked by little Rob Wilson, threatened to score again.

Amid the cheering of the Warrior fans, Bobby trotted across the field to shake hands with Buddy Rourke, who gave Bobby a rueful grin.

"You gave us a good country lickin', coach."

"Another day, you might do the same to us."

"We'll do that very thing next year. Will that black quarterback be back?"

"Sure will."

"Tell him I said he played a fine game."

Later, riding back along the lonesome Texas highway in the darkened bus with his team, Bobby felt an exhilarating happiness. His team had won a great victory with Terrance Brown as starting quarterback. He had crossed a major hurdle.

SIX

On Tuesday of the week after the game with Post, Paula met Bobby at the door as he came home from practice. She kissed him lightly on the lips as he came into the living room. Her green eyes hinted at secret information.

"Guess what happened today."

"What?" he answered playfully.

"Guess."

"You won that sweepstakes you entered?"

"Nothing that dramatic."

"You wrecked your car?"

"It wasn't something bad."

"One of your old boyfriends called?"

"No, silly. I haven't talked to any of them in years."

"I give up then."

Her eyes brightened with anticipation. "I"m going to start teaching in two days."

"That's good. Too bad it won't be but for a few days."

"It'll be for the rest of the year," Paula said exultantly.

"It's not a substitute job?"

"No. One of the teachers at the middle school just quit to go take care of her sick mother in Midland. Purvis called and offered me the job. I'm going to be teaching seventh- and eighth-grade English for the rest of the year."

"Ugh. Seventh- and eighth-grade. Those kids have the attention spans of chimpanzees. Sure you can stand it?"

"It's not my pick of assignments, but it sure beats part-time substituting."

Bobby felt glad for Paula and glad for himself. The regular job would mean more money, and might take Paula's mind away from her dissatisfaction at the move to Comanche Springs.

He pulled her to him and held her tight. He could feel the beating of her heart through her breasts pressed against his chest. He felt a sudden tenderness for her.

"I know it's been hard just sitting around the house all these weeks."

She turned her face up toward him, happy tears in her eyes. He reached up and brushed several strands of shining, red-blonde hair from her face, then kissed her. She put her head against his chest.

"It's not law school, but at least I'll be doing something useful again."

Two days later, Paula got up before Bobby, showered, and dressed herself with meticulous care. When Bobby stumbled into the kitchen for his first cup of coffee, she sat at the kitchen table wearing a sensible grey skirt, with a matching grey sweater over a white blouse. Lipstick of subdued red accented her lips and her hair curved in an imposing red-blonde wave above her forehead.

Bobby gave her an approving look. "You look great. I hope the little bastards appreciate you."

She returned a confident smile. "When they're that age, they don't appreciate anyone, but I can handle them."

"I know you can."

Bobby thought of all the people who would see Paula in her new job. He secretly felt jealousy toward the male teachers, and feared what they would say among themselves about her in the teacher's lounge. He feared her contact with other men; their suggestive looks, the temptations they might present. He knew he had no right to keep her to himself, but he secretly wished she would stay home and out of harm's way. He knew better than to suggest such a thing to her, however.

After breakfast, they left the house together. Bobby locked the door behind them. Paula drove off ahead of him in her old Chevrolet, with a wave and a bright smile over her shoulder. He drove toward the high school in his pickup, glad on the one hand that she would be working, but fearful of her increased contact with other men.

When he got home after practice, Paula's car was parked in the driveway. He smelled pizza as he entered the house. In the kitchen, Paula had set two places on either side of a familiar-looking flat pizza box. She came into the kitchen from the back part of the house, now changed into blue jeans and a sweatshirt.

"I guess this is the end of the home-cooked meals," Bobby said, with humorous sarcasm.

"If you want home-cooking, you might try your hand at a pot roast tomorrow." She stuck out her tongue at him.

"I'm not complaining. I love pizza." He went to the ice box and got out a canned Coca-Cola.

"Bring me one, too."

He got out another and took the two drinks to the table, where they both sat down to eat the pizza.

He quizzed her with his eyes.

She gave him a rueful look. "They tested me pretty well. Some of the boys threw spitballs at each other, half the kids in class talked incessantly, and I had to send a girl to the office at recess for pulling up her dress in front of a bunch of boys."

"Sounds like a normal group of seventh- and eighth-graders."

"It sure was, but I was getting the hang of how to handle them by the end of the day. I kept some of the spitball-throwers after school and read them the riot act. They didn't like it when I told them I'd be calling their parents if they didn't straighten up. I think things will go smoother when they all see I mean business."

"How are they at conjugating verbs?"

"So-so, but they'll get better at it once I get control of them."

"Sounds to me like you kind of enjoyed it."

"It's going to be a challenge, but I think I'm going to like it."

Paula's voice held more animation and interest than Bobby had heard from her since the move to Comanche Springs. She had been a good high school history teacher at Lamesa, and Bobby felt sure she would excel with the more difficult demands of teaching English grammar to middle school students.

Bobby knew she'd never be happy staying home. This new teaching job might satisfy her need for challenge for the time being, but he knew one day soon, he'd have to make good on his promise to move to a place where she could go to law school. Hers was not a character to give up a dream easily; their marriage probably wouldn't survive a prolonged failure to accommodate her plans.

◆

The next Friday, the Warriors played their first district game against the Stephenville Yellowjackets, in the pretty town of Stephenville, seventy miles southwest of Fort Worth. The Yellowjackets were not highly rated, but Bobby took nothing for granted.

In his pre-game pep talk, he told the boys to forget the good start they had made in non-district play by beating Jacksboro and Post. Those games were in the past. The Stephenville game was the first that counted for anything, and to go back to Comanche Springs and hold their heads up, they had to win it.

The Yellowjackets played well the first half, holding the Warriors to one touchdown and almost scoring themselves near the end of the second quarter. Terrance Brown started off playing erratically, calling plays that didn't make sense, throwing away passes, and stumbling several times behind the line of scrimmage on option plays before he got rid of the ball.

But he looked good on the Warriors' lone touchdown, throwing a long, perfectly spiraling pass to Lee Shaughnessey, who caught it at full speed and raced into the Yellowjacket end zone yards ahead of the nearest defender.

The next time the Warriors got the ball, Terrance bobbled the snap from center on second down. The ball bounced free for several seconds, until one of the Yellowjacket linemen covered it with a low dive across the line of scrimmage.

Inspired by the recovery, the Yellowjackets marched down the field to a position inside the Warrior's ten-yard line. Bobby felt sure the Yellowjackets would score, but Albert Walker, the savage black lineman, knocked the Yellowjacket quarterback loose from the ball, then recovered it with only a few minutes to go before the half.

Bobby sent in word for Terrance to play it safe, and the Warriors ran out the clock with a couple of straight-ahead dives through the line by fullback Rutherford McAlpin and halfback Curtis McInnes. Coach Art Bennett trotted beside Bobby as they followed the team to the dressing room for the half.

"Don't you think we'd better try Rusty at quarterback for a while? Terrance's looking pretty weak tonight."

"You may be right. I'll start Terrance again next half, but if he doesn't play better, we'll put Rusty in."

"It may be too late by then."

Bobby held his irritation in check with difficulty. Coach Bennett never had anything good to say about Terrance Brown, even when he played superlatively, and every time Terrance looked a little weak, Bennett wanted to replace him immediately.

"I think Terrance will straighten up," Bobby said. "If he doesn't, we'll put Rusty in."

"You're the boss." Bennett trotted ahead of Bobby to the dressing room.

Bobby watched Terrance closely at the start of the second half. He knew he should not bow to pressure from Art Bennett, but he also knew if Terrance did not improve soon, it would be time to replace him with Rusty. He need not have worried.

Terrance found himself during the second half. On the Warrior's first possession, he ran two nearly perfect option handoffs to McAlpin and McInnes, both for long yardage, then threw a thirty-yard pass to the tall end, Eddie Ritterman, who caught the ball on the run for a touchdown.

The Warriors kicked to the Yellowjackets, who ran a couple of runs up the middle of the line, then sputtered out and had to punt on fourth down. Back in the game at quarterback, Terrance went down on bended knee in the huddle, gesticulating with his hands as he called the play.

With a cocky smile, he rose to his feet, snapped his fingers and the team trotted briskly to the line of scrimmage. Terrance did a little stutter with his feet as he moved up behind the center.

He fell back to pass as the ends, Ritterman and Shaugnessey, sprinted down the field, followed by the halfbacks, King and McInnes, who slanted down the field, crossing each other's paths in the middle of the Yellowjacket backfield.

"Not very smart, throwing a long pass on first down," Art Bennett muttered in Bobby's ear.

Bobby nodded, knowing the play held risks the team ought not to be taking. But Terrance threw the ball in another high spiral that came down perfectly into Ritterman's outstretched hands for another touchdown.

After the two quick Warrior scores, the Yellowjackets could not even make a first down, and had to punt every time they got possession. In the third quarter, the Warriors scored every time they got the ball, and as the score mounted, Terrance Brown strutted a little more as he led the team to the line of scrimmage after the huddles.

His voice took on an insolent note as he barked the signals.

Before each play, he raised up above the center and looked over the beleaguered Yellowjacket players across from him, grinning contemptuously at them.

When the score reached 28-0, Bobby called Terrance and the rest of the first-string out of the game and substituted Rusty Stedman and the second-string team. Terrance grinned at Bobby as he trotted off the field.

"How we lookin', coach?"

"Great, Terrance! Just great!"

The fresh second-string scored two quick touchdowns against the demoralized Yellowjackets, and Bobby substituted Rob Wilson, the sawed-off junior, at quarterback, along with several other third-string backs and linemen. Even the ragtag third-string moved strongly against the weary Yellowjackets, with Wilson scoring on a keeper play midway through the fourth quarter.

Finally, the game ended with the score 49 to 0. Bobby felt sorry for Billy Tolbert, the Yellowjacket coach, as he trotted across the field to shake his hand. Tolbert, a young man with an appealing boyish face, took Bobby's hand reluctantly.

"You didn't have to run up the score so much, coach." He looked at Bobby with resentful eyes.

"I didn't try to, Coach Tolbert. We played the second- and third-string the last quarter."

"Thanks for nothing, coach," Tolbert said bitterly.

"There's no call for you to be mad. All we did was play to win."

"Oh yes, I'm sure everything was on the up-and-up, even down to that smartass black quarterback of yours. Where'd he come from anyway?"

Bobby felt his temperature rising. "He enrolled in school and came out for the team, just like all the other players."

"Sure he did, coach." Tolbert spun away without further word and followed his dejected players toward their dressing room. Bobby trotted back across the field, where he joined Coach Morris at the Warrior bench.

"Tolbert is sure being a crybaby. He claimed we intentionally ran up the score."

Melvin Morris shook his head sadly. "We embarrassed him pretty bad tonight. It'll take time for him to get over it."

As Bobby walked back to the dressing room with Morris, he

reflected on Coach Tolbert's resentment. Bobby knew the bitter experience of loss, and how easy it was to wrongfully blame the victor for winning. He'd had thoughts like that after losing a game. But there had been a dimension to the bitterness in Tolbert's voice and face that went beyond the temporary resentments Bobby had experienced. Had he made an enemy for life of Tolbert?

◆

On the Saturday morning after the game, Bobby called his father on the phone. Bobby had only called Bill a few times since he and Paula had moved to Comanche Springs. Talking to his father forced him to visualize the small, paint-peeled house of his childhood, and the lonely, arthritis-crippled old man who lived alone there in his retirement from the refinery. Bobby let the phone ring ten times. Just when he decided no one was home and started to hang up, someone picked up the receiver on the other end.

"Hello?" Bill sounded hung over and irritated.

"Hi Dad, it's me."

"You're calling awful early."

"It's almost eleven o'clock."

"I didn't know it was so late."

"Did you have a rough night?"

Bill laughed bitterly. "They're all rough, these days."

"I wanted to call to check on you."

"What's there to check on?"

"I worry about you."

"Don't waste your time."

"Heard from Linda lately?"

Bobby's sister Linda, trapped in Amarillo by a bad marriage to a used-car salesman and two squalling kids, periodically drove up to Borger to visit Bill.

"She was here last weekend, but she didn't stay long."

"How's she doing?"

"Still talking divorce, but not doing anything about it."

"We won our game last night."

"That's good. How are you liking the new job?"

"It's fine."

"I'm glad you're doing so good."

"Anything I can do for you?"

"Nope. I can take care of myself."

"I'll call you again in a couple of weeks."

"I'll be here."

Bobby hung up and sat by the phone for several minutes, churning with the same frustration he always felt after a conversation with his father.

At least he could still talk to Bill, which was more than he could say for his mother, Loraine. Her mind burned out by a stroke, she couldn't recognize anyone, and required custodial care in a nursing home in Amarillo. Anger still gnawed at Bobby when he recalled how she had left home, taking Linda with her, to divorce Bill and marry a toolpusher named Red Williams. That had been just before Bobby started high school.

She paid for it, though, Bobby told himself. Red abandoned her in less than a year, leaving her to raise Linda on her earnings as a waitress and what little child support Bill sent her. The hard life took its toll. She smoked too much and grew fat, finally suffering the stroke that had effectively ended her life at the age of fifty-three.

Linda took care of Loraine's needs and visited her in the nursing home several times a month. Bobby got by once or twice a year, although there was little point in going at all, since his mother couldn't recognize him.

She cost me my dad, Bobby thought, remembering how Bill had changed after Loraine left. We never went fishing after that. And he only came to a few of the games, even after I got to be a star. All he could think about was his beer. A six-pack almost every night, and more on Fridays and Saturdays. It's a wonder he hasn't killed himself.

In the bitterness of their separation, his mother and father had no room for him in their narrow lives. His little sister, Linda, grew up apart from him, a virtual stranger. In his hunger to belong, he turned to Coach Mattingly and the game of football. And now, even his surrogate father was gone, killed two years earlier in a head-on collision on the way to Lubbock for a coaches' conference.

I've still got Paula, Bobby thought, but for how long? When she leaves, I'll be all by myself. Maybe some men are just meant to be that way. Angry at himself for the tears in his eyes, Bobby pushed himself up from the chair by the telephone and walked purposefully out to the garage to fill the lawnmower with gas and mow the lawn.

◆

Mike Proctor called Bobby on the phone the Sunday after the Stephenville game to ask Bobby and Paula to have dinner with the Proctors at the Comanche Springs Country Club that Wednesday. Proctor's tone in extending the invitation had an imperious, condescending quality Bobby resented. He started to make excuses, then thought better of it, and told Proctor he would call him back after talking to Paula.

Paula had driven to a convenience store. When she got back to the house, Bobby told her about the invitation.

"I don't really want to go. I get mad at Proctor almost every time I talk to him."

Paula arched her eyebrows in a worldly look. "A head coach has to be a kind of diplomat. Look on it as a little necessary diplomacy."

"Looks to me like you want to go whether I do or not."

Paula shrugged her shoulders. "What if I do? We don't get that many shots at a free dinner at the country club."

Bobby shook his head in disgust and went to the phone to call Proctor back.

◆

On Wednesday night, the Proctors met Bobby and Paula in the foyer of the country club, just as the sun slipped beyond the crest of the hill rising behind the building, casting a multi-hued pink haze into the sky that swiftly faded to darkness.

Proctor wore a light-brown sports jacket and a button-down shirt with a red-striped tie. Elizabeth Proctor seemed perfectly dressed in a straight-lined skirt and filmy blouse. She held her mouth in a tightly-compressed line that made her look cold to the point of being in pain.

Proctor led them to a private dining room overlooking the golf course, where a few late golfers were making their way toward the clubhouse. Proctor nodded toward the men coming in.

"Some of these guys would play all night, if we'd light the course."

"There're fanatics in every sport," Bobby said.

They had drinks before sitting down to the dinner. Proctor ordered rack of lamb for the main course. Bobby had to concentrate to keep from wrinkling his nose as he helped himself to several of the little ribs with their odoriferous burden of meat. Paula shot him a sympathetic look. She knew he couldn't stand lamb. Proctor beamed a cherubic look around the table as he poured everybody more wine.

"Isn't this great? Lamb wasn't even on the menu until I asked them to add it. I bet there's not another country club in West Texas between Midland and Fort Worth that serves it."

"Not much demand for it, where I come from," Bobby said gruffly.

Paula kicked him under the table.

"I'm sorry," Proctor said, with an obviously insincere tone of sudden understanding, "I should have known a guy from Borger wouldn't like lamb. I'll order you a steak."

"That's okay. It's real good. I just don't eat much of it."

"You sure it's all right?" Proctor asked solicitously. "I'd be glad to get you a steak."

"It's just fine."

Proctor turned to Paula. "Do you like the lamb?"

Paula laughed. "Sure. In the country clubs of North Dallas, we ate little else."

Proctor grinned familiarly at her. "I guess lamb is kind of a big-city dish, at least down here in Texas."

Elizabeth Proctor's tightly-drawn face displayed chilly disapproval. "Haven't we worn out the subject of lamb?"

Bobby echoed the sentiment inwardly, but said nothing. Proctor flashed quick anger at his wife with his eyes.

"I suppose so, darling. What would you like to talk about?"

Elizabeth turned down her mouth in contempt. "Nothing that would be of much interest here."

Proctor bit his lips and the color in his cheeks heightened. Bobby wished he were somewhere else. He had no desire to witness a quarrel between the Proctors.

"Didn't the team look good last Friday against Stephenville?" Paula interjected diplomatically.

Proctor turned toward her, forcing a smile as he studiously avoided looking at his wife. Elizabeth picked up her wine glass and sipped at it, looking haughtily out the window.

"They looked just great," Proctor said, his voice gushing with enthusiasm. "Terrance Brown played his best game yet. I think your husband deserves a lot of credit for his courage in starting Terrance even in the face of a lot of opposition." Proctor turned toward Bobby with a patronizing smile.

An almost intolerable resentment welled up inside Bobby. Proctor had just congratulated him for doing what Proctor had urged him to do all along. Disguised in the false compliment was a message that Bobby had acted foolishly in not following Proctor's advice in the first place. Proctor had deliberately made the hypocrisy more galling by directing it to Bobby through a remark made in a familiar tone to Paula.

"I just play the best players I can find," Bobby said, his voice sullen. "Anyone who doesn't like what I do can go to hell." He gave Proctor a pointed look.

Proctor smiled back disingenuously. "That's the spirit. I like a man who follows his own path--does his own thing, as the saying goes."

"That's one thing about Bobby," Paula said, tossing back her curl of light-red hair, "he's his own man to the core."

The tension in Paula'a voice told Bobby she understood his anger, but he resented the smile she gave Proctor with her eyes.

Proctor smiled back at her. "I really appreciate that quality in your husband. For my money, he's the best coach we've ever had in this town."

Again, the compliment had the ring of an insult, but Bobby saw little point in further verbal sparring.

"I sure appreciate your confidence in me," he said, giving his voice a tone of self-deprecation as he reached for the wine bottle.

Shortly afterward, he made excuses that the next day was a school day, and he and Paula got up to leave. Paula thanked Proctor for inviting them. Bobby couldn't bring himself to echo her words.

Elizabeth Proctor favored them with a chilly smile. "We'll have to get together again one of these days."

Paula made the proper response: "We'd love to."

On the parking lot, Bobby opened the car door for Paula, then got in himself. "Do you really want to socialize again with that iceberg?"

Paula gave her head a little shake. "Can't say that I do, but it never hurts to tend neighborly fences."

"I'll leave that sort of thing to you." Savagely, he jabbed the key in the ignition and started the car for the drive home.

◆

The success against Stephenville had stilled Bobby's critics in the booster club for the time being. The team had looked so good no one could now suggest that Rusty Stedman should be starting instead of Terrance. On the practice field, Art Bennett kept his criticism to himself, and even congratulated Terrance from time to time.

Bobby knew Bennett and the others would become vocal again if Terrance made a bad slip, or played a poor game. In the meanwhile, Bobby welcomed the respite from tension and concentrated on honing the team's skills for the next game.

Several days after the dinner with the Proctors, during the middle of his ten o'clock algebra class, Bobby suddenly remembered he had left his playbook on the kitchen sink at home. He would need it during the afternoon practice to teach the team some new plays he had worked up the night before.

At lunch, he drove home in his pickup. Several mild cool fronts had mitigated the summer-strong heat of September, ushering in the languid warmth of Indian summer. Brown-edged leaves fell from the trees into the street, and the green grass of the lawns had a tired, declining look. The empty house seemed fearsome and lonely without Paula's presence. Bobby walked quickly to the kitchen, picked up the playbook, and went back to the truck.

He drove to the McKeever Steakhouse, thinking he would get a quick hamburger instead of chancing what would be left on the serving line in the school cafeteria. He parked his car and started for the door. Halfway across the parking lot toward the green-shuttered cafe, he noticed Paula's Chevrolet parked in the first line of cars near the door.

A quick, cold sense of something amiss clutched at him. He had assumed Paula always ate at school, like he usually did. She had not told him of going out to lunch before. He opened the door of the restaurant and walked in, searching the room with his eyes.

He spotted her sitting at the far side of the room, her lovely face turned in profile to him. Across the table from her sat Mike Proctor. As Bobby watched, Proctor said something with an ingratiating grin on his pink-cheeked face, and Paula threw her head back in an intimate laugh, with a toss of her strawberry-blonde hair.

Bobby read a world of meaning into the look that passed between his wife and Proctor. Quickly, he stepped behind a supporting column, so neither Paula nor Proctor could see him. One of the fresh-faced waitresses approached with a menu in her hands, wearing a welcoming smile on her young, freckled face.

"You need a table, sir?"

"I don't believe so. I was looking for a friend. Doesn't look like he's here."

"Well, have a good day." The girl turned and walked away.

Bobby stood behind the column, trying to decide what to do. He rejected the idea of approaching the pair. It seemed there could be no innocent explanation for the look he had just seen pass between them. He could not stand the thought of listening to Proctor's bland, condescending voice as he made up some lie about the meeting.

Bobby turned and walked to the door, keeping the column between the table where the pair sat and himself. Outside, be blinked in the bright sunshine as he walked toward his truck. His mind churned frantically, seeking the meaning of what he had just seen.

He passed Paula's Chevrolet, and, for the first time, noticed Proctor's big, gold-trimmed Town Car parked a few cars from it. With their cars so close, Bobby felt sure they had intentionally met each other at the restaurant. A cold feeling hit him in the pit of his stomach. What business did his wife have leaving school to have lunch with Mike Proctor?

He drove back to the school, oblivious to the fall scenery. He went to his classroom without eating lunch and stood staring out the window with his hands behind his back, painting increasingly darker mental pictures of the relation between his wife and Mike Proctor, until the first students started filtering into the room for his first afternoon math class.

All that afternoon, Bobby could hardly keep his mind on his teaching. He found himself stopping suddenly in the middle of explaining problems at the blackboard, his train of thought suddenly submerged in visions of Paula's face sharing an intimate look with Proctor. It didn't take long for the students to notice Bobby's preoccupation.

"It ain't that hard a problem, is it coach?" Cheery O'Leery asked laconically, after Bobby had stood before the board for several seconds, chalk poised in the air, the solution to the problem lost in the maze of his mind.

Bobby's consciousness snapped back to the classroom and he turned to face the class. "We all get stumped sometimes, Cheery." He forced an unfelt brightness into his voice as he started over with his explanation.

Even during the practice that afternoon, he could not concentrate on the play. He kept finding himself staring off across the fence into the pasture on the far side of the practice field, his mind lost to what the players were doing.

"You feel okay, Bobby?" Melvin Morris asked, his tobacco-plug face screwed up in concern.

"I'm a little preoccupied today, Mel. Got a little headache."

When the time came for the scrimmage between the first and second teams, Bobby turned the practice over to Art Bennett, and made a show of being interested without really contributing anything to the coaching.

At the end of the practice, Bobby showered quickly, changed to his street clothes, and drove slowly toward home in the pickup, wondering how to broach his worries to Paula. All she'd done was have lunch in a very public restaurant with a man they both knew. Bobby told himself it was not the fact she'd had lunch with Proctor that bothered him. His worries lay in that look he'd seen them exchange.

Bobby parked in the drive and went apprehensively into the house. He walked into the kitchen, where Paula stood at the stove frying hamburgers. Bobby came up behind her and kissed her on the nape of her neck.

"How was your day?" he asked softly, feeling the depth of his love for her in the pain caused by his suspicions.

She shrugged her shoulders. "It went okay. Should I open a can of beans to go with these hamburgers?"

Bobby shook his head. "Just open some potato chips." He went to the bedroom to change clothes.

At supper, Bobby sat across from Paula as he fixed his hamburger, wondering whether he should ask what she'd done at lunch. He feared her answer. So long as he asked no questions, he could still believe the lunch with Mike Proctor had been a chance meeting. If he asked and she lied about it, he could only assume the worst.

Bobby took a bite of the hamburger he had fixed. It seemed tasteless. He studied his wife's voluptuous body, her full lips, her shining hair. She and Proctor made a handsome couple. A woman like Paula just naturally looked better with a prosperous, handsome man like Proctor than she did with an unfinished bumpkin like himself. She should have married a guy like Proctor in the first place, instead of someone like Bobby who would never be more than a high school football coach, with all the financial insecurities implicit in the job.

In addition to giving Paula a standard of living equal to that of her parents, Proctor could give her the baby she wanted. Bobby's vision seemed clear. Inevitably, he was meant to lose Paula's love, and Proctor had come along at the right time to steal her from him.

"Why so solemn?" Paula suddenly asked.

Bobby looked up at her. She was looking at him with a little quizzical grin, her eyes luminous and warm.

"I was just thinking about something."

"Did something go wrong today at school?"

"It's not that."

"I understand the practices have been going really well this week. I had lunch with Mike Proctor today, and he told me all the bitching about Terrance Brown has pretty well stopped, after that great game he played at Stephenville."

Relief coursed through Bobby's soul. Paula would not have mentioned her meeting if she had reason to feel guilty about it. Bobby knew his face showed his sudden change of mood, and he bent over his plate to conceal his expression.

"That's right," he said, making his voice matter of fact, "most of the complaining's stopped. How'd you come to have lunch with Proctor?"

"He came by the school on school board business. We ran into each other in the hall and decided to go have a sandwich at McKeever's."

"Isn't the school cafeteria food good enough for you?"

"I eat it every day, but it sure was nice to get away from it for a change."

Bobby studied her face for signs of insincerity. She had an open, guileless look and she smiled the fond little satirical smile she had worn during their intimate conversations for all the years of their marriage. He sensed no duplicity.

Now convinced that there was nothing between Paula and Mike Proctor, Bobby felt rising anger at Proctor's presumption in asking Paula to have lunch with him.

"I don't like the idea of that son of a bitch having lunch with you."

Paula stopped smiling. She shrugged her shoulders in quick irritation.

"What's the harm in it?"

"It just makes me mad for him to think he's got a right to ask you to lunch."

"I've got a few rights myself." Paula drew herself straight in her chair. "After all the weeks I've spent cooped up in this house, I've got a right to talk to someone besides you for a change."

"I wouldn't ask his wife to have lunch with me." Bobby held his hands in his lap under the table, clenching and unclenching them.

Paula smiled grimly. "You wouldn't want to socialize with that iceberg anyway, would you?" She mocked Bobby with his own description of Elizabeth Proctor.

"Goddamn it, Paula, that's not the point," Bobby exploded, getting up from his chair so suddenly it crashed to the floor behind him.

"Watch it, big boy!" Paula said in sultry voice. She looked up at him with a cool smile.

Bobby felt an urge to hit her. In all the years of their marriage, he had never hit Paula.

"Don't you see how it makes me feel to think of you having lunch with Proctor?" he asked, holding his hands before him with the fingers spread in exasperation.

The mocking smile faded from Paula's face. "I didn't know you disliked him so much."

"I've never made any bones about it, have I?"

"No, I guess you haven't. Somehow, I didn't think you were serious."

"I'm serious all right. I hate the man's guts."

"Why?" Paula probed his face with her green eyes.

"For one thing, he's a rich boy." Bobby spat out the words.

"That's not a reason to hate him."

"He's a rich boy with a smart mouth who thinks he owns everybody, including me, and I can't stand to think of him messing around with my wife behind my back."

"We weren't exactly messing around," Paula said with dark humor. "All I did was eat lunch with the man. I can't really understand why you dislike him so much. He's always been charming to me."

Bobby thought his head would explode. "Goddamn it, Paula, that's just the point! He's charming to you just to spite me. He'd like nothing better than to fuck you, just to prove he can do it."

Paula's face went cold. "You crude bastard! Don't take out your insecurity by talking dirty to me."

Bobby wiped angry, frustrated tears from his eyes. "I'm sorry. That was uncalled for. But it does seem to me that's how Proctor is."

"So what am I supposed to do about it?" She got up from the table and stood several steps from him, hands on her hips, fixing him with her angry eyes.

"Next time he asks you to have lunch, turn him down."

"I should pass up a free lunch just to cater to your insecurity?"

Bobby shook his head in chagrin. "Don't make a joke of this Paula. Don't mess with the bastard."

"I'll give the matter some thought." She turned away and walked to the sink, where she made the dishes clatter angrily as she rinsed them to put in the dishwasher.

For the rest of the evening, they did not speak. Bobby stared at several shows on the television without paying any attention to them, stared vacantly at the ten o'clock news, then went into the bedroom to get ready for bed.

Paula lay on the far side of the bed, her face away from Bobby. He knew from the tautness of her body that she was not asleep. She didn't move or speak as he undressed and put on his pajamas. He turned out the light and lay on the bed, keeping to his own side, staying as far from her anger as he could.

SEVEN

The next morning, Bobby got up before Paula and went into the bathroom to shave. When he came out, she sat before the mirror on the dresser, putting on her makeup. Bobby saw her half-finished face reflected in the mirror. He tried to catch her eye, but she stared into the mirror at herself, studiously ignoring Bobby's image next to hers.

"Good morning," Bobby said, in a friendly, conciliatory tone.

Paula bent forward toward the mirror, giving all her attention to the lipstick she was putting on.

He gave an exaggerated shrug into the mirror, went out into the kitchen, and fixed himself a bowl of cereal. In a few minutes, Paula came into the kitchen, looking past where Bobby sat at the table as though he weren't there.

"Ease up, Paula." Bobby heard the growing irritation in his voice.

She fixed stern eyes on him. "What makes you think I want to talk to you?"

"I just thought it might be nice for us to acknowledge each other's presence before going to work."

"Well, I'll acknowledge your presence, but I don't care anything about chitchatting with you this morning. If I can't talk with who I want to, I just won't talk to anyone."

"I never said you couldn't talk to who you wanted to."

"You said I can't talk to Mike Proctor."

"I just said not to go out with him."

"Eating lunch with a man is not going out with him."

"For Christ's sake, Paula, can't you understand how I feel about the son of a bitch?"

She shook her head violently. "No Bobby, I really can't."

"Don't you know what people might think?"

"Have I ever cared what people thought?"

"You ought to."

"Anyone who doesn't like who I eat lunch with can go to hell." She let her eyes blaze at him.

Bobby decided to change tactics. "Okay, I give up. You can eat lunch with the bastard if you want. Just remember how I feel about it."

She gave him a scornful, bitter look. "So now I can eat lunch with him, but I'm supposed to feel guilty?"

"How you feel about it is up to you."

"Thanks for giving me such wonderful latitude." She looked at her watch. "I have to get going." She picked up her keys from the kitchen counter.

He followed her as she walked toward the front door. "Paula! Let's not stay mad like this."

"You started it!"

"I know it. I'm sorry."

Her face softened, and she turned toward him. They embraced, and he tried to kiss her.

"Not now. You'll mess up my lipstick."

"I'm sorry for what I said."

She smiled wanly at him. "I won't eat lunch with Proctor again. But I just can't stand to have anyone tell me I can't do something."

"I know. You've always been like that."

She brushed his lips with hers. "See you tonight." She turned toward the door.

Bobby heard her car start and back out of the driveway. He gathered together his playbook and teaching materials and went out to his truck. Although their differences had been mended for the moment, he had misgivings about this quarrel. He could not purge from his mind the intimate look he had seen pass between Paula and Mike Proctor in the restaurant.

◆

During the afternoon practice, Bobby submerged his lingering resentment in the heat and excitement of preparing his team for the game the coming Friday against the Graham Steers. The game would be the Warriors' second in district play.

Graham had a strong team, rated second in the district by most of the sportswriters, right behind the Warrior's archrival, the

Breckenridge Buckaroos. Even though the sportswriters had only rated his team third, Bobby knew his boys could beat Graham, then go on to win the rest of their games, including the final game against the Buckaroos.

During the scrimmage that afternoon, Terrance Brown projected supreme confidence, controlling the cadence of the practice with flawlessly executed plays. He ran powerful slants and traps behind strong blocking from the line. He ran snappy options to the halfbacks, and threw precision passes to the ends.

Other members of the team were living up to their preseason promise. Rutherford McAlpin had gained ten pounds since the season began, at the same time increasing his speed. Once he got through the line, he plowed down the field with tremendous power, frequently carrying several would-be tacklers with him. He would surely be an all-district choice, and might even make the all-state team.

Ned Chambers, now shorn of his summer flab, had become a superb center and linebacker. On defense, he made tackles all over the field, intercepted passes, and recovered more fumbles than all the linemen put together. On offense, he cleared wide holes up the middle for the backs, and centered the ball in a low, sure spiral. Chambers was a strong contender for all-district honors along with McAlpin.

The other linemen--scrappy, red-haired Bill Foster and olive-hued Freddie Alhamid at guards, 270 pound Juan Guerrero and the snake-mean black weightlifter, Albert Walker, at tackles, and tall, sticky-fingered Eddie Ritterman and the quick, sure blocker, Lee Shaugnessey, at ends--made a strong front wall, although none of them had all-state potential. The pretty boy, Curtis McInnes, and fast, fearful Joe King had improved strongly in their halfback positions.

Bobby left the practice that day with the feeling that he had never seen the team look sharper. He didn't care what the sportswriters thought, the Warriors would beat Graham on Friday. His elation took his mind away from his morbid fears about Paula and Mike Proctor. He went home and spent a happy evening finetuning the plays in his playbook, preparing for the game Friday, while Paula sat at the kitchen table planning her lessons for the next day.

◆

The Thursday before the Graham game, Bobby went to the athletic office in the fieldhouse on the lunch hour to see whether Cheery O'Leery had washed the jerseys for the game the next day. Bobby found the clean jerseys neatly stacked in the locker-room. He went into his office to check the mail.

A long envelope with the bright blue logo of the Texas Interscholastic League lay on top of the stack of mail delivered from the school office earlier in the morning. The Interscholastic League, headquartered in the State Capitol of Austin, regulated high school athletics throughout the state.

Standing at his desk, Bobby put a pencil into the flap of the envelope, tore it open, and took out and read the letter inside.

"Son of a bitch!" he swore.

Bert Mullins, the President of the League, said in the letter that Billy Tolbert, the disgruntled Stephenville coach, had filed a formal grievance against the Warriors, accusing them of recruiting Terrance Brown in violation of league rules by arranging for Royal Brown to become the preacher at the True Word Baptist Church. The charge was under investigation, and the League would inform Bobby of the outcome.

Interscholastic League rules did not disqualify a player from playing when his family moved from one town to another under normal circumstances, but if Tolbert could prove that Comanche Springs arranged a job for Royal Brown so his son would come to town to play football, Terrance Brown would be disqualified for a year, and the Warriors would forfeit all the games he had played in.

Bobby thought of the strong enthusiasm Mike Proctor had shown from the start in promoting Terrance as the starting quarterback. Was it possible that Proctor had secretly arranged for Royal Brown to get his job? Bobby reached across his desk for the telephone book, located the number of the True Word Baptist Church, and called it. A woman answered, and Bobby asked to speak to the Reverend Brown. After several minutes, the preacher answered in his deep, vibrant voice.

"Reverend Brown, this is Bobby Thompson. Something has come up I need to talk to you about."

"What would that be?"

"The Stephenville coach has accused us of recruiting Terrance by arranging for you to get your job as pastor."

"Where do they get off accusing anyone of something like that?" Brown spoke with a kind of weary anger.

"I think Stephenville is just bitter because we beat them so bad, but we have to answer the charge. If the Interscholastic League sustains it, Terrance will be disqualified for the year, and we'll forfeit all the games he played in."

"When do you want to see me?"

"Can you come in this afternoon after practice?"

"I'll be there."

After the practice that afternoon, Brown came into the dressing room after most of the boys had left for home. Terrance had driven off fifteen minutes earlier in his decrepit Ford. The preacher came across the room and shook Bobby's hand.

"Thanks for coming," Bobby said. "Let's talk in my office."

Melvin Morris stood across the room at the water fountain, discussing the day's practice with Bill Foster and Rob Wilson. He beamed a questioning look at Bobby.

Bobby shook his head. "Talk to you tomorrow, Mel," he called across the room.

Bobby held the door of the office open for Reverend Brown and followed him in, shutting the door. The preacher took one of the dented folding chairs facing Bobby's desk. Bobby sat in the scarred oak swivel chair behind the desk. He studied the face of the man across from him.

Brown had taken off his plaid-banded hat. A fringe of curly hair with a lot of grey in it rimmed his bald crown. He had a proud face with high cheekbones. A trim mustache set off his firm mouth. Bobby saw no sign of guilty knowledge in the preacher's eyes.

Bobby leaned forward, laying his forearms on the desk. "I hate having to talk to you about this, but I do have to reply to Stephenville's charge. Is there anything about the way you got the job as pastor that would make you think it had been arranged by someone?"

Reverend Brown shook his head slowly. "I don't think the Lord called me to Comanche Springs to be His preacher just so my son could play football, Coach Thompson. To tell the truth, so far as his football playing is concerned, both Terrance and I'd rather have stayed in Fort Worth, although you have given him a fair deal here."

"I appreciate your saying that, Reverend Brown. I've been very pleased with the way Terrance has played. But the people in

Stephenville seem to think your call to Comanche Springs didn't come from the Lord. How were you contacted about the job?"

Brown's folding metal chair creaked as he leaned forward.

"A committee of three men from the church here showed up at my office in Fort Worth one day. They said one of 'em heard me preach at a revival we had in Fort Worth late last spring. They said they needed a preacher here, and would I consider taking the job. My wife and I came out and looked the place over, and we decided to answer the call."

"How about the pay?"

Reverend Brown smiled. "The truth is, Coach Thompson, the pay is quite a bit better than what I was making."

"How much better?"

"About double."

"Have you figured out where it's coming from?"

"We've been taking in a good bit at the services lately, but a good part of the church budget comes from a couple of our members who have done pretty well in life, and can afford to support the church better than most."

Bobby's suspicious focused in sudden conjecture.

"Those members don't happen to be the same ones that were on the committee that came to see you in Fort Worth, do they?"

"Fact of the business is, they do, Coach Thompson. But none of 'em ever said anything about Terrance playing football."

"They didn't have to. They knew he'd play, wherever he went to school."

Royal Brown shook his head firmly. "I can't believe those men would deceive me like that."

"Maybe they didn't. Maybe there's nothing to the charge. I wish there was some way we could check it out."

"I can't come out and ask them if someone else is giving them the money for my salary. A question like that would destroy all the trust and credibility I've built up as their pastor."

"I know that. I'm going to answer the charge by saying as far as we're concerned, there's nothing to it. In the meanwhile, if you get any information to the contrary, will you let me know?"

The preacher nodded. "I sure will, coach."

When Brown had gone, Bobby dug into his cluttered desk until he found some stationery. He wrote a short note to Bert Mullins saying that Billy Tolbert's charge was groundless, and that Comanche Springs would welcome any investigation the League might make.

Bobby found a stamp and put it on the letter, turned out the lights and left the building. He would post the letter on the way home, and tell the other coaches and the school board about the Stephenville charge the next day.

◆

The Graham Steers, gaudy in their bright red and blue uniforms, made it plain they had come to town to play football. Even before the game started, they exuded a domineering air in the way they charged from their dressing room onto the field to do their pre-game calesthentics.

The Steers won the toss, and elected to receive. On the kickoff, Freddie Alhamid didn't get his foot into the ball, and it came down at the Steer fifteen yard line into the arms of Zane Turner, the Steers' all-state running back. Turner started down the sideline behind a wall of Steer blockers.

"Get him! get him!" Bobby heard himself screaming as Turner passed one yardmarker after another.

Finally, Ned Chambers flattened Turner around midfield. The Steer quarterback quickly huddled his troops and brought them up to the line of scrimmage. The play went off on the first count, catching the Warriors napping. The quarterback fell back into a well-protected pocket, braced, and threw a long pass to a long-legged end, who had gotten a few steps ahead of Joe King. The end caught the ball, stretched out his legs, and crossed the goal line seconds later. The steers converted the point-after to lead 7-0.

Terrance Brown seemed shaken by the quick score. He fumbled on the first handoff from scrimmage and barely recovered. On the next play, he threw a wild pitchout that was almost intercepted, and ended up having to punt with fourth and long yardage.

The Steers returned Alhamid's kick almost to midfield, then started a business-like march down the field, making three and four yards on the ground on almost every running play, and completing most of their passes. The drive ended with a plunge through the line into the end zone by the big Steer fullback. Again, the Steers converted, to lead 14-0 with the first quarter not even over.

Joe King made a nice runback with the kickoff, giving the

Warriors good field position near the fifty. On this series, Terrance settled down, cranking out good yardage on the ground, and completing several sideline passes to the ends. Just when it seemed the Warriors would march down and score, Terrance threw a wild pass into a nest of Steer defenders. One of them intercepted the ball, ending the drive.

"Jesus Christ, where did that boy learn to pass?" Coach Bennett raved, shaking his head angrily.

The Steers started another long drive, ending with another Steer touchdown. Again, they converted, to lead 21-0. After the kickoff, Terrance tried to move the team with less than two minutes left in the half. He tried a draw, then a screen pass, but both ended with only short gains. On third down, Terrance called a downfield pass. He got good protection from the line as the ends streaked down the field toward the Steer goal line.

Bobby saw with growing excitement that Eddie Ritterman had pulled several yards ahead of his defender.

"Throw it!" Bobby yelled.

Terrance set for the throw and heaved the ball, but his foot slipped on the turf. Instead of flying in a perfect spiral to Ritterman, the ball wobbled haphazardly and came down short. The defender who had been following Ritterman slowed down to make the interception and end the Warrior drive. The Steers ran out the clock and the teams headed for their dressing rooms for the half.

During the half, Bobby and the other coaches had a conference in the office. Art Bennett leaned against the wall, looking at Bobby with tense, angry eyes.

"We're dead if you keep Terrance in at quarterback."

Bobby loathed Bennett's handsome bronzed face. "You've given me that kind of crap every game since I decided to start Terrance instead of Rusty."

"I can't help it if you're too big a fool to see the truth."

"Fuck you, asshole!"

Bennett clenched his fists and started toward Bobby, but Melvin Morris stepped between them.

"Take it easy! How's the team gonna react if they hear the coaches having a brawl?"

"He called me an asshole!"

"Keep your voice down, Art! Sometimes you are an asshole. And

Bobby, you're an asshole too. For once, I agree with Art. It's time to pull Terrance and put Rusty in."

The reason in Morris's voice sank in. "Okay. Maybe you're both right. We'll try Rusty this half."

On the Warriors' first possession in the second half, Rusty took command of the offense and started running a series of shrewdly-called, well-executed plays that moved the team down quickly for the first Warrior touchdown on a plunge from the five by Rutherford McAlpin. The Warriors converted the extra point, making the score 21-7.

The Steers took the kickoff deep in their own territory and ate up a lot of time moving into Warrior territory before they came up with third and long yardage at the thirty. They tried a field goal that went wide, and the Warriors got the ball on their own twenty.

Again, Rusty went confidently to the helm, moved the team through two first downs, and then threw a touchdown pass to Curtis McInnes. Again, the Warriors made the point after, and the score stood at 21-14.

"Just one more series like that and we'll be tied," Art Bennett gloated.

The Steers soon obliterated Bennett's premature optimism. On the second play after the kickoff, they turned Zane Turner loose up the middle. He broke two tackles, then eluded the entire Warrior defensive secondary and led them all on a race to the Warrior goal line. This time, the Steers' big kicker missed the extra point, making the score 27-14.

The teams traded the ball between them several times without either scoring. Then, late in the fourth quarter, Rusty brought the Warriors to life again. They made long yardage on a screen pass to McInnes, then McAlpin powered up the middle for two successive twenty-yard gains. Finally, Stedman ran an option to the left, kept the ball himself, and threaded his way through the defenders for a touchdown. The Warriors converted, making the score 27-21.

Bobby looked at the clock. Less than two minutes remained in the game.

"Circle up men!" he called to the kickoff team, and the players gathered around him.

• "We gotta get the ball back! Let's do an onside-kick."

The team lined up with the kicker, Alhamid, a little short.

"Onside-kick! Onside-kick!" shouted the Steer players.

Under the rules, after the ball went ten yards on the kickoff, the team that ended up with the ball got to keep it. In the onside-kick routine, the team kicking off tried to kick the ball a bare ten yards on the ground, then cover it before the opposing team could get to it. It was a desperation measure, only used when time was short.

Alhamid approached the ball at half his usual speed. Scuttling like a crab, he clipped it with the side of his foot. It bounded end-over-end toward the Steer front wall, and into the hands of a big Steer tackle.

"Hit him!" Melvin Morris shouted.

Juan Guerrero crashed into the tackle, and the ball spurted loose onto the ground. Ned Chambers dove toward it, along with several of the Steer players.

"Jesus Christ!" Bobby swore, "did Chambers get it?"

The officials peeled the players off the pileup. In sudden joy, Bobby saw that Chambers lay at the bottom of the pile with the ball in his arms.

"Now let's score!" Bobby shouted. The clock showed just over a minute to play.

On the snap, the interior linemen surged forward, and Stedman fell back to pass while the ends and halfbacks streaked downfield. Eddie Ritterman broke away from his defender and headed for the goal line. Stedman set himself and heaved the ball, but before he could get it away, a Steer defender drove into him, and the ball wobbled upfield short and off-course. One of the Steer linebackers made an easy catch.

"Oh shit!" Bobby groaned.

Taking no chances, the Steers ran out the remaining time with no-risk plays. The game ended 27-21. Bobby congratulated the Steer coach, then followed his dejected players into the dressing room. Ray Stewart of the Courier accosted him at the door.

"Why did you wait so long to put Rusty Stedman in, coach?"

"I though Terrance deserved a chance to get things going."

"Do you think keeping Terrance in so long cost us the game?"

Bobby struggled to keep his voice civil. "It's hard to say, Ray. Excuse me, I've got some things to tend to."

Bobby turned away from the repulsive little reporter, knowing he could expect a critical story in the morning's paper.

♦

The next Monday night, Warrior fans filled the tables and lined the walls at the booster club meeting. Bobby stood at the podium, with white-maned Joe Timmons and tall, reasonable Willis Fullerton seated on either side of him. He looked out over the collection of angry, disappointed faces.

Stewart's article in the Saturday morning paper had said that Bobby's bad judgment had cost the Warriors the game. To make matters worse, someone had told Stewart about the Interscholastic League charge, and he had written a lengthy story about it in the Sunday paper.

Stewart sat with Art Bennett at a table in the middle of the room, among the fans clustered around Gerald Stedman. What a fickle little bastard, Bobby thought, playing up first to Proctor, now to Stedman.

Mike Proctor sat unsmiling at a table near the back of the room. Bobby looked around for Royal Brown, but the preacher was not in the room. Guess I can't blame him, Bobby thought. Between the Stephenville charge and Terrance's poor playing, Brown had reason to avoid this meeting.

Bobby thumped the microphone and cleared his throat. "This game video is not what I hoped it would be, folks, but let's watch it and then talk about it."

He nodded to Melvin Morris at the video console, and Morris started running the video. The audience watched in sullen silence until the first time Terrance Brown fumbled. With this mistake, a low, mean chuckle started near the middle of the room and passed from one table to another. Bobby ignored the sound and went on with his matter-of-fact narrative of the game.

"Terrance didn't look very good on that play, folks. We pretty well beat ourselves with our own mistakes the first half."

Several of the fans in the darkened room guffawed sarcastically. With each of Terrance's mistakes, the boosters laughed bitterly, vented belligerent snorts, or gave mocking applause. Finally, the video came to the play just before the half where Terrance stumbled and threw an interception instead of a touchdown pass.

"Trust a nigger to choke in a pinch!" someone in the audience shouted in disgust.

Others in the audience laughed and whistled. Bobby fervently wished Reverend Brown had come to the meeting. His presence would have stifled most of this racial invective.

The boosters liked the second half of the video, where Rusty Stedman played better than he had ever played before, brought the Warriors from behind, and almost won the game. Now the comments were approving.

"Ol' Rusty really threw a beauty that time!"

"He faked the hell out of 'em with that call!"

"Did you see the way he cut upfield on that one?"

The disembodied voices, thick with racial pride, came at Bobby from all over the darkened room. Even when Terrance played superlatively, the boosters had never given him the praise they now lavished on Rusty. With their excessive praise for Rusty, the mean-spirited voices triumphantly rejected Terrance's right to the quarterback position.

The boosters groaned in collective disappointment at the Warriors' last play from scrimmage, where the Steers intercepted Stedman's pass to end the Warriors' chance of winning.

"Let's fast-forward over the rest, Mel," Bobby said, "the game really ended with that interception."

Morris flipped the cassette player to fast-forward and turned on the room lights. The boosters blinked, gaped and stretched in the bright light.

"Well, that's it, folks. We played good the second half, but we just got too far behind to pull it out."

A big man in overalls sitting at the table with Gerald Stedman held up his hand. Bobby nodded at him.

The man stood up, looking around the room and then back at Bobby. "I got a question for you, coach."

"I'll sure try to answer it."

"Why the hell didn't you pull Brown as soon as he started screwin' up in the first half?"

Men all over the room looked at each other and nodded angrily.

"That's a good question. The answer is that you don't pull a quarterback over a few bad plays. I thought Terrance would straighten up. When he kept playing bad, I decided to change quarterbacks at the half."

A sallow-faced man in a suit raised his hand, and Bobby nodded to him.

"Wouldn't we have won the game if you'd changed quarterbacks sooner?"

Bobby kept his temper. "It's hard to say. There are so many variables in a football game, most of the time you can't say one thing caused you to win or lose."

"Bullshit!" Someone called from the back of the room.

Gerald Stedman put up his hand.

"Yes, Mr. Stedman."

Stedman rose to his feet, staring at Bobby with baleful blue eyes.

"Coach Thompson, I can understand why you would play Terrance some at quarterback, and maybe even start him in some games. The boy has played well at times. But for the life of me, I can't understand why you would keep him in so long when he kept fouling up, especially when you had another good quarterback who might have been able to win the game for us. I think blacks deserve their chance, but not the kind of favoritism you've been showing for Terrance Brown."

"Damn straight," called the big man who had spoken first.

"It's always a mistake to give a nigger shoes," called an anonymous heckler.

An amused murmur passed around the room.

Bobby felt his neck swelling. "Cut out the racial crap."

Mike Proctor suddenly got up from where he was sitting and came to the podium. He took the microphone from Bobby.

"Give the coach a break. Up until this game, there was no doubt Terrance Brown was the best quarterback. We can't fault Coach Thompson for sticking with Terrance through the first half, considering how well he's played so far this season."

"Why are you so interested in that nigger, anyway?" called the big man from the Stedman table.

Proctor's face tightened coldly. "I just believe in fair play. Terrance played great up until this game, and he didn't deserve to be pulled right away because of a few mistakes."

Gerald Stedman had remained standing during all the heckling by his supporters. Now, he spoke again, his voice shaking with passion.

"You never thought about fair play one minute in your entire life, Mike Proctor! I think there're some questions you need to answer about how Brown came to be here in the first place, and why we may forfeit all our games because of him."

"Watch who you're accusing, you son of a bitch!" Proctor's face was livid and swollen.

"That's right, Mike! Cuss me out. You've done it before. Remember the last time?"

"God damn you!" Proctor growled through clenched teeth. He jumped down from the raised speaker's platform and started for Stedman, who moved to meet him, fists raised and clenched.

Proctor threw a wild, looping punch that landed on Stedman's nose, making the blood fly. Stedman stepped back, shaking his head, and Proctor advanced, fists flailing. Stedman took Proctor's measure and got his weight into a punch that connected solidly with Proctor's chin.

Proctor fell backwards and would have landed on the floor, but two men caught him, holding his arms to his sides, just as Bill Blevins, the Methodist preacher, restrained Stedman with a bearhug from behind. At the podium, Joe Timmons took the mike from Bobby and spoke to the crowd.

"This isn't the best way to end a meeting, folks," he said, with grim humor, "but I think we'd better end it before anything else happens. This meeting is now adjourned!"

Bobby exchanged regrets for what had happened with the booster club officers, then drove home with the windows of his pickup down, letting the cool fall air play over his heated face.

Only a few days before, he had been in control of a team that he thought was headed for a district championship. Now, with a key game lost, a charge filed that might disqualify the team, and the outbreak of bitter hatred and division among the fans, both the team's future and his own seemed bleak.

At home, he told an incredulous Paula what had happened, then went to bed. Although bone-weary, he tossed about for hours, thinking about the fight between Proctor and Stedman, and wondering what ancient dispute lay between them that made them hate each other.

EIGHT

The morning after the fight between Mike Proctor and Gerald Stedman, the Courier carried a story by Ray Stewart giving all the lurid details. The teachers talked about the fight in the teacher's lounge. They tried to draw Bobby out, but he put them off with laconic comments and noncommittal shrugs of his shoulders. Before the practice that afternoon, the players stood talking together in little groups. Bobby gathered them around him.

"I know you've heard about the fight at the booster club meeting last night. It's too bad it happened, but it doesn't mean the booster club is down on the team. I want you to put the fight out of your minds, and concentrate on the Brownwood game. Just let the booster club take care of itself."

Bobby knew Rusty Stedman had won the right to start in the Brownwood game. During the practice, Rusty looked good, while Terrance moped around, glowering at the world from under his Frankenstein flattop with a demoralized scowl that seemed to justify his demotion.

Terrance avoided Bobby's eyes, not speaking except to acknowledge directions during the practice. Terrance seemed beaten, almost cowed, but Bobby still saw a magic in Terrance's moves that Rusty would never have.

After the Tuesday practice, Royal Brown waited for Bobby outside the dressing rooms.

"Have you heard any more about the Stephenville charge, coach?"

"No, I haven't. They said they'd investigate and let me know."

"I went ahead and asked Sutton, the undertaker, if anyone had put him up to recruiting me. He's the one who really convinced me to come here. If anything underhanded was going on, he'd know."

"What'd he say?"

Reverend Brown shook his head, little lines of wry amusement around his mouth. "He was mad, Coach Thompson. Asked me how I could suspect him of such a thing. Said he wouldn't let no white man tell him who to hire as preacher, even if it meant the team would get a good football player out of the deal."

Bobby nodded sympathetically. "I know it was hard for you to ask him."

"It wasn't so bad. I told him I didn't suspect anything; I just had to ask, that was all."

Bobby thought of all the heckling he had taken the night before. "We missed you at the booster club meeting."

Brown looked down at the ground. "I read about what happened, and I wish I'd been there, but I just didn't feel like coming."

"I know what happened with Terrance was a disappointment to you."

"He had an off night, coach. I don't know why. Maybe the recruiting charge upset him."

"He'll have another chance."

"Will he, coach?"

"You can bet on it. But you'd better come to the rest of the meetings."

"Why's that?"

Bobby told Brown about all the heckling Stewart had not reported in his article.

The preacher shook his head angrily. "Those yahoos would have lynched me if I'd shown up."

"No they wouldn't. Most of them would have been ashamed to say what they said if you'd been there."

"I heard some of that crap the one time I did come."

Bobby nodded. "There'll always be some of that. But it wouldn't have been as bad if you'd come."

Brown raised his eyes. "If it'll help, I'll come to the rest of the meetings."

"It'll help."

◆

The next day, Bobby lingered in his office after practice, working on new plays. When he finally started for the outside door, all the other coaches and players had gone. Cheery O'Leery stood in the front of one of the clothes driers, folding freshly-washed jerseys.

"See you tomorrow, Cheery," Bobby called.

O'Leery turned toward Bobby. "Can I talk to you for a minute, coach?" The boy's slow, laconic voice sounded troubled.

"Sure, son, what's on your mind?"

"I ought not to tell you."

"Tell me what?"

"It probably don't amount to nothin'."

"What are you talking about?"

"I found something in McAlpin's locker."

"You'd better show me."

O'Leery led Bobby over to the locker with McAlpin's name on it. The door was closed and locked with a padlock, but O'Leery lifted up slightly on the door and pulled out on it. The door popped open.

"You shouldn't be breaking into lockers, Cheery."

The boy looked at Bobby defensively. "I wanted to make sure about what I thought I seen him put in here."

O'Leery reached down and pulled a cloth bag out of the locker. He reached inside and pulled out a large hypodermic syringe of the sort used on livestock. Bobby drew in his breath. He knew players sometimes used these kinds of syringes to give themselves steroids, to quickly increase their size and physical strength.

Bobby thought of the weight McAlpin had put on since the start of the season; of how much stronger he had become. Use of steroids was against the law and banned by the rules of the Interscholastic League. If McAlpin had been using steroids, Bobby had a duty to report it, even though it would mean McAlpin's disqualification, and the team's forfeiture of all the games he had played in.

Bobby looked steadily at O'Leery, thinking of the exchange in the halftime dressing room early in the season when O'Leery had refused to get McAlpin a bottle of gatorade.

"You don't like Rutherford much, do you?"

O'Leery shook his head. "No, I don't."

"Why not?"

"He acts like he's better'n anyone else."

"You sure you're not trying to get back at him for something?"

O'Leery shook his head. "It wouldn't make no difference how much I hated him, I wouldn't do that."

Bobby studied the boy's face for several seconds. "I believe you, Cheery. Have you seen any other players with these?"

O'Leery shook his head.

"Keep your eyes open and let me know if you see any others."

"Okay coach."

"Don't say anything about this to anyone else. And don't go breaking into any more lockers."

O'Leery nodded and went back to folding jerseys. Bobby left the building and drove home, mulling over the implications of this new problem. All O'Leery had found was a syringe used to give medicine to livestock. The fact it was in McAlpin's locker didn't prove McAlpin was using it to give himself steroids.

Bobby had no basis to accuse McAlpin of anything yet. Bobby knew McAlpin's father was a rancher. If Bobby accused McAlpin, he would probably say the hypodermic was used on the ranch. Bobby decided to take no action for the time being; to keep his eyes and ears open for more evidence.

◆

On Friday, the Warriors drove on two-lane highways more than a hundred miles to the southwest, to the town of Brownwood, located in rolling ranch country in the central part of the state. Before the Graham game, the Warriors had been rated over the Brownwood Lions, but now, the small-town sportswriters of central Texas picked the Lions to win.

"You know what the newspapers are saying, men," Bobby told the team in his pre-game pep talk in the dressing room. "They're saying the Graham game proves we don't have what it takes--that we can't beat this bunch. I'm telling you that's bullshit! If each of you will reach down inside himself and find the burning desire I've talked about so often, we'll win this game, and let the sportswriters know they can roll up their newspapers and put 'em where the sun won't shine on 'em. It's up to you, men! Let's get 'em!"

Bobby trotted after the team to the playing field. As he often did just before a game, he thought of Bill Mattingly, with his loving toughness and intense enthusiasm. How would Mattingly handle all the problems that had suddenly developed with Bobby's team?

Rusty Stedman looked good on the Warriors' first possession. He moved the team down the field for two first downs and almost connected on a long pass to Ritterman that could have been a touchdown. The drive ended with a pass tipped by a rushing lineman so that it flipped crazily end over end into the hands of one of the Lion linebackers.

The Lions moved briskly up the field for several downs, then had to kick the ball back to the Warriors. Again, Stedman did a good job of moving the team for several downs, then got sacked behind the line on third down and had to punt on fourth. For all of the first quarter and most of the second, the teams traded the ball back and forth with no score.

Late in the second quarter, the Lion quarterback connected on a long pass up the middle to one of his halfbacks, who twisted through the Warrior defenders down to the ten yard line. The Lions pounded in for the score in three plays, then made the extra point to lead 7-0 with short time left before the half. The Warriors tried some long passes and a screen, but couldn't connect, and the half ended with the Lions still seven points ahead.

As he talked to the team during the halftime break, Bobby had a gut feeling he should start Terrance the second half. Stedman had done nothing wrong. He had not fumbled, or thrown any interceptions except the one tipped ball. But he had played cautiously, woodenly. He had failed to inspire and the team had failed to move.

Bobby finally decided Rusty deserved to start the second half. After all, he had played better than Terrance the week before, and might have won the game if Bobby had put him in earlier.

The Warriors took the kickoff at the start of the second half, and Joe King ran the ball back nearly to midfield. Rusty ran McAlpin up the middle for short yardage for two plays, then, on third down, fell back into a pocket of blockers and braced for a long pass. The play called for both ends to streak down the sidelines and for the two halfbacks to cross over the middle.

On Shaughnessey's side, the defensive back who should have covered him started in to cover Joe King, who was slanting across the middle of the field. By the time the defender realized his mistake, Shaughnessey had a five-yard lead. He streaked toward the goal line, looking over his shoulder for the ball.

"Nail it!" Bobby shouted.

Rusty set his feet for the throw. He had plenty of time; McAlpin, Chambers, Foster and Alhamid had dropped back to block, giving Rusty a perfect pocket of protection, but when he threw the ball, instead of flying in a smooth spiral into the arms of Lee Shaughnessey, it wobbled erratically downfield and dribbled into the ground yards short of the receiver.

"Jesus Christ, what happened?" Mel Morris asked in disbelief.

Art Bennett shook his head apologetically. "He just didn't get anything on it that time."

The Warriors punted and the Lions ran the ball back to the thirty. They went nowhere and had to kick back to the Warriors. On the Warrior's first play of the series, Rusty tried to run an option to the right, but his pitchout was short. McAlpin tried to come back for the ball, but it fell to the ground, where McAlpin covered it, ending the play. On the next play, Rusty lined up behind center with his feet planted pointed to the right.

"Doesn't he know he's giving away the direction of the play?" Bobby asked, exasperated.

Several defenders read Rusty's moves, crashing in between center and right guard to end the play almost before it started. The officials called time for the Lion manager to replace a broken shoelace for one of the players.

"Brown!" Bobby called tersely, looking toward where Terrance sat hunched up on the bench.

Terrance grabbed his helmet, putting it on as he ran up to Bobby. "Yes sir, coach."

"Get in there, get us a first down on the ground, and then open up with some passes."

"You bet, coach!"

Terrance ran for the huddle. Bobby ignored a disgusted look from Art Bennett as Rusty Stedman trotted dejectedly off the field.

Terrance handed off first to McAlpin, then to Curtis McInnes, for gains of four and five yards up the middle, and a first down. With the Warriors at midfield, he put the ball in the air on first down, connecting with Ritterman for fifteen yards, bringing up first down around the Lion thirty-five.

On the next play, Terrance ran an option to the right behind blocking from McAlpin and Foster. When the time came to pitch the ball out to McInnes or cut upfield, Terrance planted his foot and cut. Foster cut down the corner man, breaking Terrance free into the Lion secondary, where he scrambled past one tackler after another. Finally, at the five-yard line, he put his shoulder into the last defender between him and the goal and rolled into the end zone for a touchdown. With the point after, the Warriors tied the score 7-7.

The defense found inspiration in Terrance's quick score. They sacked the Lion quarterback twice and stopped one run at the line of scrimmage, forcing a punt. Within a minute and a half of playing time after the score, the Warriors had the ball again. Running out to the huddle, Terrance carried himself with cocky arrogance. Even from the sidelines, Bobby could see him chopping the air decisively with his hands as he called the play.

Under Terrance's tutelage, the Warriors marched down the field, making yardage on the ground and in the air, until Terrance connected from the twenty-five on a pass to Ritterman for another Warrior touchdown. With the extra point, the Warriors led 14-7.

For the rest of the game, the Lions spewed and sputtered, but could not get any offense going. Late in the fourth quarter, Comanche Springs scored once again, on a keeper by Terrance from the two yard line. The Warriors converted the point after and the game ended with the score 21-7.

As Bobby followed his jubilant team into the showers, Terrance trotted up alongside him, a beatific smile on his face.

"Thought I'd lost it, didn't you coach?"

"Last week, you did lose it, Terrance."

"That was last week. It won't happen again."

"That's the spirit!"

Terrance trotted on ahead. In the dressing room, Ray Stewart cornered Bobby.

"Terrance Brown sure looked good tonight, coach, but who's gonna start next week?"

"I'm gonna worry about that next week, Ray. Right now, I'm just glad we were able to pull it out."

Later, as the team sped toward home on the dark highway, Bobby sat in the back of the first bus, listening to the happy banter of the tired players. He felt good about his decision to substitute Terrance for Rusty. Terrance had clearly been superior.

With Rusty looking better one week and Terrance the next, he didn't think anyone could justly criticize him for starting either one of them the next week. He had already decided to start Terrance. The boys were equal in their strong desire, but Terrance had all the real talent.

◆

The next morning, Bobby slept late, finally getting up around 10:30. He decided to go down to the fieldhouse to do some paperwork. When he tried to start his truck, the battery was dead. He asked Paula to drive him down to the school and pick him up in two hours. He could get the battery fixed later in the afternoon.

Paula let him out in front of the fieldhouse. She bent toward him, brushing his lips in a parting kiss. Bobby unlocked the building and went inside. He opened several windows for ventilation, then started on his work.

He had been working about half an hour when he heard a car drive up and stop outside the building. Thinking one of the other coaches had come down to do some work, he kept looking over his papers for several minutes. When no one came into the building, Bobby got up, walked to the front, and looked out one of the windows he had opened.

Rutherford McAlpin stood just outside, next to his sporty new Ford. He stood with his hands in his pockets, looking expectantly toward the street. His pale blue eyes clashed incongruously with his conceited dark face.

After several minutes, a battered grey pickup pulled into the parking lot of the fieldhouse and stopped next to McAlpin's Ford. Mike Proctor got out and walked toward McAlpin. A shiny green bruise around one eye recalled the fight at the booster club meeting. What was Proctor doing driving an old truck Bobby had never seen before?

"That's sure a pretty eye!" McAlpin said familiarly.

"Go fuck yourself," Proctor answered.

McAlpin returned a malicious grin. "Did you get the stuff?"

"Don't I always?"

The two walked to the back of the truck, where Proctor pulled a burlap bag out of the bed and held it open.

McAlpin looked inside. "That looks like plenty."

"It oughta be. My foreman ordered it for the herd on the south ranch. He'll wonder what happened to it."

"What he don't know won't hurt him."

Proctor stepped away from McAlpin and looked him over. "This stuff seems to be working pretty good for you."

"I've gained more than ten pounds, and it's all muscle."

Proctor nodded approvingly. "The others are looking pretty good, too. Can you get their share to them this weekend?"

"No problem."

"Good. Be careful though. Don't let anyone else know what you're doing."

"Don't worry about it. No one will know except the other guys."

Proctor smiled grimly. "Be real careful not to let Coach Thompson catch you with this stuff."

"I know better than that."

"He's such a do-gooder, I believe he'd turn you in even if it cost the team the championship."

"I'm sure he would," McAlpin said disdainfully.

Proctor started walking toward the grey pickup. "Make sure that stuff gets to the others, and call me when you run out again."

"I sure will, Mr. Proctor." McAlpin hoisted the burlap bag on his shoulder and walked to his car, where he put the bag in the truck.

Proctor got in the pickup and drove away. Within a few seconds, McAlpin pulled out behind Proctor, revved his engine, and sped away from the parking lot.

Bobby moved back from the window and sank into the chair at his desk. The pulse in his temples pounded and sweat saturated his shirt under his arms.

"Dirty cocksuckers!" he said aloud.

Should he have rushed from the building to confront the rich fan and corrupt player who were violating the ethics of the game? That had been his impulse, but he had restrained himself. He needed witnesses, and more evidence. He needed to know what players were involved.

Which of the other players would receive syringes and bottles of steroids from McAlpin? Had the corruption spread to Ned Chambers, Bill Foster or Eddie Ritterman? With sinking heart, Bobby thought of Terrance Brown. It seemed certain Terrance must be on the list. Otherwise, why would Mike Proctor have touted the boy so strongly all season?

Proctor must have recruited Terrance by arranging for Royal Brown's job, then encouraged Terrance, Rutherford, McAlpin and other players to use steroids, all so Proctor could warm his own ego in the radiant glory of a successful team.

An hour later, when Paula pulled up in front and honked the car horn, Bobby still sat at the desk, the work he had come to do forgotten. His head ached with conflicting thoughts. Anything he did would be wrong and fraught with potential disgrace. Paula honked again, with two impatient beeps. He got up, closed the windows, and went out to the car.

"Didn't you hear me honk?" Paula asked, as he got into the car.

Her voice came at Bobby as though from a distance. "What's that?" he asked.

"Didn't you hear me honk the first time?"

"Oh, sure. I was just putting up the paperwork."

She looked curiously at him. "Are you okay?"

"Sure. Why wouldn't I be?"

"You look like you're in a fog."

"I've been concentrating on some things."

As they drove toward home, Bobby debated whether to tell Paula what he had just heard. She had proven in the past she could be close-mouthed when it was needful, and he longed for her reaction.

He thought of the look he had seen pass between Paula and Mike Proctor in the restaurant. Bobby still feared the intimacy he had seen in that look. Mistrustful of Paula's relation with Proctor, he decided he would not share anything with her for the time being.

At home, he went to the bedroom and stretched out on his back on the bed. Should he call Melvin Morris or Art Bennett? How much did they know about what was going on? Did either of them suspect that team members were using steroids? Or were they involved themselves?

Finally, Bobby decided it would be better to keep his own counsel, until he found out what other players were involved. For the rest of the weekend, he tried to think of a way to get more information without tipping off Proctor or McAlpin that he knew what they were doing.

◆

The fans packed the booster club meeting at the McKeever Cafe on Monday night. Mike Proctor, bruise still visible, sat on one side of the room, and Gerald Stedman his nose swollen and red, sat among his supporters on the other side. This time, Ray Stewart took up a politic position in the middle. Royal Brown slid in late and sat at the back, just as Joe Timmons, his big gut jiggling over his Texas-shaped belt buckle, called the meeting to order.

"Let's keep things under control this time," he said. "It doesn't set a good example for the team for the adult leaders of the community to fight among themselves."

Bobby gave a running commentary on the Brownwood game video. When he came to the point where he substituted Terrance Brown for Rusty Stedman, several fans hissed, but Royal Brown's presence inhibited further heckling.

"That's it, folks," Bobby said, as the video came to an end. "We didn't play a super game, but we did win, and that's what it's all about."

One of the men sitting with Gerald Stedman raised his hand.

"Are you ever gonna settle on one starting quarterback?"

"That's a fair question. The fact is, we have two good quarterbacks, and both of them are capable of doing a real good job. I can't say for sure which one will start the rest of the year, but it does look like both of them will be playing a lot."

"Who's gonna start this week?"

"Probably Terrance Brown. It all depends on how the practices go the rest of the week."

There were more low hisses. Gerald Stedman put up his hand.

"Yes, Mr. Stedman."

"What about the Stephenville charge? Are we going to forfeit all our games over that?"

At the back of the room, Royal Brown put up his hand, and Bobby nodded to him.

Brown stood up. "Maybe I can answer that question, Mr. Stedman. I understand the charge to be that someone offered me my job as pastor so I'd come here and Terrance would play football for Comanche Springs. I can assure you no one ever said anything like that to me."

Stedman swung around in his chair to face Brown. "You're new here, Reverend Brown. You don't know how this town works. You may have been recruited for the job and not even know it." Stedman looked toward Mike Proctor.

Proctor jumped to his feet. "What are you insinuating?" he shouted.

"I'm not insinuating anything, Mike. You must have a guilty conscience."

At the podium, Joe Timmons took the mike from Bobby.

"Let's not start that stuff again. Sit down, Mike!"

Proctor sat down, still glaring across the room at Stedman.

"We'll just have to see what kind of evidence Stephenville has," Timmons said. "No point in getting worked up over the issue until then."

Timmons called on the Baptist preacher to dismiss the meeting with a prayer, and the pastor exhorted everyone to remember they were all children of God and should love each other.

Later, Bobby drove home from the meeting with a good feeling in spite of his worries about steroid use. He had actually enjoyed the friction between Stedman and Proctor. Serves both the assholes right, he told himself.

♦

On Wednesday night, Bobby went back to the athletic offices after supper, to finish the paperwork he had left undone on Saturday morning. As he tried to sort through the stack of papers, his mind kept straying from his task. Several times, he found himself leaning forward, elbows on the desk, as he pondered his problems.

At nine o'clock, he shoved the remaining papers away, and got up to leave. He caught a glimpse of himself in one of the locker-room mirrors, and stopped to look more closely. Was it possible he was beginning to put on a little spare tire? He still had a long, youthful face, and thick, curly brown hair, but his haggard brown eyes made him look middle-aged.

On the way home, he stopped at a red light where the road from the stadium intersected with the highway going out of town. As he waited for the light, several cars passed through the intersection on the green. Just as the light changed, a battered grey pickup came through the intersection, headed out of town. A streak of light fell across the face of the driver, and Bobby saw that it was Mike Proctor.

Impulsively, Bobby turned and followed Proctor. He felt sure Proctor had not seen him at the light. Why was Proctor driving the dented old pickup again, instead of his Town Car? Several miles out of town, the seedy, decrepit buildings of an old tourist motel squatted in a mesquite grove beside the highway. A flickering neon sign said it was the Cactus Flower Motel. Bobby had noticed it before, and wondered who would stay there.

As Proctor approached the villainous-looking place, he slowed, turned in, and pulled up to a paint-peeled cabin with a sign advising it was the office. Bobby drove by, taking care not to change speed. He looked toward the motel as he passed. The grey pickup sat in shadow several feet from the door of the office. Through an open window of the building, Bobby saw Proctor talking to a slovenly-looking man with a bald crown surrounded by a fringe of grey hair.

A light movement in the front seat of the pickup caught Bobby's eye. He looked toward the truck, and saw a shadowy figure seated on the passenger's side. Why had he not seen the passenger when Proctor passed him at the signal light?

Bobby passed the motel and drove a quarter of a mile beyond it, where he turned around in a ranch driveway and drove back toward the motel. As he approached, Bobby saw Proctor's truck parked under the carport of the cabin farthest from the road. Proctor had gotten out and was walking toward the door of the cabin. The passenger stood in the shadow of the unlighted carport. With a sudden shock, Bobby realized it was a tall, graceful woman, waiting for Proctor to get the door of the cabin open. Bobby could not see her well enough to make out her features.

Bobby drove several blocks down the road, and turned around again. As he passed the Cactus Flower for the third time, light shone through the windows of the rear cabin. The grey-haired man stood at the open blind in the office. Was he wondering why Bobby kept going back and forth in front of the motel? Bobby sped up and drove toward home.

Ten minutes later, when he pulled into the driveway, Paula's car was gone. He went quickly into the house, where he looked for a note that would explain her absence, but there was none. Demons of jealousy tormented him with suspicions of the worst. He turned on the television and tried to watch the news, then turned it off with a quick, angry motion.

"Shit!" He spat out.

Just after eleven, he heard Paula's car turn into the driveway. He turned the television back on and sat down, pretending to watch the late movie. Outside, Paula fumbled with the door key. The door opened and she came into the room, carrying a sack of groceries.

She beamed a bright look at Bobby. "Hi, honey. Did you get all the work done?"

He kept his voice calm. "I worked on it for a couple of hours then gave up and came home. Where have you been? I've been worried."

She tossed her curl of hair back from her forehead. "I went over to the all-night Kroger's on the Abilene highway and picked a few things for breakfast."

"You could have left me a note."

"I didn't think I'd be so long."

"Why were you?"

She frowned impatiently. "I drove around town a little before coming home. For Christ's sake, what is this? The third degree? All I did was go buy some groceries."

Bobby kept his voice flat and passionless. "I was just worried, that's all."

"Well, you can stop worrying now. I'm home, all safe and sound."

Her smile was too bright, her tone too gay. She had the nervous, defensive manner of someone who was lying. Later, Bobby lay in bed, listening to the sounds of Paula taking a shower. If she had done what he suspected, she would not wash away her guilt so easily. When she came out of the bathroom in her nightgown, he feigned sleep. She moved around the room for a few minutes, then turned off the lights and lay beside him.

Soon, Paula's even breathing told him that she slept. He turned on the bedside lamp, and looked at her placid features. Could a woman who slept with such an untroubled face be as guilty as he imagined? He asked himself the many variations of that question for over two hours, until sleep finally came to him around 2:00 a.m.

NINE

The next day, Bobby could not concentrate on teaching math. He found himself standing at the blackboard, chalk in hand, unable to even add simple figures. Finally, he had several of the students write a series of problems on the board for the class to work at home.

While the students wrote the problems, Bobby sat at his desk, preoccupied by his growing conviction that his wife had been the woman with Proctor. Once again, Bobby compared himself to Proctor, and Proctor came out the winner. He had money, looks, possessions, and a glib style that went well with a sophisticated lady like Paula. How could Bobby blame her if she preferred Proctor?

But a part of Bobby championed Paula's innocence. What real evidence was there that she had been with Proctor? There was none, other than the presence of a woman of Paula's height at the motel, coupled with her absence from home.

Then he remembered the nervous air Paula had when she came home, and her vague explanation that she had gone to the grocery store, then driven around town by herself. He remembered her over-bright manner, the furtive look in her eyes, the flippancy in her voice. His demons again convinced him that there could be no doubt about it, Paula was having an affair with Mike Proctor.

During the pep rally held after lunch to fire the team and the students for the game the next night against the Decatur Eagles, Bobby sat woodenly through all the rousing marches and fight songs. Even the dark, flashing legs of Angie Zamora, as she somersaulted across the gym floor with the other cheerleaders, could not whet his interest.

He gave a short inspirational talk encouraging the students to come to Decatur for the game, but he knew the speech lacked his usual exuberance. At the end of the rally, he reluctantly walked back to his classroom for the tedium of the afternoon. At the bell signaling the end of his last class, he walked quickly to the field house, and put on his practice clothes for the final practice of the week before the game the next night.

Decatur had a lukewarm team that the sportswriters expected the Warriors to stomp, but Bobby took no chances. He and the other coaches drilled the boys carefully, looking for the little flaws in play that could make the difference between winning and losing. Terrance Brown moved the team around the practice field like a seasoned general. His good performance at Brownwood seemed to have cemented his confidence.

Rusty Stedman ran the second-string with grim intensity, taking Bobby's directions with a sullen, unhappy face. When they talked, Rusty looked beyond Bobby with his blue eyes. He started affecting a cocky, wide-shouldered swagger. In spite of these exhibitions, Rusty did his job at second-string without outright insubordination.

◆

At home that night, Bobby watched Paula closely as she fixed supper, reading guilt into every change of her expression, every action. She had burned the hamburgers and forgotten to heat the beans.

"Too many things went wrong at school today," she explained. Her eyes glistened with unshed tears.

"I know you must have a lot on your mind," Bobby said coyly.

Paula put the partly-ruined meal on the table, and they sat down across from each other.

"What happened that was so bad?" Bobby asked.

"A couple of the boys kept talking and wouldn't shut up. Every time I turned my back, they threw spitwads at me. When I took them to the office, that ass, Prissy Puryear, implied it was my fault for not taking firm enough a hand with them, as she put it."

Bobby nodded in understanding. He had met the elementary school principal, Priscilla Puryear, at a teacher's meeting several weeks earlier. An ambitious woman in her mid-thirties with a robust build and straight blonde hair worn in a ponytail, Ms. Puryear had opinions on everything, and announced them in an imperious tone, implying that those who didn't agree with her were fools.

"That's a mighty frustrating woman."

"I can't stand the bitch."

"Try not to argue with her."

"Don't worry, I know better than that."

Bobby decided to change the subject. "Are you going to drive to the game tomorrow with Wanda?"

Paula shook her head. "I've been feeling bad the last several days, like I was coming down with something. Would you mind if I sat this one out?"

Cold suspicion gripped Bobby. Paula and Wanda had driven together to all of the other out-of-town games. Did Paula really feel bad, or was there some other reason she didn't want to go? "I like for you to go to the games."

"I know honey, but would you really mind my missing this one? I really do feel under the weather."

Bobby gave a quick, angry shrug of his shoulders. "Suit yourself."

He sat with his elbows on the table, staring morosely at his half-eaten food. After several minutes, he got up and went into the bedroom. For the rest of the evening, he deliberately avoided speaking to Paula.

◆

On Friday afternoon, the school dismissed the football players early for the bus ride to Decatur. The team members arrived at the fieldhouse around 2:30 in the afternoon and started packing up for the trip. Mike Proctor drove into the parking lot and parked his Town Car next to one of the buses. He got out and came to the rear of the bus, where Bobby was supervising the loading operations.

"Are you ready to go get 'em, coach?" Proctor asked patronizingly.

Bobby looked up at Proctor, guarding his own expression to conceal his dislike. Proctor's bruised eye was almost healed. His smirking mouth seemed to mock Bobby.

"I believe we're ready for 'em, Mr. Proctor."

"What's this 'Mr. Proctor' stuff? You oughta know by now to call me Mike."

"Sorry, Mike. I forgot."

Proctor smiled and clapped Bobby on the back. "I came by to see the team off, but I'm not gonna make this one."

"Why's that?"

"I've got to drive to Fort Worth tonight so I can see a guy early in the morning about some cattle I'm buying."

Cold anxiety struck Bobby like a knife in the pit of his stomach. The bastard wouldn't miss a game for business that could be done another time. Proctor stood looking at Bobby with a superior air. Bobby clenched and unclenched his fists, wanting to drive them into Proctor's conceited face.

With a wary look, Proctor look a step backward. "You seem awful tense, coach."

Bobby straightened his fingers and put on a false smile. "I'm always this way before games."

"You won't have any trouble with this one. I'll be there for the last two. There's no way I'll miss the one against Breckenridge."

Bobby curbed his angry passion. "Good luck with the cattle," he said blandly.

"Thanks. Score a touchdown for me."

Bobby tormented himself with thoughts of Paula fornicating with Proctor most of the way to Decatur. Would they do it on the living room couch, or back in Bobby's own bed? Or would they go to the Cactus Flower again? That would be safer, because the neighbors wouldn't see Proctor's car in the drive. Finally, Decatur came in sight and Bobby pried his mind away from morbid worries and started thinking about the game.

The town sat high on a hill, and the ornate turrets of the 19th-century Wise County Courthouse, thrusting above the lower buildings of the business district, appeared on the horizon when the bus was still miles away. When they entered the city limits, Bobby started giving the driver the directions to the stadium he had gotten over the telephone from the Decatur coach earlier in the day.

The Warriors took command of the game that night early, building up a fourteen-point lead in the first quarter, and adding another touchdown midway through the second. With the score, 21-0, Bobby sent Rusty Stedman in with the second string. They held the Eagles to no score, and scored once more before the half.

Bobby could not concentrate on the game. His mind kept turning to what was happening in Comanche Springs. When the ball was in the air during a long pass, Bobby suddenly visualized the lurid lights of the Cactus Flower. While the team churned out yardage on a long run, Bobby thought of Proctor's smirking face. Was he copulating with Paula at this very moment?

The Decatur team never challenged the Warriors. In the third quarter, after Stedman marched the team down the field for another touchdown, Bobby started substituting third- and fourth-string players.

Finally, the hapless Eagles scored on a long pass, and connected on the extra point, but they could not hold back even the Warrior scrubs. Under little Rob Wilson, the ragtag mix of third- and fourth-stringers marched down the field to score once more, and the game ended with the final tally 35-7.

As the bus rolled back across the darkened prairie toward Comanche Springs after the game, Bobby brooded over what he would find at home. Would he know by Paula's face that she had made love with Proctor in his absence?

Forcing his mind away from his worries, Bobby reflected on the game. The Warriors had dominated a Decatur team that had been considered pretty good early in the season. Many Warrior players who had not played in earlier games had seen some action, and Rusty Stedman had played for a substantial part of the game at the helm of the second string. There was nothing in tonight's performance to draw complaints from the booster club.

◆

Bobby pulled into the driveway around 1:30 a.m.. He parked next to Paula's Chevrolet. As he walked past the car, telltale cracking noises coming from under the hood told him that the car was cooling down after being recently driven. He put his hand on the hood. It was still warm.

"Jesus Christ!" he swore softly.

He walked to the front door and let himself in with his key. Paula had left a lamp burning next to the television. Bobby walked back to the bedroom. He turned on the bedside lamp. Dressed in a nightgown, Paula lay on her back in the bed, her mouth slightly open. Her chest rose and fell naturally with her breathing.

He reached down and shook her shoulder. "Paula! Wake up!"

She stirred, closed her mouth, and opened her eyes. For a moment, her eyes held a dreamy, disoriented look, then she focused on Bobby and smiled.

"I heard we won the game." She sat up in bed.

"What's that to you?"

She arched her eyebrows in surprise. "Are you still mad because I didn't go?"

"Why should I be?" He looked down at the floor, fixing his eyes on a spot on the carpet.

"I went up to the stadium and waited for you to get back, but I came on home after one."

Bobby thought of the several carloads of students who had been waiting when the bus pulled in. "Was there anyone else there?"

She nodded. "Lots of kids, but I didn't know any of them. What's the big deal, anyway? I don't have to account for where I am every minute."

Bobby nodded grimly. "That's right. You sure don't."

Paula stood up. Hands on her wide hips, she faced Bobby. "What's wrong with you tonight?"

He looked at her with sick anger. "There's nothing wrong with me. It's just I thought you were too sick to leave the house."

"I never said I was sick, just that I felt bad."

"What's the difference?"

"I just didn't feel like going to the game."

"But you did feel like getting out of the house while I was gone?"

Paula's face turned red. "What's that supposed to mean?"

Bobby compressed his mouth in a harsh, accusing line. "I think you know what I'm talking about."

"No, I don't. What the hell are you getting at?"

How could she look at him with such outraged innocence?

"Just seems to me if you were well enough to leave the house, you could have gone to the game. I'd have appreciated the support."

She looked at him incredulously. "You're impossible tonight."

She walked purposefully out of the room, into the front part of the house. Bobby went to the bathroom. When he came out, she had turned out all the lights in the house except the one in the bedroom. Bobby snapped on the hall light and went into the living room. By the light slanting in from the hall, she saw that she lay on the couch, sobbing softly.

He flipped off the hall light with an angry click, then went to the bedroom, where he threw himself fully clothed on the bed and turned off the bedside lamp.

◆

Bobby got up the next morning with a grimy feeling that came of sleeping in his clothes. He went to the bathroom, shaved, and changed into blue jeans and a T-shirt. He walked out into the kitchen, looking for Paula. He looked through the window in the kitchen door, and saw her sitting pensive and unsmiling in a lawn chair in the back yard.

Bobby went into the front yard, where he retrieved the morning paper from the driveway. He brought it into the house and sat on the living room couch to read the sports page.

Ray Stewart had written an article about the win over Decatur. Uncritical for once, Stewart gushed with praise for the team and all the key players. Bobby turned quickly to the stories about the other games in the district.

He read with excitement that Mineral Wells had beaten Graham in a close game, while Breckenridge was now the only undefeated team in the district. Next Friday night, the Warriors would be up against Mineral Wells, while Breckenridge would be playing Graham.

The Warriors could not win district just by winning all the rest of their games, unless some other things happened. Since Graham had beaten them, if the Warriors won all their games, and Graham won all their games, both teams would have lost only one game, and district honors would go to Graham, because they had beaten the Warriors.

But if Breckenridge beat Graham, and the Warriors beat Mineral Wells and went on to beat Breckenridge in the final game of the schedule the following week, the Warriors would take the championship, because the Warriors and Breckenridge would be the only teams in the district to have lost only one game, and the championship would go to the Warriors because they beat Breckenridge.

Bobby knew it would be hard for his team to win the last two games. Mineral Wells had proven itself by beating the tough Graham team, and Breckenridge was regarded by the sportswriters as one of the best teams in the state. Bobby thought Breckenridge probably would beat Graham. If they did, and the Warriors could beat Mineral Wells, the district championship would ride on the outcome of the

Breckenridge game the week before Thanksgiving.

◆

Throughout the morning, Bobby and Paula didn't speak. Toward noon, she came through the living room where Bobby was sitting. She had her purse on her arm.

"I'm going to the store," she announced in a sullen monotone.

Bobby nodded coldly. "See you later."

During the hour and half she was gone, he tortured himself with his suspicions. He imagined her having coffee somewhere with Proctor, or maybe even engaging in a little daytime sex at the Cactus Flower. He kept looking at his watch. It seemed she had been gone too long just to be buying groceries.

Finally, she returned, and he helped carry in the sacks. Unsmiling, she tolerated his help. He stayed out of her way the rest of the day and evening. She went to bed early, complaining of a headache. She slept with a wet towel over her eyes. Bobby watched movies on television until nearly midnight, then turned off the light and slept in his clothes again, this time on the couch.

The next morning, they did not go to church. All morning, the two of them moped around the house, punishing each other with resentful looks and sullen silence. During the afternoon, Bobby watched the Dallas Cowboys lose a close one to the Washington Redskins. Just after the game started, Paula retired to the bedroom with another splitting headache.

When the game ended, Bobby turned off the television, then lay on the sofa with his hands behind his head. He stared at the ceiling, thinking dark thoughts. Paula came into the room and stood next to him.

She looked down at him with forgiving eyes. "Let's stop this silly crap."

Her wave of red-blonde hair lay lusterless across her forehead; swollen patches underscored her green eyes. Were these symptoms of her guilt?

His resentment quickened. "The whole thing started because you wouldn't go to the game. Don't you think a man deserves a little support from his own wife?"

"I told you I didn't feel good."

"Isn't that just an excuse for something?"

"There was a reason for it."

"I bet there was."

"I was going to tell you yesterday, but you didn't give me a chance."

"Tell me what?"

"I went to the doctor Friday afternoon."

A cold blade of concern sliced through Bobby. "What did you go to the doctor for?"

"I've been nauseated in the mornings several times the last week, and I've been having dizzy spells. I asked Wanda to refer me to someone, and she got me an appointment with her doctor."

"What did he say was the matter?"

"'Nothing's the matter. It turns out that, after all these years, I'm pregnant." She ended her words with a gentle, triumphant smile.

Bobby returned a look of cold doubt. Why had she become pregnant now for the first time?

"Did you tell the doctor about all the trouble we've had?"

"I sure did."

"What was his explanation of why you suddenly got pregnant?"

"He said sometimes it just happens that way."

"Sure it does."

Her eyes widened in outrage. "You've been saying crap like that for several days now. What are you getting at?"

He looked up at her angry face. Was the hurt in her eyes real? All his doubts came together in remembrance of the look of complicity he had seen pass between her and Mike Proctor in the restaurant. He had a bitter, sick feeling in his heart.

"I'm not getting at anything in particular," he said deliberately. "I'm just wondering if the baby's gonna look like me."

Shock passed across Paula's face, and she stepped backwards. "You son of a bitch! You think I've been making love with someone else?"

"The thought has occurred to me."

"You bastard!"

She turned and went to the bedroom. In several minutes, Bobby heard the sounds of drawers being opened and banged shut. He sat on the couch, frozen by cold anger. She came back into the living room, carrying a suitcase, hastily closed so that some article of bright clothing stuck out from the side. She walked quickly through the room to the door.

"Don't try to find me, asshole!" She went out the door, banging it shut behind her.

Bobby heard Paula's car start. He heard the sound of it backing out of the driveway and driving away. Then he heard nothing except the angry pulse pounding in his head. He sat on the couch without moving for almost an hour.

Finally, he forced himself to get up. "To hell with her!" he announced loudly. His words echoed unnaturally through the house.

Outside, the sun was going down. The wall clock read 6:30. Bobby went out to his truck and drove to the Dairy Queen. He saw Bill Foster and Freddie Alhamid sitting inside at a table with some girls. He didn't want to exchange pleasantries with anyone, so he went to the drive-through and bought a hamburger and french fries, then drove far into the country, eating the food and trying to think what would come next.

Around 8:30, he pulled back into the driveway. He had hoped to find Paula's car there, but it was still gone, and the house lay in darkness. Inside, he turned on the television and tried to watch a movie. After half an hour, he had no idea what had happened on the screen.

He turned the set off and went to the bedroom, where he flopped down on the bed and lay for more than two hours, listening for the telephone, or the sound of Paula's car pulling into the drive. Finally, he reconciled himself to the fact that she would not return that night. He took a shower and returned to the bed, where he tossed awake for many hours, before finally falling into troubled sleep in the early hours of the morning.

◆

At school that morning, Melvin Morris met Bobby as he came out of his first period class. Morris's dark, seamed face showed concern.

"What's going on with you and Paula?" he asked with characteristic bluntness.

Bobby resented the inquiry, but at the same time, he felt glad that Morris knew about his problem.

"News gets around fast," he said sarcastically.

"Paula called Wanda last night and told her she'd moved out," Morris explained. "What's the damn deal?"

"We just had an argument. I don't really want to talk about it."

Morris nodded. "Is there anything I can do?"

Bobby tightened his mouth stoically and shook his head. "It'll blow over. I'm just waiting for her to call so we can talk about it."

"Let me know if I can help." Morris gave Bobby a sympathetic look and walked away.

Bobby realized how much he had come to like his obscene little assistant. He remembered how resentful Morris had seemed when Bobby first took over as head coach. All the hostility between the two of them had gradually evaporated. Always a loner, Bobby had few close friends. For the first time, he knew that Melvin Morris was one of them.

During his free period just before lunch, Bobby went into the teacher's lounge to get away from the clamor of the halls. The room was empty. Thank God for small favors, he thought, glad he would not have to parry pleasantries with other teachers. He took a seat in a worn easy chair at a coffee table near one of the windows, leaning back in the chair with his hands behind his neck.

In several minutes, he heard the door open. Why can't they leave me alone, he thought irritably. He looked over his shoulder and saw that Lola Cochran, an English teacher, had come into the room.

She nodded pleasantly to Bobby, and took a chair across the coffee table from him. She fumbled in her purse for a cigarette, lit it with a plastic throwaway lighter, leaned back in her chair and inhaled deeply. She let the smoke trickle from her nostrils.

"How's things with the team, coach?" She looked at Bobby with a cynical air.

"We played a good game this week."

"So I heard." Her mouth carried a coy smile.

About forty, Lola had a sallow, unhealthy complexion, high cheekbones setting off hungry brown eyes, and high, pert breasts displayed to their best advantage by a foundation garment that thrust them against the fabric of the half-open blouses she wore. Bobby had heard she was a childless divorcee.

"Did you go to the game?" he asked.

She shook her head. "I've been to a couple of the home games, but I'm not enough of a fan to drive to Decatur just to see a bunch of clumsy kids maul each other."

"Seems like you don't have a very high opinion of the team."

Her smile deepened. "I don't have much interest in football, Coach Thompson, but I've been very impressed with the way you've brought the boys around this year. And I've been following all the trash you've been taking over your decision to start Terrance Brown instead of Gerald Stedman's spoiled brat."

Lola's patronizing praise discomfited Bobby. "I sure appreciate the support."

Lola leaned forward and knocked the ash from her cigarette into an ash tray on the coffee table. She looked at Bobby with invitation in her eyes.

"We don't have many real men in this town. You're one I'd like to get to know better."

Bobby looked uncomfortably at his watch. "I sure appreciate that, Mrs. Cochran, but right now, I'd better get going." He stood up.

"Just a minute, Bobby." She used his first name for the first time.

He stood awkwardly beside the coffee table while she fished a small note pad from her purse and wrote something on it.

She handed the note up to him. "Here's my phone number. Call me sometime."

Bobby took the note and stuffed it in his shirt pocket. "I'll think about it."

The door opened as several other teachers came into the room. Bobby took advantage of their entrance to make his escape. For the rest of the afternoon, thoughts of Lola Cochran, her pert breasts, and her exciting availability, kept intruding into Bobby's mind, superimposing themselves over his worries about Paula.

◆

At the booster club meeting that night, the players looked good on the video. Terrance Brown's moves seemed almost professional, but Rusty Stedman had played well too. The Stedman fans had plenty to gloat over in Rusty's performance. For the first time since the Stephenville game, the fathers of the third- and fourth-stringers had something to talk about.

Bobby avoided looking at Mike Proctor during the meeting.

Once or twice, Proctor caught Bobby's eye. His insincere smile seemed to mock Bobby. Seething inwardly, Bobby could barely keep his voice calm as he addressed the boosters.

"We played a fine game, folks. Decatur wasn't as tough as I thought they'd be, but there is some good talent on their team, and it was no cinch to beat them."

He outlined the status of the teams still in the running for the district championship, explaining that if the Warriors beat Mineral Wells and Breckenridge beat Graham, the championship would hang on the final game of the season against Breckenridge.

"Mineral Wells is gonna be tough. Lots tougher than Decatur. This will be our toughest game since the Graham game, but there isn't any doubt we can win it, so all ya'll come to Mineral Wells this Friday night and give us the moral support we need to win."

As Bobby drove home after the meeting, his excitement about the team faded as he approached his dark house. Again he lay awake for hours, assuaging his self-pity with thoughts of sex with Lola Cochran.

◆

On Tuesday, Bobby went to school, taught all day, got through the afternoon practice, and returned again at sundown to his empty house. He wondered where Paula was living. How many times had she made love with Mike Proctor since she left Bobby? Lonely and resentful, Bobby thought of Lola Cochran and her arousing availability.

He thought of the cigarette smoke curling seductively from her nostrils, of her thrusting breasts and open blouse. With her aging skin and slatternly hips, she had no beauty, only an appealing lewdness. Bobby wanted her with a growing morbid intensity. Finally, he could stand the pressure no longer.

"Go to hell, Paula," he said aloud.

He went into the bedroom and found the little slip of paper with Lola's phone number. He returned to the living room and sat on the couch next to the telephone table. His heart pounded with guilt and desire as he dialed Lola's number.

"Hello," Lola answered, her voice deep and seductive.

"Hi, Lola, it's me, Bobby," Bobby clutched the receiver tightly, conscious of his sweating palms.

"Hi, Bobby. I've been hoping you'd call. What's on your mind?"

"When we talked yesterday, you said you'd like to get to know me better."

"That's right."

"I'd like to get to know you better, too. Could we get better acquainted tonight?"

"I'm here by myself. Come on over."

Lola gave Bobby directions to the garage apartment she lived in near the central business district. Bobby told her he would be over in half an hour. He showered, dressed, combed his hair carefully, so he would look good even for Lola Cochran, and headed out the door, almost forgetting to lock it behind him. He drove in his pickup toward Lola's apartment.

He turned left onto the highway into town and drove for several blocks. It widened to four lanes near the business district. Stopping for a red light, he glanced at his watch. It was 8:30. Several other cars were stopped at the light with him. The group of cars hung together for the first half-block after the light changed. Bobby drove in the right-hand lane, with the other cars just to his left.

Suddenly, Bobby recognized Mike Proctor's old grey pickup approaching from the opposite direction. The truck passed even with Bobby's at a point in the road brightly lighted by overhead lights and neon lights from roadside businesses.

Through the window of the car next to him, Bobby saw Proctor at the wheel of the grey pickup. He was headed in the direction of the Cactus Flower Motel. Was Paula crouched down next to him? Or was she waiting for him at the motel?

What difference does it make, Bobby asked himself bitterly. If Paula wanted to make love with Proctor, there wasn't anything Bobby could do about it. Lola Cochran was waiting just a few minutes ahead. Diversified sex was a game two could play.

But Bobby's anger rose at the thought that, within minutes, Mike Proctor would be making love to Paula. He pushed Lola Cochran out of his mind, turned around in a service station driveway, and started following Proctor out to the Cactus Flower.

"Showdown time!" he said aloud.

The grey pickup was out of sight by the time Bobby got turned around. He drove out of town until the garish lights of the Cactus Flower came into view. Slowing down, he passed the motel. Looking between the buildings, he saw the pickup already parked at the rear unit.

Bobby looked around for Paula's car, but he didn't see it. He drove past the motel and pulled to the side of the road. A clump of mesquite trees, clinging to their foliage despite the lateness of the season, stood along the road. He pulled behind them, cut the motor and lights, and got out of the car.

He shivered in the cool air as he walked slowly back toward the motel. As he approached the driveway, he saw the course-faced manager through the windows of the office. The man sat on a sofa watching television. Quickly, Bobby crossed the drive and stepped into a patch of shadow by the office.

He edged to the back of the building and looked around the corner. The lights of the rear unit where Proctor's truck was parked glimmered through the blinds. Should he get close to the room and try to see what was going on? Bobby recoiled from the thought of sneaking around like a thief.

"Nothing like the direct approach," he muttered.

He stepped out of the shadow and walked purposefully toward the rear unit. Pulse pounding, he stepped up to the door and rapped sharply on it. After several seconds of silence, he rapped again.

"What is it?" Proctor's muffled voice sounded irritated.

"Manager," Bobby said loudly, in a rough and surly tone.

"Go away, goddamn it!"

"I got to check the room. Smoke coming from somewhere."

"Just a minute, then."

Bobby waited. In several seconds, he heard Proctor fumbling with the inner latch. Bobby stepped a little to the side. The door opened a few inches, then caught on the inner chain.

"Do you have to check in here?" Proctor asked.

"Yep, roof may be on fire."

"Okay, then, but don't look at the lady in the bed."

"Don't worry, I won't."

Proctor lifted the chain and opened the door a few feet. He wore nothing but a pair of slacks. His eyes widened as the light from the room fell across Bobby's face.

"You!" he said in disbelief.

He tried to close the door, but with force bred of fury, Bobby put his shoulder into it and knocked it wide open, throwing Proctor across the room. Bobby pounced into the room like a wildcat. A low lamp burned beside the bed, and in the bed lay a long form covered from head to foot with the bedspread. In two long steps, Bobby was at the head of the bed. Sick with dread, he put his hands on the top of the bedspread and jerked it cleanly away.

He stepped back in sudden confusion. He saw before him the cowering, naked form of a woman, but not of his red-haired wife. Instead of Paula, Angie Zamora lay before him, her dark skin and glossy black hair in high contrast with the white of the sheets.

TEN

Angie Zamora sat up in bed, her eyes flashing with fear and anger. She crossed one arm across her breasts. With her other arm, she pulled a sheet around herself. Mike Proctor picked himself up from the floor and stood glaring at Bobby. Dusky rage distorted his face.

"God damn you, Thompson," he growled through gritted teeth.

"Have a seat, Mr. Proctor," Bobby commanded with mock respect. He motioned toward a chair by the bed.

With hate-filled eyes, Proctor went over to the chair and sat down.

"You're finished here, Thompson," he said, his voice choked with anger.

Bobby looked contemptuously at Proctor. Did the man think his money would justify him in everything?

"Don't you have things a little bit backwards, Mr. Proctor?"

The color in Proctor's face slowly receded. His look became guarded and calculating. He shook his head. "I don't have things backwards, you do."

"How're you gonna explain what happened here tonight?"

"I'm not gonna have to explain anything, because you're not gonna tell anyone."

"Seems to me I've got some responsibility along those lines. The president of the school board doesn't have any business taking under-age cheerleaders to cheap motels."

Proctor smiled grimly. "Nobody's gonna believe you if you tell a story like that. How about it, Angie? We haven't been going to any cheap motels, have we?" He turned to the girl.

She shook her head. "Don't tell anyone about this, Coach Thompson. If you do, I'll deny it ever happened." Her face and voice held fear and defiance.

Proctor smiled and spread his hands. "See how it is, Bobby? You can't tell anyone about this. Angie and I will both deny it. Who do you think the town will believe, you or us?"

"You're a despicable bastard!" Bobby looked at Proctor with loathing.

Proctor nodded. "Maybe so. But no one's gonna take my life away without a fight, and when I fight, I go for the nuts. What business of yours was it to follow us here and break in this way?"

Proctor looked at Bobby with a little cynical half-smile, as though he knew the reason Bobby had followed him to the Cactus Flower. Could Proctor be having affairs with Paula and Angie Zamora at the same time? It was possible; some men were insatiable.

Bobby wanted to believe it had been Angie at the motel with Proctor the first time Bobby had seen the truck pull into the place. He wanted to believe he had been wrong all along about Paula. But he could not be sure. Proctor's face showed he saw the doubt in Bobby's eyes. He continued looking at Bobby with his amused look.

Bobby decided to raise the ante. "Actually, Mr. Proctor, I didn't come in here expecting to find you with a woman."

Proctor raised his eyebrows. "Did you think I'd be having sex with a man?"

Bobby shook his head. "No, that wasn't it, either."

"You're gonna have to enlighten me, then."

Bobby decided to string the game out. "You use that truck outside on your ranch, don't you?"

"Obviously."

"And you use it to come to town when you want to be inconspicuous."

"Sometimes."

"Do you ever carry medicine for your livestock in it?"

Proctor's smart smile faded, and the pink spots on his cheeks brightened. "Sure. So what?"

"Sometimes you carry steroids for the livestock, don't you?"

Proctor's eyes narrowed. "What does that have to do with anything?"

Bobby paused, wondering how far to play the hand. The only football player he had seen receive steroids from Proctor was Rutherford McAlpin, and Bobby couldn't prove McAlpin had ever used them. Rutherford would lie if confronted. Bobby didn't even know the names of the other players involved. He could not let Proctor know how little he really knew.

He took a step toward Proctor, looking him directly in the eye. "I know some of those steroids never made it to the herd. I know you've been supplying them to the football players. I know some of the names, but not all of them. That's why I followed you tonight. I thought I'd find you delivering steroids to some of the boys."

Proctor's face went grey and cold. He got halfway out of his chair, then sat back down. He looked up at Bobby, his mouth a thin, bitter line.

"That's the most preposterous story I've ever heard."

"You and I both know it's true."

"Bullshit! What proof do you have?" Doubt dominated the bluster in Proctor's voice.

"You'll find out in due course."

"What are you gonna do?"

"Report what I know to the other members of the school board and the Interscholastic League."

A look of calculation and resolve passed over Proctor's face. "You know, it's a shame what happened out here tonight." He shook his head sadly.

"It sure is."

"I don't mean what you think happened with Angie and me. You were mistaken about that. Angie wasn't even here. I mean the way I drove in here and caught you making love with some whore who drove off in a car. I guess I'll just have to report what I saw to the full school board. I'd better call an emergency meeting to discuss the situation. I know Paula's gonna be surprised and disappointed."

Bobby nodded his head slowly. "So that's the way it's gonna be."

He turned to Angie Zamora, who sat in the bed with her back against the headboard, still holding the sheet across her body.

"You're not gonna go along with a lie like that, are you, Angie?"

Tears streaked the girl's face. "It's like Mr. Proctor says, Coach Thompson. I don't know nothin'."

Bobby gave both of them a bitter smile. "I guess it's a Mexican standoff, then. But I do think the other members of the school board and the Interscholastic League will be interested in what I have to say."

"Don't be a fool, Bobby," Proctor said, speaking slowly to emphasize his words. "Don't throw your entire career away over this deal. If you piss in the wind, it's gonna blow back on you."

Bobby looked down on Proctor. "Thanks for the advice." He turned to Angie. "Can I give you a ride home?"

She shook her head. "Mr. Proctor will take me."

"I'm sure he will." Bobby turned to the door. "Let me know when you call that meeting," he called over his shoulder to Proctor as he left the room.

Bobby walked quickly past the office, keeping in the shadow so the scruffy-looking manager would not see him. He walked along the shoulder of the highway to his truck. As he drove back into town, he quickly scanned the events of the evening, trying to decide on a course of action.

I still don't know who's using steroids, except for McAlpin, he told himself. And who'll believe me if I accuse Proctor of having sex with Angie Zamora? I don't have proof of anything. This town'll take Proctor's word over mine every time. They'll even believe him when he tells them he caught me having sex with someone, instead of the other way around.

I'll have to raise the steroid issue with the school board, even though I don't have proof. I could demand that the players be tested for steroids, but I doubt the board will go along with that, when I don't even know who to suspect, except for McAlpin. He'll probably say there's no reason to test him, and I can't make him be tested unless the board backs me up. Why do all these problems have to come to a head just when I'm trying to get ready for two big games?

And what about Paula? Looks like I may have been wrong about her. It was Angie Zamora, not Paula. But how can I be sure? Proctor's the kind of guy to have more than one woman on his string. I sure need to talk to Paula. I've got some crow to eat if I was wrong. Will she forgive me?

He drove quickly home. As he entered the house, the phone was ringing. The clock on the living room wall read 11:15. The call might be from Paula, or from Mike Proctor. With pounding pulse, Bobby picked up the receiver.

"Hello?"

"Bobby, I thought you were coming over here." Lola Cochran's husky voice sounded angry and disappointed.

Bobby had not thought of Lola since he had turned to follow

Proctor to the Cactus Flower.

"I'm sorry, Lola," he said diplomatically, "I was on my way over and had a flat tire. I didn't have a spare, and by the time I got it fixed at the gas station, it was too late. I was just fixin' to call you."

"It's not too late. I'm still here."

"We've both got to get up and go to school in the morning. Let me take a rain check."

"Okay, Bobby. Call again soon."

Bobby hung up and quickly punched Melvin Morris's number. After eight rings, Morris answered.

"Hello?" Morris sounded sleepy and irritated.

"Mel, it's me, Bobby."

"Jesus Christ, Bobby, do you know what time it is?"

"I'm sorry to call so late, but this is kind of an emergency."

"What's the deal?"

"I've got to talk to Paula tonight, and I don't know how to get hold of her."

"Why does it have to be tonight?"

"I've found out some things that may help to patch things up between us, but there's some shit coming down she needs to hear about from me first."

Morris hesitated several seconds, then spoke. "Okay, Wanda has her number. I don't want you two to get into a fight, so Wanda'll call her, and I'll call you back in a few minutes."

"Thanks Mel." Bobby hung up and waited with churning stomach for almost ten minutes. Finally, just when he was on the verge of calling again, Morris called back. He said Paula did not want to see Bobby alone, but she would see him at Morris's house.

"Come over in half an hour. We'll put some coffee on. Doesn't look like we're gonna get much sleep tonight, anyway."

Just after midnight, Bobby pulled up in his pickup in front of the yellow-painted frame house several blocks from the high school where the Morrises lived. Paula's old Chevrolet was parked in the drive. Bobby walked to the front door with his heart in his throat, wondering if Paula's pride would let her listen to him. He rang the bell and waited.

Wanda Morris opened the door. Her angular face softened in a smile.

"Come in, Bobby." She held the screen door open for him.

He walked into the living room. Mel Morris sat in a worn easy chair, sipping from a cup of coffee. Paula sat on the sofa next to him, face cold, eyes fixed on the floor.

"I ain't gonna be worth a crap at practice tomorrow," Morris said, his seamed, dark face screwed up in a scowl. "You oughta be ashamed causing a guy to lose his beauty sleep."

"You'll get over it."

Morris got up from the chair. "You two need to talk, so Wanda and me'll clear out."

Paula looked up quickly at Morris. "I'd rather you both stayed."

"Don't be that way, Paula," Bobby said. "I've got some things I need to tell you alone."

She shot a baleful, green-eyed look at him. "I don't even want to talk to you at all, asshole."

"We'll be in the kitchen," Wanda said. "I'll bring you both some coffee."

Bobby sat in the easy chair Morris had vacated. Paula sat a few feet away, eyes studiously averted from Bobby's earnest look. Wanda brought two steaming cups of coffee in from the kitchen. She handed one to Paula and one to Bobby.

"Call us if you need anything else." She turned and left the room.

Bobby continued looking at Paula for almost a minute. She sipped her coffee, keeping her eyes fixed on the top of the coffee table in front of her. Her wave of red-blonde hair hung over her forehead. The color in her cheeks told Bobby to be wary. She wore jeans and a white blouse under a fuzzy red sweater Bobby had bought her for Christmas the year before.

He opened with a compliment. "That sweater always did look good on you."

She twisted her mouth bitterly and gave him a sideways look. "What do you care what a shameless tramp like me looks like?"

"I never called you a tramp."

"Yes you did. You said I made love with someone else. You said the baby I'm carrying isn't yours." She put her hand to her face and wiped away several angry tears.

"I thought I had reason to think that way. Now I'm pretty sure I don't."

She looked him full in the face for the first time, her red lips curled in outrage.

"Well, isn't that just great? You drag me over there in the middle of the night to tell me you're now 'pretty sure' I haven't been screwin' around on you. What changed your mind, stud?"

"Something that happened tonight."

"What earth-shaking event was that?"

"I followed Mike Proctor out of town to the Cactus Flower motel. I expected to find him making love to you, but when I got into the room, he had someone else in the bed."

A shock passed over Paula's face.

"Who was it?"

"Angie Zamora"

Paula's eyes narrowed and her mouth drew into a tight line. "That son of a bitch!"

Was it jealously or outrage that suddenly clouded her eyes?

"I saw Proctor going into the motel a couple of weeks ago, and he had a woman with him then. I couldn't tell who it was. When I got home, you were gone. That's what made me think you were having an affair with him."

Paula twisted her mouth bitterly. "It's incredible how much confidence you have in me."

"Was I wrong to suspect something?"

Paula looked away, her face a guarded mask. "You ought to know better than to ask that."

"I'd like to have your answer."

"I don't have to answer a question like that." She kept her eyes averted.

Bobby wanted to press her further, but he feared her response. Her evasion suggested guilt. All his queasy doubts returned. He sat in silence for several seconds, studying her hardened face.

"There's more you should know," he finally said.

She looked toward him again, raising her eyebrows.

Bobby told her about the meeting between Proctor and Rutherford McAlpin at the fieldhouse; how Bobby had later followed Proctor to the motel, thinking he was making a steroid delivery, and seen him going into the rear motel unit with a woman obscured by the shadows. Finally, omitting the detail that Bobby had been on his way to meet Lola Cochran, he told how he had again followed Proctor to the motel and caught him in the room with Angie Zamora lying nude in the bed.

"I told Proctor I was going to report both the steroids and his affair with Angie. He and Angie both said they would deny everything. Proctor's gonna call a school board meeting and tell everybody I was at the motel with a woman to cover his own ass. I wanted to tell you about it before you heard it from someone else."

Paula cocked her head to the side in a quizzical look. "Of course it isn't true?"

"Of course what isn't true?"

"You weren't having sex with a woman at the Cactus Flower tonight?"

Bobby thought guiltily of Lola as he shook his head. He looked Paula directly in the eye. "No, I wasn't."

"Why should I believe you? Maybe Mike did catch you out there with someone. How do I know you're not the one making up stories?"

"You'd believe that asshole over me?"

"If you were with a woman, you'd have a good reason to lie about it."

Frustrated, bitter anger swept over Bobby.

"I should have known better than to try to talk to you."

He got to his feet. For several seconds, he stood before Paula, looking down at her proud, aloof face. He vented his frustration in angry words.

"Just go to hell!"

He turned away, walked to the front door, and left the house, closing the door decisively behind him. He drove home with bitter, recriminatory thoughts.

I wasn't wrong after all, he thought. She is having an affair with Proctor. I gave her a chance to deny it, and she didn't. She may ditch him now that she knows about Angie, but that doesn't help me. How can we ever reconcile? I'll be damned if I'll be responsible for another man's baby. This damn town's gonna cost me my wife and my career at the same time.

◆

The next morning, Bobby met Melvin Morris in the coaches' office in the fieldhouse during their free period. Bobby apologized for leaving the Morrises' house so abruptly the evening before. He told Morris about overhearing the conversation between Proctor and Rutherford McAlpin, and about what had gone on at the Cactus

Flower Motel the night before. When Bobby had finished, Morris shook his head slowly in anger.

"I always thought Proctor was a dirty cocksucker and now I know it."

"Did you ever suspect anything like this was going on?"

Morris looked down at the floor with narrowed eyes, then back up at Bobby. "I didn't dream Proctor was screwin' a cheerleader. I did have some suspicions about the steroids."

"What caused them?"

"Even last year, Proctor seemed to be a little too close to McAlpin, and Rutherford seemed to be getting bigger and stronger way too fast. Coach Winslow told me he saw the two of them meeting up here once or twice on Saturdays. I know he was concerned about the situation, but he never got any proof."

"Why didn't you mention this to me?"

"No point in stirring up trouble."

"Do you have any idea what other players might be involved?"

Morris shook his head. "Winslow never said anything about anyone except McAlpin."

"Maybe I'd better talk to Winslow."

"I'll give you his number in Dallas."

"What are my chances at this school board meeting, Mel?"

Morris studied the floor for a few minutes. "I believe every word you say. I've always thought Proctor would do stuff like this, but that doesn't mean other people will believe you. There are people like Gerald Stedman, who will want to believe you because they don't like Proctor, but unless you can prove what you say, most of the people in this town will believe him."

Morris concluded in a somber tone. "It's gonna be tough. He's been in this town all his life. Half the people here owe him something, one way or another."

"Maybe I oughta just pack up and leave."

Morris set his leathery jaw. "Fuck that shit. Spit in the bastard's eye and let the chips fall where they may. I'm with you all the way."

"Thanks Mel."

"If we lose, we can leave town together."

◆

Late that afternoon, just before football practice, Principal Leon Purvis brought a letter to Bobby in his class room. The prim little man waited just inside the door until all the students left, then walked up to Bobby and put the letter in his hand.

"This just came by hand delivery from the administration building." Purvis' high-pitched voice vibrated with tension. "I got one too."

Bobby deliberately opened the envelope, took out the letter and read it. It informed him his presence was required at a special school board meeting the Monday after the final game of the season with Breckenridge. Mike Proctor had signed the letter as President of the School Board.

"What can it mean?" Purvis asked anxiously.

Bobby calmly yawned to conceal the excitement he felt. "Probably just the usual financial emergency."

"It must be something more serious than that. It says a delicate personnel matter will be discussed."

"I guess we'll find out at the meeting."

Purvis left the room, shaking his little head from side to side in agitation. After the practice, Bobby showed the letter to Melvin Morris.

Morris smiled without humor. "The shit's fixin' to hit the fan. We better line up some ammunition."

"I've been thinking about going to the sheriff and telling him about Angie Zamora."

Morris shook his head vehemently. "It won't do any good to take that story to Sheriff Wallace. He owes his election to Proctor. It's nothing to the good sheriff that Proctor's screwin' some Meskin gal."

"What about the district attorney, or the police?"

"Proctor's in tight with all of them, too."

"What can I do then?"

"See what Coach Winslow can tell you about the steroids. If he doesn't know anything, then just pray for a miracle."

◆

At home alone that night in his empty house, Bobby pulled Mel Morris's note with Winslow's number on it out of his shirt pocket, picked up the receiver and dialed the number. Nervously, Bobby waited for someone to answer. He had never met Coach Winslow, and didn't know how the man would react to his call.

After several rings, a woman answered.

"Is Bob Winslow there?" Bobby asked.

"Just a minute."

Bobby heard the sounds of the receiver being laid down, then the woman's voice called, "It's for you, honey!"

Thumping sounds indicated someone was picking up the telephone.

"Hello." Winslow's voice sounded faintly irritated.

"Coach Winslow, this is Bobby Thompson, out at Comanche Springs."

After a short pause, Winslow answered, his voice now affable.

"Good to hear from you, Coach Thompson. From what I read, you're doing pretty good with the team."

Bobby said the team's success was due more to Winslow's groundwork the preceding year, and the natural talent of the boys than to any special ability on Bobby's part.

"Don't sell yourself short. I never thought they'd come this far so fast. You must be doing something right."

"I lucked into a good quarterback."

"You sure did. Where did that kid come from, anyway?"

"His father came out from Fort Worth to be the new preacher at the True Word Baptist Church."

"That was sure lucky for the team. Rusty Stedman plays well at times, but he's not consistent enough to be a really good quarterback."

"Some of the other teams are mad about Terrance. Stephenville has a charge against us, claiming we recruited Terrance by getting his father the job."

"Those folks have always been sore losers."

"I think the Stephenville charge is just sour grapes, but I'm worried about it. There are a lot of people that want to believe it, including some of our boosters who're mad because I've been starting Terrance over Rusty."

"I bet Gerald Stedman's fit to be tied." Winslow sounded grimly amused.

"He and his group are the main problem."

"It doesn't help that Terrance is black."

"That's just like salt in the wound to Stedman. The Stephenville charge is bad enough, but what I called about is an even bigger problem. Mel Morris thought you might be able to help me with it."

"What is it?"

Bobby described the meeting he had witnessed between Proctor and McAlpin. "I don't even know what players are involved, except for McAlpin. Coach Morris thought you might have some information about it."

After several seconds of silence, Winslow answered in apprehensive, evasive voice.

"I did suspect Proctor was giving McAlpin steroids, but I finally decided I was just imagining things. I sure never suspected any other players."

"I found some notes you wrote last year about McAlpin that made me think you might have something on him."

"McAlpin's a remarkable asshole for such a young man, but that's about all I was ever able to say about him. I'm sorry. I can't help you."

Winslow's voice had a final sound, like the closing of a door.

"Well, I'd sure hoped you'd know something, but if you don't, you don't. Thanks for talking to me."

"You're welcome," Winslow answered brusquely. "Good luck."

After Bobby hung up, he sat by the telephone for almost an hour, trying to think of other options, but there were none. The people of Comanche Springs would believe Proctor's charges. The football season would close with Bobby losing his wife and his career. Why should he even worry about the last two games of the season? He was finished.

Suddenly, he remembered Bill Mattingly, and the words he had had for Bobby and his high school teammates.

"Remember, men, you can't help getting beat sometimes, but you can help being a quitter. Give the game your all, and you can always walk off the field with your head up."

Bobby clenched his teeth in determination. He would not be a quitter. Whatever else happens, I'll win these last two games for 'em! he told himself.

◆

On Friday night, the buses taking the Warrior team to the game against the Mineral Wells Rams pulled into Mineral Wells in late afternoon. They drove past a little mesa covered with mesquite and prickly pear into the downtown. The old Baker Hotel building, a defunct relic of the days when Mineral Wells had been a spa where people from Fort Worth and Dallas came to take mineral baths, dominated the business district.

They ate at a downtown restaurant, then drove to the stadium, where the team suited out, then trotted toward the playing field. As he followed the team onto the field, Bobby glanced over the nearly full stands. He wondered if Paula had come to the game. In spite of everything, he wanted her to be there. He saw Angie Zamora cartwheeling before the fans with the other cheerleaders. Was she thinking of sex with Mike Proctor even while she gyrated so gracefully?

The Rams played a tough game, taking the lead for most of the first half. Just before the half, Terrance connected on a touchdown pass to Ritterman to put the Warriors ahead for the first time. They led by a narrow margin for the rest of the game.

The second half was like a war of attrition, with both teams grinding out yardage for a few downs, then giving the ball up with a punt. Never ahead by more than one touchdown, the Warriors held grimly onto their lead, and the final whistle blew with the score 21-19 in their favor.

Bobby shook hands at midfield with the dejected Mineral Wells coach, then trotted toward the dressing room. The red-haired reporter, Ray Stewart, met him at the dressing room door.

"Great game, coach. Win the one next week and we've got it all."

Bobby's heart jumped. "Did Breckenridge beat Graham?"

Stewart nodded exultantly. "14-0. I just heard it on the radio."

"That's just great!" Bobby entered the dressing room to share the news with his happy team.

ELEVEN

The Saturday morning after the Mineral Wells game, the telephone in the living room rang at 8 a.m. Bobby woke up with the first ring. At first, he rolled over in bed and covered his head with a pillow, trying to ignore the nagging sound. After five or six rings, he rolled out of bed and looked at his watch.

"Too damn early," he muttered as he stumbled through the house to the phone.

"Hello?" Bobby answered with a surly voice.

"Hello, coach, this is Ray Stewart."

Stewart's sweating, pimpled face intruded unpleasantly into Bobby's mind.

"I might have know it was you, Ray."

"Why's that?"

"No one else would have the gall to call this early."

Stewart laughed gratingly. "Gall's part of my territory."

"What can I do for you?"

"What's the deal on this school board meeting a week from Monday?"

"Why don't you ask Mike Proctor?"

"I did. He implied it had something to do with you."

Bobby remembered his suspicions that Stewart was in Proctor's pocket. Stewart probably already had the full details of Proctor's accusation.

"Ray, I expect the meeting does have something to do with differences between Proctor and me, but I'm not gonna talk about it now. I'm gonna save my talking for the meeting. I wish Proctor would do the same."

"I just wanted to give you a chance to tell your side of it, coach."

"That must mean you already have Proctor's side."

"He has told me a little bit about what the charges involve."

"I just bet he has. I'm still gonna wait till the meeting to say what I have to say. I will give you some advice, though, Ray. Keep your powder dry on this story."

"What do you mean?"

"Come to the meeting and find out."

The front page of the Courier the next morning carried Stewart's story about the meeting. "Thompson Accused of Misconduct," ran the headline. In the story, Stewart said that a source within the administration who spoke on condition of anonymity had confirmed that the meeting had been called to discuss charges of an extremely serious nature against the Warrior coach. The source declined to give the details of the accusation. They would be discussed at the meeting.

◆

On Monday afternoon, Bobby gathered the team around him on the practice field before the start of practice.

"I know you've read the stories in the paper about the meeting next week, men," he said, looking over the uplifted young faces around him. "I don't want to talk about the charges against me now. I'll have a lot to say about them at the meeting, but for right now, I don't want anything to get in the way of your getting ready for the Breckenridge game. This is our last district game, men. If we win it, we go on to bi-district. Some reporters are picking Breckenridge to win state. That means if we beat them, we can win state. So don't worry about my problems, men. Just concentrate on the game Friday, so you can give it all you've got."

Bobby sent the players to start their calesthentics. As he walked toward where the captains were forming the men up in lines, Mel Morris fell in beside him.

"What rumors are going around about what I'm accused of?" Bobby asked.

Morris grinned sardonically. "Some nice person's been leaking all the details. One story is that you were smoking dope and having sex with two teenage girls at the same time. In another version, you were drunk as a skunk and doing obscene things with some woman hitchhiker you picked up on the highway."

"No telling what they'll be saying by the time of the meeting."

"No telling. Did you call Bob Winslow?"

"Yep, but he couldn't tell me anything."

"I was afraid of that."

With difficulty, Bobby focused his attention on the details of the practice. He and the other coaches put the boys through their drills, then concluded the session by scrimmaging the first string against the second. Bobby watched Terrance Brown and Rusty Stedman closely. At the end of the practice, he concluded that Terrance would be his pick to start the Breckenridge game.

As he drove home after the practice to get ready for the booster club meeting, he thought of Paula with bitter longing. He had not seen her or talked to her since they had met at the Morrises. He did not even know if she had gone to the Mineral Wells game. It seemed certain they could not reconcile. After the Breckenridge game, he would see a lawyer. Although no divorce would be granted until after the birth of the baby, at least, he could get things started.

At the booster club meeting, Bobby looked over the crowd as Joe Timmons called the meeting to order. With his silvery pompadour, turkey-wattle jowls and large gut straining the front of his flowery western-style shirt, Timmons was the caricature of a West Texas rancher. Serious-faced and owlish in his horn-rimmed glasses, banker Gerald Stedman sat with Coach Art Bennett and others of his camp at a table near the speaker's platform.

Mike Proctor, pink-cheeked and broad-shouldered, sat with freckled, pimply Ray Stewart, and other Proctor groupies at a table across the room from Stedman and his group. Mel Morris was near the middle of the room at a table with school board members Willis Fullerton and Ned Zablonski. Fullerton wore his usual plaid sports coat. His face carried a laid-back, humorous smile. Dark and serious in grey khaki work cothes, Zablonski sat between Morris and Fullerton.

While Timmons was going through the opening business, Royal Brown came into the back of the room and took a seat at one of the rear tables. He gave Bobby a little nod as he took off his plaid-banded grey felt hat and sat down. When the waitresses had served the last dish of cherry cobbler, Timmons called on Bobby for his report. The room grew quiet as he went to the speaker's stand and adjusted the microphone. He knew the fans were thinking as much of the charges against him as they were of the team.

"We've come a long way this year, folks," he said. "Just a few weeks ago, I wouldn't have believed it possible that the district championship would be riding on our game with Breckenridge this week, but we've won some key games and had a little luck, and now, we've got a real chance at winning district. And since Breckenridge is one of the best-rated teams in the state, if we beat them, there's no telling how far we can go. If we beat them, we'll have a real good shot at the state championship."

Spontaneous applause broke out all over the room. Some of the fans whistled and cheered. Bobby had the hollow feeling that he was deluding the boosters by holding out hope for a championship. If his charges of steroid use by the players held up, they would negate all the Warrior's victories, but he couldn't tell the fans that now. He waited for the noise to die down, then went on.

"In spite of the good position we're in, there are some serious clouds hanging over us. I'm sure you've read about some charges that have been made against me. Some of you are involved with those charges, and those of you on the school board will have to judge those charges. I'm not gonna say anything about them tonight, except to assure you I've done nothing wrong. I believe I'll be able to make my position clear at the school board meeting next week. I'd invite all of you to come and hear me out at that time."

One of the Proctor groupies, a bland-faced man named Ned Stapleton who owned a dry cleaners, held up his hand, and Bobby nodded to him.

"I got a little problem with those charges, coach. If half of what I'm hearing is true, you oughta be resigning, instead of talking about coaching the team in this game."

Bobby held Stapleton's eyes with a level look. "If half of what I'm hearing about myself was true, I'd agree with you, but talk is cheap. Why don't you wait until the school board meeting to judge the right and wrong of the situation?"

Stapleton shook his head. "All I'm saying is, if there's any truth to what I'm hearing, you're not fit to be coaching the team."

Willis Fullerton stood up, faced the crowd, and spoke with a voice of level tolerance. "Folks, a man's innocent until proven guilty. Let's not judge Coach Thompson until we've heard all the evidence."

Murmurs of approval came from several parts of the room, and Stapleton sat down. Bobby glanced toward Mike Proctor, who was leaning back in his chair with his hands behind his head, looking at the ceiling with a self-satisfied smile. Bobby had an intense desire to smash Proctor's head on the floor. Gerald Stedman held up his hand and Bobby recognized him.

"What about the Stephenville charges, Coach Thompson? Are we going to win the district championship just to lose it by being disqualified?"

"I said we had some clouds hanging over us, and that's one of them. I haven't heard anything from the Interscholastic League, but I continue to think there's nothing to the charges."

"I'm not so sure about that, myself." Stedman looked meaningfully toward Mike Proctor, who straightened up in his chair and turned toward Stedman with an angry face.

"I'm getting awful tired of you and your insinuations, Gerald!"

Joe Timmons moved quickly to the podium and spoke into the mike.

"Please, folks, if we ever needed unity, it's now. Everyone cool off, and let's put aside our differences and start concentrating on supporting our team."

"Thanks for those words, Mr. Timmons," Bobby said. "We shouldn't be having dissension when we have to much to gain by pulling together. We can win this game, but we need your support. Ya'll all come to the game and root for the team. Let's put our problems aside for now, and just concentrate on beating Breckenridge."

Bobby called on the Methodist preacher, Bill Blevins, to dismiss the meeting with a prayer. While Blevins spoke his words of reconciliation, Bobby said a silent prayer of his own, for his team, for the town, for Paula, and, most of all, for himself.

◆

Dry-mouthed, Bobby watched the Breckenridge Buckaroos warming up across the field as the Warriors went through their own preliminary drills. Only a few fall insects flurried around the floodlights bathing the field and a cold northern breeze demonstrated the lateness of the season.

Fans filled the stands on both sides of the field. On the Breckenridge side, a fight song blared from the green-and-white uniformed band. The Comanche Springs cheerleaders were doing a yell in which the girls stood on the thighs of the boys, who held their legs while they leaned forward exhorting the fans.

The Buckaroo team started a passing drill. Bobby saw their big quarterback, Bob Abernathy, drilling passes to the players running downfield from two lines alongside the center. Big and smart, lightning-quick at 210 pounds, Abernathy was a strong contender for the all-state team. The Buckaroo fullback, Hunter Boyd, fired off from the line, sprinted downfield, and cut smartly to the inside, where he nailed the pass Abernathy drilled to him. A lean 225 pounds, he ran the 100-yard dash in less than ten seconds.

Bobby mentally contrasted the well-publicized might of the Buckaroos with the unheralded talent of his own team. Billy Wayne Fox, the handsome, curly-headed, insufferably arrogant Buckaroo coach, had been quoted in the paper making disparaging remarks about the Warriors. He said they had been lucky to come as far as they had because they had no real talent. He had hedged his remarks by saying he was taking nothing for granted, that his team was preparing for a tough game, but his cockiness irritated Bobby.

Just before 8 p.m., the teams went back to their dressing rooms to get ready for the kickoff. While Cheery O'Leery bustled about putting on a few last bandages and packing up more bottles of gatorade, Bobby stood before the players and reached down inside himself to pull out the inspiration the team would need to win.

"How many of you read the paper this morning?" he asked, and about half the hands in the room shot up. "Those of you who did know what this pretty-boy coach of theirs, Billy Wayne Fox, thinks of you. He says you're not even in the same league with his team. He says none of you has any real talent. He says you've just been lucky to come this far.

"He's used to winning, and he's used to having the press tell him how good he is. That goes for the Buckaroo players, too. That big fullback, Boyd, and that quick-steppin' quarterback, Abernathy, think they're sure bets for the all-state team. Just think of what the press has said this year about you guys. Up until we popped Mineral Wells last week, no one thought we had any chance at winning district. Even now, they're not taking us seriously."

Bobby held up the sports page of the Abilene paper, spreading it out so all the team could see it.

"See what they're saying: 'Breckenridge Picked by 21 Points'. Can you believe that? With all the great playing we've done, the sportswritrs don't think we can even stay within three touchdowns of this crew.

"Well, they've got another think coming. The Buckaroos have a nasty surprise in store for them. You guys are better than they are. You haven't got the recognition, and you haven't got the publicity, but you're better, just the same. All you've got to do is search your souls for that burning desire I've been talking about all season.

"If you can find that, we can take the hide right off this bunch of smart-asses, and let the sportswriters in Abilene know that all their newspaper is good for is to take to the outhouse when you're short of toilet paper. This is it, men! Remember everything you've learned this year; play tough and smart, and we'll bring that championship home where it belongs. Now, let's go get 'em!"

With a guttural, determined roar, the Warriors clattered to their feet and trotted toward the field.

The Warriors won the toss and elected to receive. With misgivings, Bobby watched the gusty north breeze tearing at the American flag posted over the stadium. Had he made the right choice in going for the ball? The wind was going to be a real factor in this game.

Joe King pulled in the Buckaroo kickoff just inside the end zone. He did an indecisive little dance to the right, then reversed himself and started back to the left.

"Make up your mind, Joe!" Bobby called in exasperation.

King finally started straight up the middle of the field, but his blocking had all lined up to the right. One of the Buckaroo defensive backs straightened him up at the ten. Then, two of the big defensive backs smashed him into the ground. The Warriors had the ball, but with poor field position and a strong north wind in their faces.

Terrance Brown ran a fullback slant over right tackle and McAlpin churned out three yards before going down. On the next play, Brown handed off to Curtis McInnes, but the preening canary didn't go anywhere. One of the Buckaroo linebackers met him on the Warrior side of the line of scrimmage and threw him down for a yard loss, bringing up third and eight.

Playing it safe, Terrance elected not to pass into the wind. He tried an option around right end, keeping the ball himself and trying to make the cut up field for first down yardage, but the Buckaroo defensive end caught him at the line of scrimmage and threw him down for no gain.

Mel Morris screwed up his dark face in disgust. "Their linemen are wiping the field with our asses."

With fourth and long yardage, Alhamid dropped back to punt. He got a good foot into the ball, but it shot into the air at a high angle, where the strong wind caught it, blowing it back over Alhamid's head toward the Warrior goal, with three or four Buckaroos in hot pursuit.

"Shit! shit! shit!" Bobby's words hissed through his teeth.

McAlpin and Terrance Brown chased the ball with the Breckenridge players until it came down at the Warrior five-yard line. All the players in the vicinity dove for the ball at the same time, piling on top of each other. When the officials had peeled the players off the pileup, Boyd, the big Buckaroo fullback, came up with the ball. The Bucks had a first and ten at the Warrior four-yard line.

Art Bennett shook his noble head. "We're giving it to 'em on a silver platter!"

"Time! Time!" Bobby yelled toward the field.

Ned Chambers glanced toward the Warrior bench, and Bobby held his hands up together in a "T".

"Time!" Chambers yelled at one of the officials, and the official called a timeout.

Bobby motioned the defensive team over to the sideline. "It's gonna be tough, men, but we've been in tough places before. They're gonna try to bull it up the middle with that big fullback. Jam 'em up, and make 'em fumble. Let's get the ball back and get going!"

Back on the field, the Warriors formed a tight defensive formation, with Chambers and the feisty, red-haired offensive guard, Bill Foster, playing right up in the gaps from their interior linebacker positions. The Buckaroos came up to the line and Abernathy, the quarterback, called a quick snap. As Bobby had predicted, Hunter Boyd came charging up the middle, taking the handoff from Abernathy and plowing into the line right over the tail of the Buck's center.

Juan Guerrero met him at the line of scrimmage and straightened him up. Chambers and Foster hit him high and drove him back, and the play ended with no gain.

"Way to go! Way to go!" Bobby yelled.

The next play, Abernathy handed to Boyd again, this time on a slant over left tackle, but Albert Walker and Lee Shaughnessey got loose from their blockers and hit Boyd together, stopping him for no gain. On third and goal, Abernathy tried an option around right end, keeping the ball himself and trying to make the cut in for the touchdown, but Eddie Ritterman and Joe King cut him down as he tried to turn the corner, bringing up fourth down and still goal to go.

"Watch for the pass!" Art Bennett yelled, and the defense loosened up a little.

Bobby watched as the Buckaroos trotted up to the line for their fourth and final try for the score. The Warriors had held the Bucks for three downs. Could they do it again?

This time, Abernathy dropped back into a pocket while the Buckaroo ends ran a crossbuck pattern into the end zone. Rutherford McAlpin and Terrance Brown covered them man for man as the Warrior interior line attacked the pocket of blockers protecting Abernathy.

Just as Juan Guerrero broke through the blockers and charged Abernathy, rushing with his arms up like an attacking bear, the end Terrance was covering got a step ahead of him. Abernathy drilled the ball to the end with a perfect lead, and the boy made a good catch. Bobby took no consolation in seeing Guerrero, unable to check his momentum, crash into Abernathy and knock him to the ground. The Buckaroos had drawn first blood. Boyd kicked the extra point, and the Bucks led 7-0.

McInnes ran the Buckaroo kickoff back to the thirty before going down, giving the Warriors better field position than on their first possession. Brown ran a halfback dive to Joe King for two or three yards, then another to the left to McInnes for four yards, bringing up third and about four. The next play could be either a run or a pass. Bobby hoped Terrance would stay on the ground. The Warriors were still too close to their own goal to be passing into the treacherous north wind.

When Terrance took the snap from center and started to fall back, Bobby knew he had called a pass.

"Don't take any chances, Terrance!" Bobby muttered to himself.

The line gave good protection, and Terrance had plenty of time to pick a target. At first, all the receivers were covered. Just as several of the Buckaroo defenders broke through the blocking and charged Terrance, Eddie Ritterman pulled away from his defender and cut across the middle, hands extended for the ball.

Terrance planted his feet to drill the ball downfield, but just as he threw it, one of the Buck defenders knifed into him from the side, and the ball wobbled across the line out of control, where the wind blew it into the arms of one of the oversized Buckaroo linebackers.

"Get him! Get him, goddamn it!" Mel Morris yelled.

McAlpin and Albert Walker hit the big man, one high, the other low. Stumbling, he shook them loose, broke across the line of scrimmage, and headed for the goal line. Terrance nailed him at the one, but his momentum carried him into the end zone for the second Buckaroo touchdown. Again, the Bucks converted the extra point to lead 14-0 with several minutes to go in the first quarter.

As the teams lined up for the kickoff, Art Bennett edged up to Bobby.

"Terrance has fucked up twice already. Isn't it time for a change?" Bennett's voice had a disdainful edge to it.

Bobby answered angrily. "I wouldn't say he fucked up."

"He let that boy get ahead of him in the end zone, and that cost us a touchdown. Now, he's thrown an interception."

"The interception wasn't his fault, and anyone's gonna get beat on defense sometimes."

Bennett grinned a bitter, supercilious grin. "Don't say I didn't warn you."

Bobby reviewed his options. The game threatened to become a rout. Should he pull Terrance now and send in Rusty? The move would be popular with many fans and would still certain criticism if the Warriors lost. On the other hand, Terrance had not looked bad; he had simply been the victim of bad breaks. Bobby decided to leave him in for the time being.

The wind caught the Buckaroo kickoff and carried it completely out of the end zone. The Warriors took the touchback on their own twenty and started grinding out yardage on the ground. Bit by bit, they grimly trudged up the field. McAlpin made good gains up the center of the line. McInnes made several gains of six to eight yards over the blocking of Alhamid and Walker. With his scared-jackrabbit style, Joe King sliced through the right side of the line several times for good yardage.

The first quarter ended with the Warriors at the Buckaroo forty. With the change in the wind, Bobby decided to open the game up. He called Terrance Brown over to the sideline.

"You're going good on the ground, but now that we've got the wind, let's keep 'em honest with a few passes."

"You got it, coach!"

Terrance ran two more running plays that gained ground to the Buckaroo thirty-two. On third and one, he dropped back to pass. McAlpin and McInnes dropped back to block, while Joe King and Lee Shaughnessey ran a crossbuck pattern across the middle. Eddie Ritterman at right end bumped the Buckaroo defensive end, then streaked for the goal line.

The Buckaroo defensive backs had started coming up when they saw Shaughnessey and King running the crossbuck. Ritterman flew past the last two defenders. They turned to follow him, but he maintained the several steps he had gained on them. Behind perfect blocking, Terrance set himself and got the ball off in a perfect parabola toward Ritterman's outreaching arms.

Wild with excitement, Bobby saw that the pass would come down just as Ritterman crossed the goal line. But the catch was not to be. At the last split second, Ritterman suddenly stumbled and sprawled on the grass, and the ball hit the ground several yards ahead of him.

"God damn it to hell!" Bobby swore bitterly.

On the field, Terrance fell to his knees, pounding the turf with his fists. Recovering, he got to his feet and huddled up the team.

With fourth and one, Terrance ran a dive up the middle to McAlpin, but two of the huge Buckaroo linemen hit the big fullback at the line and stopped him for no gain, and the ball went over to the Bucks on downs.

"Shoulda stayed on the ground," Art Bennett said knowingly.

Ritterman came running over to the sideline, tears streaking his face.

"What happened?" Bobby asked.

"One of my shoes came untied and I tripped on the string."

"Shake it off, son! No use crying over spilled milk."

The Buckaroos took the ball around their own twenty-five yard line and started a meticulous march down the field. Wisely, they avoided the vagaries of the gusty wind, and stayed entirely on the ground, running first to one side of the line, then another, then up the middle, usually for good yardage. Bobby kept looking at the clock as the seconds of the first half kept ticking maddeningly away. His anxiety increased when the Buckaroos crossed into Warrior territory and threatened to score again.

"Tighten up, defense!" he shouted toward the field.

With several minutes to go in the half, Abernathy ran an option to the right, tossing the ball out to Hunter Boyd, who caught it without breaking stride and turned on all his speed as he crossed the line of scrimmage. Ritterman bumped him hard at the Warrior forty, but could not get hold of him. Boyd made a cut and headed back to the inside of the field. He brushed past Juan Guerrero before the big man could grab him, made another cut, and headed for the goal line.

Suddenly, Ned Chambers, running with speed Bobby had never seen before, came flying across the field and caught Boyd with a flying tackle at the thirty. Boyd hit the ground with a solid thump, and the ball squirted out of his arms, bouncing crazily across the field with both Warriors and Buckaroos after it.

Running low to the ground, Albert Walker dove in ahead of the others and wrapped himself around the ball so tightly that he still had it, even after the officials peeled off the players of both sides from the ensuing pileup. Bobby looked at the clock. Less than two minutes remained in the half. He pulled Terrance Brown to the side.

"We've got the wind, but don't take any chances. Don't pass unless you can get across the fifty. Let's get on the scoreboard."

"Right on, coach!"

Brown ran a couple of slants, a fullback dive, and a draw up the middle to McAlpin for over fifteen yards, taking the Warriors across the fifty for a first down.

On first down, he fell back into a deep pocket and lobbed a long pass to Lee Shaughnessey, who caught it at the Buckaroo twenty-five, amid cheers from the Warrior stands. On the next play, Terrance tried another pass, this time to Joe King, who had run a buttonhook pattern down to the ten.

The ball flew straight and true toward King, but at the last second, Bob Abernathy swept across the field and intercepted the pass, halting the Warrior drive.

"Lord, give us a break!" Bobby said disgustedly.

"That's three fuckups now for Terrance," Art Bennett taunted Bobby.

Bobby gestured obscenely with his finger, and Bennett turned his comely face away with a condescending smile.

Taking no chances, the Buckaroos ran out the time with long counts and running plays, and the half ended with the Bucks ahead

14-0.

In the dressing room, Bobby looked around the room at his grim, silent players. The team had a weary, careworn look, as though the fight had all drained out of them. Had they come so far only to ignominiously lose to the cocky Buckaroos?

"Listen up, men." Bobby paused until all eyes were turned toward him. "There's nothing to cheer about in the first half. The wind hurt us, and bad breaks hurt us, but I'm not gonna blame what happened on bad breaks or the wind. You can overcome bad breaks by playing at the very peak of your ability. We haven't been doing that, but the game's not over yet.

"It's hard to spot a team like this bunch fourteen points and come back and win, but we can do it. Burning desire, men! That's what it takes--burning desire. How many of you can really say you've felt that kind of desire in this game so far? If you find that desire and play like you've never played before, the score will take care of itself."

Bobby went to the blackboard and started outlining defensive positions and offensive plays. He showed the players the weak spots and told them how to tighten up.

"Terrance, this half, I want you to run along the line on the option like you were always gonna keep the ball yourself. Last half, I could tell when you were gonna pitch out by the way you pussy-footed out to the corner. These Buckaroos are smart. If I can read you, so can they. Let's fool 'em better this next half."

Terrance answered with a tight, fierce nod of his head.

"Chambers, I can tell when you're gonna rush the passer, and when you're gonna hang back. Keep 'em guessing this half. Make 'em think you're gonna rush every time."

"Right, coach." Chambers set his jowly jaw in resolve.

"On your feet men!" Bobby said when he had finished his critique. "Time to go get 'em. If we've got the ball, we're gonna keep it. If they've got the ball, we're gonna get it back. And we're gonna win this football game!"

The Buckaroos elected to take the ball, giving the Warriors the increasingly strong north wind at their backs for the third quarter. A norther was moving in, and the temperature was dropping by the minute. Alhamid's kick flew beyond the end zone and the Buckaroos had to settle for taking the ball on their own twenty. They tried running up the middle, but Chambers, Foster, Alhamid, big Juan

Guerrero, and snake-mean Albert Walker presented a solid front and stopped the Bucks cold for three downs.

On fourth down, the Buckaroo kicker caught the ball solidly and it took off at a perfect angle for a long punt, but then the wind caught it. The ball seemed to hover in the air, then actually moved backward, toward the Buckaroo goal. Ned Chambers was under the ball when it came down.

He caught it, wrapped his arms around it, and started lumbering downfield. He had only gone a few steps when several Buckaroo defenders caught up with him from behind and brought him down, but he had returned the ball to the Buckaroo twenty-five. The Warriors had the ball with good field position and the wind to their backs.

"Now it's their turn to sweat," Bobby crowed to the other coaches.

Terrance took the team down to the fifteen with slants and dives into the interior line by McInnes and McAlpin. On first and ten, he called a short pass play. The two ends, Ritterman and Shaughnessey, crossed over the middle, while Joe King ran down and out into the end zone. He fooled his defender with a quick swivel of his hips, and cut across the middle.

"Hit him! Hit him!" Bobby yelled.

Terrance threw a smooth spiral right into King's arms for the first Warrior score. Alhamid converted the point after, and the score was 14-7. While the officials were setting up the kickoff, Bobby called the defensive team over to the side of the field.

"Hit 'em hard men. Don't give 'em any breathing room. Force a punt so we can get the ball back while we've still got the wind."

Again, Alhamid put the ball out of the end zone, and the Buckaroos started out on their own twenty, with the goal eighty yards away.

The Warrior wall grudgingly gave the Buckaroos a few yards on the first two downs. If the Warriors held one more down, they would force a punt into the increasing wind. On third down, Abernathy ran an option to the left. When he got to the point where he would have to decide whether to keep the ball or pitch it out to Hunter Boyd, Eddie Ritterman shook loose his blocker, charged across the line, and hit Abernathy at the belt line.

Keen joy swept over Bobby as he saw the Buckaroo quarterback start to go down. But at the last split second, Abernathy twisted his body and got the pitchout off to Boyd, who caught the end-over-end ball and charged across the line.

The Warrior defenders had all slowed down when they saw Abernathy start to go down. Pouring on his legendary speed, Boyd headed for the far sideline. McInnes and Terrance Brown followed on angular courses, trying to cut Boyd off, but they were too late.

Brown made a desperate flying leap and got a hand on Boyd at the fifty, but Boyd broke the tackle and galloped off down field with no one near him. In seconds, he crossed the goal for the third Buckaroo touchdown. Bobby turned away from the field, holding his head in his hands. The Buckaroos missed their extra point try, but the 20-7 lead seemed insurmountable.

The Warriors lined up for the Buckaroo kickoff with minutes left in the third quarter. The wind kept the Bucks' kick out of the end zone. Joe King caught the ball on the five yard line and made a nice runback to the thirty-five before going down. The Warriors pounded out two first downs with runs through the interior of the line and short passes, crossing over into Buckaroo territory just as the gun sounded for the fourth quarter.

Bobby looked up at the American flag behind the scoreboard. The wind had it stretched out flat like a piece of cardboard.

He turned to Mel Morris. "We'll have to stay on the ground now."

Morris nodded. "It's gonna be tough."

Terrance Brown brought the team up to the line of scrimmage at the Buck forty-five. He ran an option to the right, kept the ball himself, and made his cut up the field. He picked up three yards before one of the big defensive linemen put a bear hug on him. Terrance twisted his body desperately, breaking loose from the tackle, but before he could turn and start running again, Hunter Boyd came flying at him from across the field, crashing into him from the side and knocking him hard to the ground.

Bobby heard Terrance's head hit the ground with a sickening thud. Hunter Boyd got up from where he had fallen, but Terrance lay still and unmoving on the field. Cheers and catcalls came from the Buckaroo side of the stands. One of the officials called time and Bobby and Cheery O'Leery ran out to where Terrance lay. Just as they got to him, he sat up.

"You okay, Terrance?" Bobby asked.

Brown didn't answer. He sat on the ground with his hands

behind him. O'Leery mopped Terrance's face with a towel.

"What's your name?" Bobby asked.

Brown shook his head several times, then looked up at Bobby.

"Terrance Brown." His eyes again held intelligence.

"See if you can get up." Bobby put his hands under one of Terrance's arms while O'Leery did the same thing on the other side.

Haltingly, Brown got to his feet. Bobby and Cheery loosened their holds. Brown took a few faltering steps, then walked forward with more confidence.

"We'd better give you a rest," Bobby said.

Terrance turned quickly toward Bobby, eyes fully alert. "I'm okay, coach."

"You sure?"

Brown nodded emphatically.

"Let's get 'em, then."

With misgivings, Bobby ran off the field while Brown formed the huddle for the next play.

Art Bennett approached Bobby with eyes of outrage. "That boy's in no shape to play."

Bobby shrugged. "He looks okay to me. We'll watch him."

For the first several plays, Brown called the snap unevenly, and stumbled as he executed the plays. He ran a halfback dive to the right, then to the left, and the team made a first down.

Mel Morris watched the field with concerned face. "He acts like he's dizzy."

Bobby nodded. "I'll pull him if it keeps up."

On first down, Terrance pulled back as if to pass, but Bobby knew he had laid the ball deftly in McAlpin's gut. Rutherford delayed until one defender rushed by him, then took off up the field. He bowled over one of the Buckaroo linebackers and broke into the secondary, threading through the minefield of defenders.

He brushed aside the last Buckaroo back at the fifty and turned on all his speed in a sprint downfield. He crossed the goal line amid a roar of approval from the Warrior stands. Alhamid connected on the extra point and the score was 20-14 with almost eight minutes still to play. Suddenly, the game seemed in reach again.

The Buckaroos returned Alhamid's kickoff to the thirty and began a methodical drive with the discipline of a team that played well when the chips were down. With runs and short passes, they

made one first down after another, eating up the precious minutes of
the clock, until, with first and ten on the twenty and the wind behind
them, they threatened to score once more with only two minutes left
in the game.

Abernathy dropped back to pass, set himself, and heaved the
ball into the end zone with a perfect lead for his intended receiver.
Bobby's heart sank as he saw the ball flying toward what seemed a
certain catch. Then, seemingly out of the very ground, Terrance
Brown rose up before the ball, raked it in at the one yard line, and
headed for the Buckaroo goal almost one hundred yards away.

Walker and Chambers cut down the two nearest defenders; then
Terrance was on his own. He took off on an angle away from the
defenders, and outdistanced all of them except Hunter Boyd, who
gained on him with an angle calculated to bring him down around
midfield.

Just as Boyd dived for his legs, Terrance put out one arm,
stiffarming Boyd into the ground. Terrance tucked the ball under his
arm, put his head down, and ran with longlegged strides toward the
Buckaroo goal, crossing it ten yards ahead of the nearest defender.

"20-20," Bobby shouted jubilantly. He held up his hands in a "T"
for a time out; Chambers repeated the sign, and an official called
time.

Bobby called Alhamid over to the sideline. "The game's riding on
your toe, Freddie."

Alhamid narrowed his dark eyes in concentration. "No sweat,
coach."

The snap from Chambers to Brown came back low and hard.
Brown caught the ball and held it upright. Alhamid took two choppy
steps and caught the ball squarely. It flew toward the goal post at a
good angle, but then a gust of wind caught it and blew it to the side.
For a long, agonizing second, Bobby thought the ball would go wide,
but it passed just inside the uprights to put the Warriors ahead for
the first time in the game with less than two minutes to go.

The Buckaroos took the Warrior kickoff with just time for one
series of downs. They ran one desperation pass after another, but the
buoyed-up Warriors defended fanatically. On third down, Abernathy
tried a long bomb downfield, but he underthrew the ball, and Joe
King got under it to make the interception. The Warriors ran the
clock out with safe plays and the game ended with the score 21-20.

The Warriors had won the district championship.

Bobby ran across the field to give his commiseration to Billy Wayne Fox, but the Buckaroo coach saw Bobby coming, turned contemptuously away, and trotted toward the Buckaroo dressing room. Ned Chambers and Bill Foster caught Bobby as he came back toward the Warrior side and rode him off the field on their shoulders through a triumphant sea of students.

Jubilant fans filled the steamy Warrior dressing room. The players joked and cut up as they took their showers and changed to their street clothes. Ray Stewart pushed his way through the crowd to where Bobby stood talking to a group of boosters.

"Congratulations, coach!" Stewart put out his bony hand.

Bobby shook Stewart's clammy paw. "Thanks Ray."

Across the room, Bobby saw Mike Proctor talking to Rutherford McAlpin and several players. Implacable anger clutched at Bobby's bowels. What right did this corrupt man have to be sharing in Bobby's victory? Bobby carefully avoided approaching Proctor. As the players finished dressing and the last of the congratulating fans cleared the room, Mel Morris walked up to Bobby.

"How about coming over to the house for a few beers?"

Sad regret gripped Bobby. Even in the triumph of the moment, he had nothing to celebrate. Paula, the centerpiece of his life, had left him, and the school board meeting Monday would probably end his career.

He shook his head. "Thanks, Mel, but I just don't feel like it."

"It'd do you good to let down for a while."

"The way I feel, two beers would do me in."

Morris nodded in understanding. "I'll see you Monday, then."

Bobby thought of Paula as he drove toward home, picturing her generous smile, her wave of strawberry-blonde hair, the high color in her cheeks when they made love. She had been both his lover and best friend. With her gone, there was no one to share his victory. The fickle fans counted for nothing. When they heard Proctor's false evidence, they would turn on Bobby and drive him out of their town.

Bill Mattingly's benevolent face came into Bobby's mind. His old coach seemed to be looking at him with an approving grin, as though Bobby had just made a good block or tackle.

Bobby spoke his thoughts aloud in the dark car. "Whatever else happens, coach, we won their damn championship for 'em!"

TWELVE

As Bobby lay in exhausted sleep in the early morning hours after the Breckenridge game, the telephone started ringing insistently. Groggily, he sat up in bed and turned on the bedside light. The alarm clock next to the light read 3:30 a.m. Who could be calling at this hour?

He stumbled into the living room and picked up the phone. "Hello?"

"Bobby, it's me," came his sister's tense voice.

A chill of apprehension gripped him. "What's up, Linda?"

"I just got a call from the nursing home. Mama's dead."

Bobby drew in his breath. "What happened?"

"It was another stroke. About an hour ago."

"I'll come right up."

"Wait until morning. You can get here by early afternoon. I'll go ahead and make the funeral arrangements."

"When are you thinking of having it?"

"Early Monday morning. There aren't many people to notify."

"I'll get started as soon as it's light."

"It's a blessing, Bobby. She wasn't doing any good."

"I know."

Bobby went back to bed, but couldn't go back to sleep. His mind boiled with recollections of the mother who had loved him as a baby, sung to him, read to him, taken him to the zoo and other places. He seethed with the bitter recollection of the betrayal he had felt when she had taken Linda and left home. Now she was gone for good, and Bobby would never speak to her the words of reconciliation he had wanted to say for so long. It didn't matter though. She had really died several years earlier when she lost her mind to her first stroke.

With the first soft grey light of morning, Bobby shaved, dressed and ate a bowl of cereal for breakfast. He packed the few things he would need for the weekend and took the suitcase to the car. Back in the house, he called Mel Morris on the phone.

"Sorry to bother you so early, Mel, but something's come up."

"Nothing can bother me, after that game yesterday. What's the problem?"

"My mama died. I've got to go to Amarillo to help with the funeral arrangements."

"I'm sorry, Bobby. Anything I can do?"

"There's nothing much to do, Mel. Just line up a substitute for my Monday classes."

"I'll be glad to do that. You want me to call Paula?"

Bobby wanted Paula to know. He needed her understanding. But bitter pride kept him from admitting his need. Paula was practically out of his life anyway.

"Don't call her, Mel. She might feel obligated to come to the funeral. I'd hate that."

"You're the boss. What about the school board meeting Monday?"

"The funeral's gonna be Monday morning. I can get back for the meeting."

"They'd have to reschedule it, if you asked them to."

"I want to get that meeting behind me. Let's leave it like it is."

"Call me if there's any problem."

"Thanks Mel."

◆

The small collection of mourners sang the last hymn of the funeral service and the preacher directed the people to come forward to view Loraine's body. Bobby helped his father to his feet and the two of them followed Linda and Ray, her car dealer husband, and their two boys down to the front of the church and past the open casket.

The undertaker had done a good job. Loraine looked younger than her fifty-five years. She had color in her cheeks and a peaceful expression on her face. All the angry confusion resulting from her first stroke had softened in the serenity of death.

So this is what it comes to, Bobby thought. This woman, his mother, old before her time, then crippled in mind and body, no longer had to contend with earthly worries. Her sins, such as they were, no longer had any importance. Bobby remembered how pretty

she had been at the age of thirty-nine, the summer she had left Bill
to marry Red Williams. Then, Loraine had lively brown eyes, smooth
creamy skin, and wavy auburn hair. Bobby adored her.

One summer night, during a week when Linda was away at girl
scout camp, Bobby and Bill went on a fishing trip to Lake Meredith,
west of Borger. They were supposed to stay for the whole weekend,
but bad weather moved in. At 1 a.m., rain started dripping on them
through a hole in the tent.

"To hell with this," Bill said.

They packed up and headed back for town. As they approached
their house, Bobby saw Williams's car in the drive.

"What the hell is Red's car doing in my drive?" Bill's voice shook
with anger.

He pulled into the drive next to the other car, jerked the car door
open, and ran to the house. Bobby followed slowly with dread in every
fiber of his body. When he came inside, he heard his father shouting
back in his parent's bedroom.

"Get out of my bed, you goddamn son of a bitch!"

"Don't blame me, Bill. If you can't satisfy her, someone's gonna
do it." Red mocked Bill even in his fear.

Bobby heard the sodden sound of blows. Loraine screamed.
Bobby ran back to the bedroom and through the open door. Inside,
Red lay stark naked on the floor with Bill astride him, pummeling his
face.

Loraine sat in the bed with a sheet pulled across her body. "Stop
him! Stop him!" she screamed.

Tears streaming down his face, Bobby took his father by the
shoulders and pulled him off of Red. A week later, after many bitter
arguments, Loraine moved out. Eventually, Bill divorced her and she
married Red. Bill and Loraine gave the kids their choice of who to live
with. Linda picked Loraine, and Bobby stayed with Bill.

As Bobby moved past his mother's body, he saw tears in his
father's eyes. Outside the church, Linda daubed at her eyes with a
handkerchief while her two little boys peeked shyly around her. Her
husband Ray, red-necked from selling used cars outdoors, stood
awkwardly off to the side.

Linda pushed back her wave of curly auburn hair, tipped with
grey in places even though she was only twenty-eight. She smiled
wanly at Bobby and her father.

"We've still got the graveside service to get through."

Bobby looked at his watch. "I'd better skip that part of it."

"What time's your meeting?"

"7:00."

"You'd better get going."

"Let me talk to dad a minute."

Bobby drew Bill to the side. Although in his early sixties, Bill looked seventy. He had thin arms, a sallow grey complexion, and a persistent cough. Crippled by arthritis from his years of oilfield work, he could hardly walk.

"I worry about you, daddy," Bobby said.

Bill shook his head impatiently. "Don't waste your time. One of these days, I'll be gone like your mother in there and we'll all be better off."

"Don't talk like that."

"Why not? It's a fact."

"I won't argue with you. Are you glad you came?"

Bill nodded. "It was good to see her one more time."

"She didn't treat you right."

Bill wiped more tears away with the back of his hand. "That doesn't make much difference now. I wish I'd patched things up with her. She didn't care nothin' about Red."

"It probably wouldn't have worked."

"Maybe not, but I wish I'd tried."

"We can't change what's past, daddy."

"I know that."

Bobby looked at the forlorn man beside him with understanding he had not had before. All these years, Bill had loved Loraine in spite of what had happened between them. The thought of these two people living apart in their lonely pride seemed too sad to bear.

""I gotta go daddy," Bobby said gently. "I'll get back up to see you in a month or so."

"Don't worry about me, son. I been taking care of myself for a long time."

◆

Dead tired after the funeral in the morning and the long drive back to Comanche Springs, Bobby sat at the side of the high school auditorium stage looking out over the crowd assembled for the school board meeting. Several folding tables had been placed in the center of the stage and covered with tablecloths. The school board members had taken their seats at chairs placed on the side of the tables away from the audience, so that they faced the people. Microphones on the tables assured everyone would be heard.

Mike Proctor sat facing the crowd, flanked by Willis Fullerton and Ned Zablonski. Fullerton looked toward Bobby with a benign nod. He wore the same plaid sports coat he had worn to all the booster club meetings. Bobby wondered if he ever had it cleaned. Zablonski stared morosely at the table in front of him, looking as if he carried the troubles of the world on his shoulders.

Gerald Stedman sat toward the end of one of the tables, as far away from Mike Proctor as he could get. At the far end of the other table sat the board's only woman member, Annabelle Grimes. Two years earlier, she had retired as principal of one of the elementary schools. Prissy Puryear had replaced her.

After retiring, Miss Grimes won a seat on the school board, running on a platform of academic excellence, discipline, and fiscal responsibility. She wore her graying hair in a tight, efficient little bun, and had little use for the frivolity of athletics.

Bobby scanned the auditorium, looking for Paula. He saw Mel and Wanda Morris seated in one of the front rows. Further back, a group of the football players sat together. Ned Chambers, Rusty Stedman, Bill Foster and little Rob Wilson sat on one row, with Juan Guerrero, Freddie Alhamid, Albert Walker and Rutherford McAlpin right behind them. A few rows back, Cheery O'Leery, Eddie Ritterman and Lee Shaughnessey had taken seats near one of the rear doors.

Bobby saw other team members scattered around the room. On the back row, Terrance Brown sat with his father and several other black men. The prim, prissy principal, Leon Purvis, occupied a prominent position on the front row. On the far side of the room, Bobby saw Lola Cochran waving at him. He raised his hand to acknowledge that he saw her so she would stop. Big-gutted Joe Timmons stood halfway up the left aisle talking with Ray Stewart and Art Bennett.

Fans and townspeople, among them the mothers and fathers of many students, continued to stream into the auditorium. Bobby looked at his watch. It was a quarter of an hour before the seven o'clock meeting time. At the rate the people were coming, the room would soon be packed.

Bobby concluded that Paula had not arrived. He wondered if she would come at all. He yearned to see her, but he did not want her to witness his degradation, which now seemed inevitable. No last-minute evidence had developed. No one would vouch for Bobby's testimony except Mel Morris, who had no personal knowledge of what Bobby had seen.

Bobby convinced himself he had almost no chance to prove his innocence to the school board. Most of the people in the room would laugh at his charge that Proctor had supplied steroids to the team. They would find an accusation that Proctor was having sex with Angie Zamora so incredible that Bobby had decided it would only damage him to bring it up. The great majority of the people would almost certainly believe whatever the smiling, popular, rich Mike Proctor wanted them to believe.

At 7:00, Proctor thumped the microphone, then leaned toward it, beaming a golden smile out over the audience.

"Let the meeting come to order."

The hum of conversation died as the people turned their heads to the front.

"Let's open with the Pledge of Allegiance."

Proctor stood up and turned around, facing the flag at the back of the stage with his hand over his heart. As Proctor led the people in the patriotic words of the Pledge, Bobby thought bitterly what blasphemy it was for Proctor to say those proud words while holding in his heart the lies he intended to speak.

When the Pledge was finished, Proctor turned back toward the people and motioned them to sit down. He cast his face in a sorrowful expression and began to address the audience.

"Friends, I have called this meeting with great regret to address a matter of great moral importance. It seems particularly sad that I must make my accusation against Coach Thompson just when he has led us to our first district championship in many years, but that can't be helped. The charges I must bring to you tonight are very serious, and must be addressed without further delay."

Willis Fullerton held up his hand and leaned toward the microphone in front of him. "Let me stop you there, Mike. I hate to raise this point, but I think I'd better. This meeting involves a personnel matter. Shouldn't we be taking it up in executive session?"

Proctor turned toward Fullerton, glaring displeasure. "I think the people of this town need to hear these charges."

"There'll be time enough for that, Mike, but don't you think at least initially, we oughta go into executive session?"

"You should have thought of that before we got all these people here in this open meeting."

"Shut up, Fullerton," came a voice from the audience.

"We want to know what's going on," someone else shouted.

Bobby got up from his chair at the side of the stage. "I don't have anything to hide. Keep the meeting open."

Fullerton leaned back in his chair with a look of resignation and Proctor continued.

"Several weeks ago, on Wednesday, the twenty-third of October, I received a call late in the evening from Buster Blodgett, who operates the Cactus Flower motel out on the Mesquite Flat Highway. He told me he had just rented one of his cabins to Coach Thompson, and that he was concerned about the situation because he had seen a young girl get out of the car and go in the room with coach.

"I got in my car and headed out to the place. When I got there, Buster and I went back to the room and Buster opened the door with his pass key. Just as we came into the room, Coach Thompson came toward us from the bed with nothing on but his underwear, while a partly clad girl ran out the back door of the unit."

The audience murmured indignantly.

"Who was it?" Ned Zablonski asked, angry-voiced.

Proctor shook his head. "All I saw was her back as she went out the door."

"What about Blodgett? Did he see her?"

"I'd better let him tell you what he saw."

Proctor waved his arm, and a shapeless, slovenly man with blue stubble on his cheeks rose from a seat near the front of the auditorium. Bobby recognized the man from the Cactus Flower. Blodgett went to the stairs at the side of the stage and walked up to the table where the school board members sat.

Proctor motioned for Blodgett to take the microphone. "Buster, I'd like you to tell the folks what prompted you to call me to come out to your motel that night."

Grinning familiarly, Blodgett took the microphone from Proctor and turned to face the audience.

"Like Mike said, I thought it was unusual for Coach Thompson to be renting a room out at the motel, since I knew he lived in town, but when I saw a young girl get out of the car and go in the room with him, I knew I had to do something about it, so I called Mike.

"While he was on the way out, I went out to the unit and looked thorough the window. The shade was pulled down, but by looking between the bottom of the shade and the window sill, I could see that Coach Thompson and the girl were lying nude together on the bed. When Mike got out to the motel, I let him in the room.

"The first key I tried didn't fit. I guess they got part of their clothes back on while I was finding the right key, because when we finally came into the room, the coach had his shorts back on and the girl was headed out the back door wearing her panties, with her other clothes under her arm."

Annabelle Grimes cocked her head back in a little bird-like motion. "Did you know the girl?"

Blodgett shook his head. "She was young, maybe sixteen or seventeen, and had black hair. That's all I can say."

Miss Grimes tightened her mouth grimly. "Did you look for her after she ran out the back door?"

"I looked all over the place for her, but never did see her again. She must have run off several blocks, put the rest of her clothes back on, and walked back into town."

"What did Coach Thompson have to say about all this?"

Blodgett turned to look accusingly at Bobby. "He didn't say much of anything. Cussed us both out for meddling in his affairs, got in his truck and drove off."

Bobby clenched his teeth to keep from venting his rage. What practice this man must have had to lie so convincingly!

"Thanks Buster." Proctor nodded to Blodgett and he left the stage and walked back to his seat.

Proctor faced the audience with the mike in his hand and a sincere face. "That's about it folks. I don't know who the girl was, so I can't bring criminal charges, but I did think I oughta ask Coach Thompson to discuss this matter with the school board."

Willis Fullerton leaned forward again. "I'd like to hear what Coach Thompson has to say about what happened."

Proctor nodded approvingly. "He has every right to speak his piece." Proctor turned toward Bobby. "You can tell your side of it now,

Bobby."

Bobby rose from his chair and walked slowly over to the micro-phone. He passed his eyes over the seated board members, then turned toward the audience. He clenched his hands into fists, feeling the cold sweat of his palms, then unclenched them. How could he convince the people that Proctor's carefully contrived story was a complete fiction?

"Folks," he began, "you don't know me as well as you know Mike Proctor, so I'm at a disadvantage, but you've gonna have to believe me anyway. I swear before God almighty that there is not one word of truth in what Mike Proctor and Mr. Blodgett have just told you. Everything they have said is a pack of lies."

A collective gasp came from the assemblage, followed by an excited murmuring. Zablonski pulled his mike toward him in a quick movement.

"Coach Thompson," he said, angry warning in his voice, "you won't help yourself by accusing Mike Proctor of lying. Why don't you stick to telling us what happened out there?"

Bobby turned toward Zablonski, looking directly into his eyes. "I can't sugarcoat this pill, Mr. Zablonski. I was never out at the Cactus Flower Motel with a girl, I did not rent a room from Buster Blodgett, and both Proctor and Blodgett have intentionally concocted up this story to try to discredit me."

"Why would they do that?"

Bobby hesitated. Should he tell what really happened at the motel? He decided against it. These people were not ready to believe that Mike Proctor was guilty of what he accused Bobby of.

"What's your answer, Coach Thompson?" Zablonski asked again.

Bobby turned to half face the people in the auditorium, keeping his eyes on Zablonksi.

"They made up the story because I told Mike Proctor I knew he had been supplying steroids to some of the players, and I was going to turn them all in to the Interscholastic League."

Guffaws of disbelief came from all over the auditorium, and for almost a minute, an angry, outraged drone filled the air. Proctor stepped up to the microphone again.

"Come to order, folks. Let's hear Coach Thompson out."

The drone subsided, and Zablonski leaned forward again.

"Where did you get an incredible idea like that?"

Bobby answered Zablonski's hostile stare with one of his own.

"To answer that question, I've got to go back about a month, to a Saturday when I was doing some work up at the athletic office. I heard two cars drive up in front and then I heard two people talking through an open window. When I looked out, I saw it was Mike Proctor and Rutherford McAlpin. I saw Proctor deliver a bag of steroids to McAlpin and heard Mike tell Rutherford to make sure they got to all the other players."

"That's a lie!" came a shout from the audience.

Bobby turned toward the sound and saw Rutherford McAlpin standing in the aisle, his conceited, handsome face twisted in anger.

"It's no lie, Rutherford," Bobby answered into the microphone. "I heard every word both of you said. I even heard Mike tell you to make sure I didn't find out what was going on."

"You heard wrong," McAlpin shouted. "I did get some steroids from Mr. Proctor, but they were for my father's cattle."

Gerald Stedman picked up the microphone at his end of the table. "Coach Thompson, you say Rutherford was supposed to deliver these steroids to other players. What other players were involved?"

Bobby shook his head. "I never did find out."

Stedman gave Bobby a steely-eyed look. "You mean to tell me you're bringing these accusations against your own team with no more evidence than a single chance conversation you overheard?"

Bobby met Stedman's gaze. "There is a little more to it than a single conversation. A few days before I saw Mike and Rutherford talking, I found a hypodermic syringe in the locker room that had fallen out of Rutherford's locker. I checked with Coach Morris, and he told me he had thought Rutherford might have been using steroids last year."

"For Christ's sake, the steroids were for our cattle," McAlpin shouted in an exasperated tone.

Willis Fullerton tipped the mike in front of him toward his face. "Is that all the evidence you have?" he asked gently.

Hot tears of frustration brimmed in Bobby's eyes. He had counted on the moderate Fullerton to believe him. If Fullerton wasn't convinced, no one would be.

Annabelle Grimes darted her head forward toward her microphone. "Coach Thompson, I'm trying to straighten all this out for myself. Are you saying that Mike Proctor and Mr. Blodget made up this story about you and the girl at the motel just because you told Mike you had seen him giving McAlpin some steroids?"

"That's exactly what happened."

"And they did this even though Rutherford had a perfectly logical explanation for the steroids--that they were for his father's cattle?"

"I know what I heard, Miss Grimes. The steroids were for the players, not the cattle."

Miss Grimes shook her head grimly. "Yet you can't name a single player who you claim was involved except for Rutherford himself?"

Out of the corner of his eye, Bobby saw one of the back doors of the auditorium open. Half turning his head, he saw Paula come in the door, followed by Angie Zamora. A sudden glad surge swept over Bobby. Paula had cared enough to come to the meeting. But what was she doing coming in with Angie Zamora?

The audience collectively followed Bobby's eyes to where the two women stood. Turning, they slipped along the back wall and sat in two seats on the very back row. Bobby looked toward Mike Proctor. The oilman's face was bland, smooth and relaxed. Did he know why Paula and Angie had come to the meeting together?

Bobby turned to face Annabelle Grimes again. "That's about the size of it, Miss Grimes. After I told Mike I was going to report the steroids to the Interscholastic League, he called this meeting and started spreading this story around that he's told you tonight."

Annabelle Grimes frowned decisively. "Sad to say, it seems to me a lot more likely that you're the one making up a story. After all, you have more reason to lie about it than Mike does."

An approving mutter spread around the auditorium. Miss Grimes had summed up the feeling of the people. Bobby felt his shoulders slump in defeat. The board would rule against him; he would have no choice but to tender his resignation.

"Just a minute!" Paula's voice reverberated through the auditorium.

All eyes in the room turned toward her. She stood at her seat along the back wall with her chin thrust forward. The high color of her cheeks matched her wave of light red hair.

"What is it, Mrs. Thompson?" Proctor asked with a condescending voice.

"Angie Zamora has something she wants to say." Paula put her hand on the girl's shoulder.

"I don't think we need to hear from her," Proctor said smoothly. "I think everyone knows how things stand."

"Wait a minute, Mike," Willis Fullerton said laconically. "We've heard from everyone else. We might as well hear from Angie, too."

Her face taut with fear, Angie got to her feet, pushed past the people sitting on her row to the aisle, and started walking toward the front of the room. Bobby knew from the anguish in Angie's face that Paula had persuaded her to tell the truth. Compassion for the girl tempered Bobby's renewed hope.

Proctor's face flashed alarm. As Angie mounted the stairs to the stage, Bobby saw Proctor catch Buster Blodgett's eye. Proctor gave a barely perceptible nod to Blodgett, whose face displayed sudden understanding. He jumped to his feet.

"That's her!" he shouted. "That's the girl at the motel with Coach Thompson!"

Angie stopped at the top of the stage and looked toward Blodgett in confusion.

"That's it, of course." Proctor said. "That's what you want to tell us, isn't it, Angie? That it was you at the motel with Coach Thompson the night Buster called me out there."

Angie turned to face Proctor, a dumbfounded look on her face. With trembling lips, she opened her mouth as if to speak. Instead, she suddenly buried her face in her hands and started sobbing uncontrollably. Proctor came around the table and put his arms around her shoulders.

"There, there," he said. "It's all right. We all understand how hard this is for you."

Angie's anguished sobbing seemed to confirm Proctor's version of her story. The audience started droning again, with new and more vicious anger. Comments started flying toward the stage.

"Cradle robber! Pervert! The bastard oughta be lynched!"

Suddenly, Angie's eyes rolled back in her head and she fainted, slipping from Proctor's arms and collapsing in a heap at the front of the stage. Mike Proctor looked out over the audience.

"Doctor Gehrhard, can you come up here?"

Doctor Edward Gehrhard, a silver-maned physician of some fifty-five years of age, got up from his seat in the third row and walked quickly up to the stage, where he bent over Angie's inert form. Bobby knew Gehrhard had been Proctor's personal doctor for many years. Angie shook her head and sat up. Dr. Gherhard put his arms under hers, helped her to stand, and led her to a chair at the back of the stage. Proctor picked a mike up off the table and spoke to the audience.

"It's too bad this had to happen, but at least we know the truth now." The audience answered with a hum of approval.

"Bullshit!"

Everyone turned to the back of the auditorium. Paula stood there with her hands on her hips, her green eyes blazing in fury.

She spoke again, loud enough for all to hear, her voice bristling with angry contempt.

"Mike Proctor, you know perfectly well Angie was not going to accuse Bobby of being with her at the motel."

Proctor gave Paula a sorrowful look. "I'm sure she'll speak for herself when she's able, Paula."

"Why can't we hear from her now?"

Doctor Gehrhard moved forward and took the mike. "Miss Zamora has hyperventilated and gone into shock. I'd advise against any further stress for her tonight. I'm going to take her to the clinic and give her a sedative."

He handed the microphone to Proctor and went back to Angie. Putting his arm under hers, he helped her get up and led her out one of the rear doors of the stage.

Proctor spoke again. "I think we'd better adjourn the meeting, at least for tonight. Contrary to what Mrs. Thompson says, I'm sure Angie will confirm that she was at the motel with Coach Thompson. I intend to refer the matter to the district attorney for prosecution."

Proctor turned to face Bobby. "In the meanwhile, Bobby, I think it only appropriate that you take a leave of absence until this question is resolved. I'm sure Coach Morris and Coach Bennett can get the team ready for the bi-district game."

Bobby set his jaw and took a step toward Proctor. "I'm standing on what I said before. This whole thing is a pack of lies. I'm not agreeing to anything. If you want me to step aside, you're gonna have to vote on it."

"Very well, Bobby," Proctor replied. "We'll vote on it. Do I hear a motion that Coach Thompson be placed on leave of absence?"

Ned Zablonski held up his hand. "So moved."

Annabelle Grimes nodded her head. "Second."

Bobby knew what the vote would be. No one on the board could vote with him and keep any credibility in the town. Grimly, he stood waiting for the inevitable. But before Proctor could call for the vote, one of the rear doors of the auditorium opened and a large middle-aged man with a close-cropped rim of hair around a balding crown marched into the room. All eyes turned toward him.

"Coach Winslow!" Mike Proctor sounded surprised. "What brings you here?"

The big man walked quickly toward the stage. "I need to talk to Coach Thompson," he said impatiently.

Proctor nodded toward Bobby. "This is Coach Thompson."

Winslow came up on the stage and walked to where Bobby stood. Winslow put out his hand, and Bobby shook it.

"Am I too late to testify?" Winslow asked.

"Pretty near," Bobby said. "They're fixin' to vote me out of a job."

Winslow turned toward Proctor. "I want to say something before you vote, Mike. Give me a few minutes with Coach Thompson first."

Proctor shook his head angrily. "This meeting's lasted long enough already."

Annabelle Grimes cocked her head toward Proctor. "It won't hurt to hear what he has to say, Mike."

Proctor looked at his watch, then shrugged his shoulders. "We'll break for a few minutes, then hear from Coach Winslow."

While the board members and the people in the audience got up from their seats and gaped and stretched, Winslow drew Bobby to the back of the stage.

"I would have been here earlier, but I had car trouble. Tell me what's been said so far."

Bobby summed up what had happened. When he had finished, Winslow looked at the ground, shaking his head, then looked up at Bobby with angry eyes.

"Proctor's an incredible lying bastard, and he winds these people around his finger like pieces of string. That's the way he did me, and that's the main reason I left. When you called, I didn't want to get involved. I had put this place behind me. But I read in the paper about the charges against you and my conscience started bothering me. I knew what you were up against, so I decided to come out and try to help you."

"Let's get this meeting over," Mike Proctor called. The school board and audience started taking their seats as Bobby and Coach Winslow walked back to the front of the stage.

"We'll hear what you have to say now, Coach Winslow," Proctor said.

Winslow stepped up to the microphone and looked out over the audience, then started speaking in a full, confident voice.

"Last week Coach Thompson called me on the telephone and asked me if I knew anything about steroid use among the players last year. I really didn't want to come back out here, so I didn't give him a straight answer. But when I read in the paper about the charges against him, I figured I'd better come out and tell what I know."

Willis Fullerton straightened in his chair. "You're not going to tell us there was steroid use on the team last year, are you Coach Winslow?"

Winslow nodded. "I can't prove it, but I think there was."

"What makes you think so?"

"On three separate occasions, I saw Mike Proctor giving sacks of something to Rutherford McAlpin after practice. The third time, I walked up to them and asked what was going on. Proctor winked at me and told me he was giving Rutherford some steroids for his father's cattle."

Fullerton put his elbows on the table in front of him, cupping his chin in his hands and frowning thoughtfully. "Did you ever check to see if that was true?"

Winslow shook his head. "I should have done something about it, but I didn't. I didn't want to rock the boat. But I was so sure the steroids were for Rutherford and other team members that I quit rather than go through another season of worrying about what was going on."

Proctor triumphantly grabbed a microphone and confronted Winslow with a contemptuous smile.

"You haven't added a thing to what we already knew, Coach Winslow. Rutherford's already told the people what the steroids were for. I can't see what on earth you made the trip out here for, except to engage in a personal vendetta against me."

Winslow's face blazed. "You're not entirely wrong in that thought, Mike. I did come back out to expose you. But I wouldn't call it a vendetta. I'd just call it telling the truth for a change."

Ned Zablonski spoke, he face darkened with anger. "I'm surprised at you, Coach Winslow. When you quit, you said you were leaving to take advantage of a business opportunity in Dallas. You never said anything about Mike doing anything wrong. Now you come back out here to tell us you think he was supplying drugs to the team, but you don't have an ounce of proof."

Winslow gave Zablonski a scathing look. "Anyone that wasn't a complete fool would be able to put what I've said with what Coach Thompson has told you and know the truth, but I guess that's expecting too much."

"You always did have a smart mouth."

"The problem is, I didn't use it enough. I saw other things going on I didn't like, and kept quiet about them, too."

"Like what, for instance?"

"Like grade fixing, for example. At the start of the season last year, Guerrero and Shaughnessey were ineligible because they'd flunked several courses in the spring. Miraculously, just before the season started, their transcripts suddenly changed to show they'd passed everything."

On the front row, Leon Purvis popped up like a jack-in-the-box. "What are you implying?" His high-pitched voice shook with outrage.

Winslow turned toward Purvis with an amused look. "I don't wonder to see you jumping up so fast, Leon. Those grades couldn't have been changed without your knowing about it."

"You'd better watch yourself. You'll hear from my lawyer."

"I'm sure I will." Winslow turned back to face Zablonski again. "I don't have any hard proof of any of this. But I can tell you one thing: the Comanche Springs athletic program is so fishy you can smell it all the way back to Dallas. You people oughta wake up to what's going on around you."

Zablonski leaned forward, narrowing his eyes meanly. "Did Coach Thompson tell you about the charge he was in a motel with a teenaged girl?"

"No, he didn't."

Proctor nodded his head contemptuously. "It doesn't really look like Coach Winslow knows much about anything. Let's get on with the business before us. I'm sure the school board will want to check out the charges Coach Winslow has made, but in the meanwhile, we have a motion on the floor we need to consider. Is there further discussion?"

Winslow walked to the side of the stage, where he stood next to Bobby. Proctor looked inquiringly from one board member to another.

"Hearing no discussion, I'll call the question. The motion is to suspend Coach Thompson pending further investigation. All in favor say aye."

"Wait," came a voice from toward the back of the auditorium.

All the people looked to see who had spoken. Ned Chambers stood at his seat, looking toward the school board, his heavy face deeply troubled. Proctor stiffened in anger.

"Sit down, Ned," he commanded.

Chambers shook his head. "I can't let you do this, Mr. Proctor."

Rutherford McAlpin leaned forward, half-rising out of his seat and grabbing Chambers by the arm. "Sit down, you fool!"

Chambers angrily shook loose, moved along the row of seats and out into the aisle, where he started walking toward the stage.

"It would be best if you didn't speak, Ned." Proctor spoke with a threatening undertone.

"Why do you say that, Mike?" Willis Fullerton asked.

"There's been enough discussion. It's time to vote."

"I think we'd better hear what Ned has to say."

Proctor looked around the table. Annabelle Grimes and Gerald Stedman were nodding in agreement with Fullerton.

"Okay, but it's a waste of time."

Ned Chambers came up the stairs of the stage to the table where the board sat. He took the microphone from Proctor and turned to face the audience.

"This is really hard," he said, his face contorted as he struggled for composure, "but I just couldn't let it go any further. Coach Thompson is telling the truth about the steroids. I know because I'm one of the ones who has been using them."

A shocked silence fell across the room. For ten or fifteen seconds, no one said anything. Then Willis Fullerton spoke in a gentle voice.

"How did this happen, Ned?"

Chambers turned to face Fullerton. Tears streamed down his cheeks.

"At the first of the season, I was in pitiful shape. I'd gained a lot of weight, and I couldn't even run windsprints. On the first day of practice, I fainted and had to be helped off the ground. Afterward, Rutherford told me he could get me some steroids to help me get in shape. I knew he'd been getting them from Mr. Proctor. I didn't think it would hurt anything."

Mike Proctor looked grimly down at the ground, not meeting the sudden collective stare of the audience. Gerald Stedman drew himself up self-righteously, looking angrily at Chambers.

"I'm not surprised to hear about Mike Proctor's role in this, and I can even understand how Rutherford McAlpin or someone like Terrance Brown could be involved, but how could a natural leader like you be involved in something so despicable?"

"Terrance Brown wasn't involved, Mr. Stedman, but there were others besides me and Rutherford."

"Who else, then?"

Chambers looked down at his shoes, then answered hesitantly. "Juan Guerrero, Albert Walker, Joe King---and Rusty."

Stedman's head jerked back as though he had been shot. He looked inquiringly toward where Rusty sat in the audience.

"Is this true, Rusty?"

Rusty's voice broke as he answered. "Yes, it's true."

Stedman turned away from his son with a stricken look. Slowly, he swung his head toward Mike Proctor.

"God damn you to hell, Proctor!"

Proctor returned a quick smirk. "That's mighty strong language for a holy Joe like you, Stedman"

Stedman's face flushed angrily. His chair turned over with a clatter as he leaped up and started for Proctor. Willis Fullerton pushed his own chair away from the table and stood between Stedman and Proctor.

"Not now, Gerald!"

Stedman stopped and stood looking at the ground, clenching and unclenching his fists. He turned, picked his chair up from the ground, and again took a seat at the table. Shock had drained the blood from his face.

"There's one more thing I need to tell you." Chambers spoke in a barely audible voice.

"What's that, son?" Fullerton asked. He had assumed control of the meeting.

Chambers looked toward Bobby. "I know Coach Thompson is

right about not being at the motel with Angie that night."

"How do you know that?"

"Because I saw Angie getting into Mr. Proctor's pickup on the back parking lot of the bowling alley that night."

The audience gasped as Fullerton turned toward Proctor with an accusing stare. "How about it Mike? Was it you at the Cactus Flower with Angie instead of Coach Thompson?"

Proctor looked at Fullerton with a contemptuous, twisted smile. "I don't know why you're paying any attention to this drivel, but I'm through with this charade." He got up and started walking toward the stairs at the front of the stage. He turned his head over his shoulder toward Fullerton. "You pissants better not mess with me. I'll sue your asses."

The audience let forth a derisive rumble. As Proctor passed by where Bobby stood, he could not resist a gibe.

"I hope your hired liar does better than you did."

Proctor's face tensed in rage. "Asshole!" He gritted the word out through clenched teeth.

He turned and sprang at Bobby, knocking him down. As Bobby lay on the floor of the stage, Proctor stood over him kicking him in the side. Coach Winslow grabbed Proctor in a bear hug, pinning his arms. Bobby got up and faced Proctor, crouching.

"Let him go!"

With a look of primeval understanding, Winslow dropped his arms. Proctor sprang forward again. Bobby staggered him with a hard right to the jaw. Proctor stumbled across the stage, crashing into the table where the school board members sat. The table fell over, throwing Fullerton, Zablonski, Stedman, and Annabelle Grimes, with her prim little bun of grey hair, to the floor. They all scrambled away from the fallen table as Proctor pushed himself up and turned to face Bobby.

Proctor charged again, his rage venting in an inhuman screech. Bobby aimed another right, but his fist glanced off Proctor's cheek, and Proctor connected with a blow to Bobby's nose that sent the hot blood flying. Bobby shook his head as Proctor backed away in a crouch. The audience roared with blood lust.

The two men circled each other, each looking for an opening. Proctor closed, grabbing Bobby around the middle and trying to lift him off the ground. Bobby twisted free and swung his elbow forward into a crunching collision with Proctor's jaw. Proctor's eyes clouded and lost their focus. Slowly, his knees buckled and he sank to the floor, where he lay on his back with confused eyes looking at the ceiling.

Bobby stood over Proctor, looking grimly down at his fallen enemy. "You oughta lay off the lamb at the country club and spend a little time trotting around your ranch to keep in shape. Or maybe you could use a few steroids."

Proctor lay on the floor gasping for breath. Coach Winslow handed Bobby a handerkerchief, and Bobby started cleaning the blood from his face. Willis Fullerton picked up one of the fallen microphones and faced the audience.

"Mr. Blodgett, could you come up here and help Mr. Proctor get home?"

Buster Blodgett slunk out of his seat and up onto the stage where he lifted Proctor to his feet. He supported Proctor on one side as the two of them walked toward the steps leading down from the stage.

Fullerton spoke again. "Mr. Blodgett, after you've helped Mr. Proctor, you might want to go home and give some serious consideration to picking another town to live in."

Blodgett acknowledged the advice with a snarl over his shoulder. He continued to support Proctor as the two of them walked along the side aisle of the auditorium, past the contemptuous faces of the townspeople, and out the back door.

Fullerton addressed the audience again. "There was a motion on the floor," he said sardonically, "but in light of what's happened, I don't think we need to vote on it. This board has a lot of thinking to do, and a lot of adjustments to make, but now isn't the time for them. This meeting is adjourned!"

THIRTEEN

When the rear door of the auditorium had closed on the departing Mike Proctor and Buster Blodgett, Coach Winslow turned to Bobby and put out his hand.

"Congratulations, coach. I'd say you've been fully exonerated."

Bobby looked at Winslow dubiously. "I can't take any satisfaction in it."

Winslow twisted one corner of his mouth. "Yeah, I know what you mean. You've lived with this team all season, and now it's shot to hell. But don't worry about it. That's not your fault."

Bobby held up the blood-stained handerchief Winslow had given him.

Winslow laughed. "Keep it. You may need it again."

Bobby stuffed the handerchief in his jacket pocket. "Can I buy you a cup of coffee?"

Winslow looked at his watch and shook his head. "No thanks. If I get on the road now, I can get back to Dallas sometime before the sun comes up."

"Thanks for coming out."

"I'm glad I did. I didn't do you much good, but it was worth the trip to see the look on Proctor's face when Chambers blew the whistle on him."

"I'm going to report what you said about the grades last year to the Interscholastic League."

Winslow nodded. "Do that. I'll be glad to talk to them. I should have reported it myself."

"Thanks again."

Winslow turned and walked away, leaving the auditorium through the rear door of the stage. Several feet away, Willis Fullerton stood waiting expectantly. He walked up to Bobby with a look of wry sympathy.

"I'm sorry we gave you such a rough time, coach." He put out his hand.

Bobby shook Fullerton's hand. "I knew I didn't have enough evidence to convince the board."

"We were too quick to believe Proctor. What will happen to the team?"

"I'll have to report everything to the Interscholastic League. We'll forfeit the district championship."

Fullerton nodded. "The town will take it hard, but it can't be helped."

"I appreciate the way you tried to be fair all through the meeting."

"The charges against you had a bad smell to them from the first, but I couldn't see the truth until Chambers spoke up."

"Proctor and Stedman would've gotten into it if you hadn't stopped them."

"They used to be friends."

"Why do they hate each other so much?"

"Because of a bad business deal. When the oil bubble burst, Stedman's bank held a loan on one of Proctor's ranches. Proctor couldn't pay, so Stedman foreclosed. Turned out Proctor had disposed of most of the collateral. Stedman tried to get him prosecuted, but the DA worked out a deal where Proctor could make payments on the judgment."

"Proctor told me the oil bust didn't hurt him."

"He lies a lot."

"So I've found out."

Fullerton looked up at the clock on the wall. "It's almost eleven. I'm gonna go home and think things over. This has been one hell of a night."

He walked down the stairs and mingled with the buzzing, milling people crowding toward the exits. Toward the rear of the auditorium, Gerald Stedman and Rusty faced each other in anguished confrontation. In one of the aisles, Rutherford McAlpin and Ned Chambers stood arguing among a group of players. Chambers had his mouth set in a bitter line as McAlpin harangued him with a face of haughty contempt.

Bobby thought he should thank Chambers for speaking out. He walked down the stairs from the stage and stood behind the crowd waiting to leave the auditorium. He could not get through the crowd to Chambers. As he stood waiting for the people to thin out, several of the townspeople standing near him glanced at him, then looked quickly away, confusion on their faces.

No one come up to congratulate him or even to acknowledge his presence. The crowd kept easing toward the rear. Chambers and McAlpin passed through the rear door, still gesturing angrily toward each other. Just before Bobby got to the exit, Mel and Wanda Morris worked their way to him along a row of vacated seats.

Mel Morris took Bobby by the arm. "You showed the cocksuckers!"

Bobby smiled thinly. "Doesn't seem to have done me much good with this crew." He gestured with his hands, indicating the people waiting to get out of the auditorium.

Morris showed his teeth in a wolfish smile. "What do you expect? You upset their applecart and destroyed one of their idols. But that's tough shit. They'll get over it."

"I wonder."

As the three of them passed through the exit door into the open air, Bobby saw Paula standing under a light standard looking toward him. Her red-blonde hair had a day-glow sheen from the light of the overhead vapor lamp. She wore the same fuzzy red sweater she had worn at the Morrises.

"I see someone I need to talk to."

Morris followed Bobby's look. "Why don't we all go somewhere and have a couple of beers?" he asked.

Wanda took her husband by the arm, pulling him away from Bobby. "Don't be silly, Mel. That's the last thing they need."

"Thanks, Wanda," Bobby said. "I'll talk to you tomorrow, Mel."

Mel nodded and allowed himself to be led away. Bobby walked to where Paula stood waiting under the lamp. She had a solemn look on her face, but the ends of her mouth curved in subtle amusement.

"Hello, stanger," she said.

"Are you going my way?"

"Can I trust a man with a smashed nose?"

Bobby put his hand to his nose, then quickly took it away. "It's starting to hurt."

Paula moved closer, concern in her eyes as she surveyed Bobby's damaged face. "Shouldn't you go to the doctor?"

He shook his head. "It'll be okay."

"Can we talk somewhere?"

"Let's get a cup of coffee out on the highway."

Together they drove in Bobby's pickup through the darkened streets of the town. Bobby stopped for a red light and looked toward Paula. She sat looking pensively ahead. He wanted to hold her reassuring warmth close against himself. Would she resent his arm around her shoulder? Best to wait, he decided.

"My mama died Friday night," he said.

She turned her head toward him. Hurt shone in her eyes. "Why didn't you let me know?"

"Wasn't sure you'd care."

She shook her head in exasperation. "Of course I care. What was it, another stroke?"

He nodded.

"When's the funeral?"

"It was this morning, in Amarillo."

"You went to Loraine's funeral this morning, then drove back here for that awful meeting?"

"I wanted to get it over with."

Tears brimmed in Paula's eyes. "I'd have gone with you."

"I'm sorry I didn't get word to you."

At the truck stop, they sat in a booth surrounded by other booths filled with rough-and-ready truckers, and ordered pie and coffee.

"Why are you such an insecure bastard?" Paula asked.

Bobby shook his head. "I don't know. I guess I'm too afraid of losing you."

She smiled ruefully. "Last week at the Morrises, when I asked if you had been with a woman at the motel, I didn't mean to be taken seriously. You stormed out before I could let you know I believed you."

"Why didn't you call me later?"

"Because you pissed me off. I decided to let you stew in your own juice for a while. In the meanwhile, I called Angie on the phone. We met together, and I convinced her to tell the truth."

"Do you think she would have tonight?"

Paula looked down at her pie. "She would have if she hadn't broken down. I don't know what would have happened if Proctor had had a chance to work on her. She was scared to death of what her father would do. She kept telling me she'd have to leave home."

"It's too bad she got involved with Proctor."

"He promised her everything and made her feel like a grown-up woman."

"Filthy bastard."

"How could you think I'd go to a motel with that man?"

Bobby fixed Paula's green eyes with his. "One day, about a month ago, I had to go home at lunch to get my playbook. On the way back to school, I decided to grab a sandwich at the McKeever Cafe instead of going through the line at the school cafeteria. When I walked in the door, I saw you and Proctor having lunch together."

"I told you I had lunch with him. Why didn't you just come over to the table?"

"When I spotted the two of you, Proctor was leaning across the table toward you, and you were looking at him like he was your lover."

Paula leaned toward Bobby, her eyes glistening. "Why didn't you tell me you saw that?"

"I didn't want to sound paranoid."

"So you've been stewing over that all these weeks?"

He nodded, taking another drink from his cooling coffee. She sat looking at him with a strange little smile and an almost unnatural brightness in her eyes.

"I guess your thinking I was having an affair with Proctor was partly my fault."

"What do you mean?"

"I never made love with Proctor, but it wasn't because he didn't ask."

Quick anger coursed over Bobby. "I thought so. When was it?"

"The first time was when I had lunch with him that time. He gave me a real line of bullshit. Seems his wife is cold and doesn't understand his needs. He said he wanted to be my lover. I told him I was flattered, but that I loved you too much to cheat on you."

"You sure looked like you were thinking of cheating when I saw the two of you talking in the cafe."

She shook her head angrily. "Nothing happened. Not then or any other time."

"Not even back in Lamesa?"

She looked at him incredulously. "You thought I was screwing around with someone in Lamesa?"

"I suspected it."

"You really are insecure."

"I can't help it."

Paula threw her head back with a sardonic smile.

"Look, honey, I've never cheated on you. I've thought about it at times. I'm only human. Don't you ever think about it?"

Lola Cochran flashed through Bobby's mind, followed by the lithe form of Angie Zamora in her cheerleader's outfit, and the alluring face of a cocktail waitress he had met at a bar one time when he had been in Austin for a coaches' meeting.

"I think about it," he admitted.

"So do I, and neither one of us can do anything about that. But whatever I may think, nothing like that's ever happened."

She's telling me the truth, Bobby thought. If she was lying, I'd know it. Why didn't I ever talk to her like this before?

He took a sip from his coffee. "What other time did Proctor ask you?"

"The night of the Decatur game. He called up about eight o'clock and asked if he could meet me somewhere. I told him no. He called again around 9:30 and said he was coming over. Even though I didn't feel good, I got in the car and drove around town for a couple of hours to avoid him. Then I went to the school and waited with the kids for the team to come in, but I went on home before you got there because I was getting dizzy."

"That son of a bitch!"

"He paid dearly tonight for being such a bastard."

Paula gazed pensively down at the table top. Under the red sweater, her full breasts thrust forward provocatively. Strands of her strawberry hair lay across her forehead. Love and passion swelled inside Bobby. How could he have considered having sex with the slatternly Lola Cochran? Paula's presence across the table from him made manifest her superiority to any other woman Bobby had ever wanted.

He believed implicitly that she had been attracted to Mike Proctor, yet had rejected him. Damn, Bobby thought, I read the signs all wrong. I thought she was being evasive to hide her guilt. All she was doing was trying to keep me from finding out Proctor was bothering her. Bobby shuddered slightly, thinking of the gross mistake his own insecurity had led him to.

"Where are you staying?" he asked gently.

She raised her eyes to his, returning a look of tolerant amusement.

"Why should I tell you that? You might come around and disturb my new single lifestyle."

"Isn't it about time you moved home?"

She cocked her head humorously, throwing the wayward strands of hair back over her shoulder.

"I don't know about that. I've come to value my independence."

"Paula!" he pleaded.

She chuckled wickedly. "I've already made plans to go to law school next semester."

Tears welled in Bobby's eyes. Was Paula joking or serious? "Don't torture me any more."

She leaned forward, touching his forearm gently with her fingers. "I'm sorry. I just couldn't resist that."

"Will you come home?"

She nodded. "Let's go get my things."

Together, they drove to the motel on the Abilene highway where Paula had been staying, and checked her out. Back in town, they drove to the high school parking lot, where Paula got in her car and followed Bobby home. Bobby thrilled with elation as Paula pulled into the drive beside him. They got out of the cars and walked toward the door.

"Seems like I oughta carry you into the house," Bobby said.

"Cut the melodrama." She went ahead of him to open the door.

Inside, Bobby deposited Paula's suitcase in the bedroom. The house seemed full and happy again. Paula came into the bedroom and stood facing him, a little half-smile on her face. Her eyes glistened in the light from the bedside lamp.

She brushed her hair back from her forehead. The movement of her arm stretched the fabric of her sweater over her breasts. Bobby pulled her to him and gave her a long kiss. He pressed himself into her groin, kneading her buttocks with his hands.

"Aren't you tired?" she asked.

He shook his head emphatically. "Are you?"

"Hell no," she whispered.

He sat on the bed and pulled her onto his lap. Soon, her fuzzy red sweater, along with her white blouse and skirt and all of Bobby's clothes, lay in a pile on the floor. Lying naked on top of the covers, they pressed their bodies together with a yearning intensity born of the bitterness of their separation.

More and more quickly, they thrust themselves together, until the sweet, reassuring ecstasy of release completed their reunion. Spent, they lay in each other's arms.

Bobby ran his fingers through her hair. "It was hell here without you."

"How do you think I felt, out in that little dinky motel room by myself?"

"I'm glad you're back."

"So am I."

"Let's stick together from now on."

"Just don't be such an insecure bastard."

"Sometimes I can't help it."

Bobby lay awake almost an hour after Paula fell asleep. He kept switching on the bedside table, so he could see the calm repose on her sleeping face. Finally, he turned out the light for the last time, curled his body around her reassuring warmth, and fell asleep.

◆

The next morning, Bobby handled his classes as if nothing had happened the night before. He called the roll, put problems on the board, and asked questions as though there had been no meeting. The students stared in fascination at the discolored bruises on his face. All the faces in his classes looked pensive. No one cut up, or joked. Bobby knew they wanted him to talk about the team, but he avoided the subject.

He saw that Ned Chambers stared sullenly at the floor, his face turned away from the other football players. Angie Zamora was absent. Bobby pitied her for the grilling she must have taken from her parents. After class, Bobby pulled Chambers aside.

Bobby looked directly at the boy until he met Bobby's look. "I wanted to tell you I appreciated your honesty," Bobby said.

"You're about the only one who does." Chambers spoke bitterly.

"What did the others think--that everything could be kept quiet?"

Chambers nodded. "McAlpin says we should have stuck together."

"And let me get fired and maybe prosecuted over a pack of lies?"

"McAlpin says you should have kept your mouth shut, too."

"Fuck McAlpin." Bobby knew his words would not meet with school board approval.

Chambers smiled slightly. "That's how I feel about it."

"You did the right thing. Don't let anybody tell you different."

"Thanks, coach." Chambers turned and left the room, his mouth still transfixed in a harsh line of worry.

On his off-period, Bobby walked over to the athletic office, where he locked himself in the office and dialed the number of the Interscholastic League in Austin. He told the secretary who answered he wanted to talk to Bert Mullins, the President of the League. Bobby held for a few minutes, then Mullins came on the line.

"Hello, Bobby, how've you been?" Mullins's voice carried a bluff affability.

"Pretty good."

"I was just fixin' to call you about that Stephenville charge on your black quarterback. What's his name?"

"Terrance Brown."

"Oh, yeah. I've got good news for you. We've fully investigated Coach Tolbert's charge that you illegally recruited Terrance, and we didn't find any evidence in support of it."

"I didn't think you would."

"Well, we didn't. Reverend Brown got a perfectly legitimate job offer and took it. That's all there is to it. Tolbert just got upset because you beat him so bad. And it didn't help for Terrance to be so cocky during the game."

"Tolbert wouldn't have made a fuss about it if Terrance had been white."

"That's probably true. Anyway, you're all clear."

"I'm afraid we're not."

"What do you mean?"

Bobby told Mullins what had happened at the meeting the night before. When Bobby had finished, he heard Mullins suck in his breath.

"Jesus Christ, Bobby, what a mess! There's no doubt about the steroid use?"

"No."

"Then you'll have to forfeit the district championship.

Breckenridge will get to go on to bi-district."

Bobby thought with loathing of the insufferable Breckenridge coach, Billy Wayne Fox, with his sneering, conceited face.

"That'll make Coach Fox real happy."

"It can't be helped."

"I know. What about Coach Winslow's information about grade fixing last year?"

"We'll make a full investigation. I'm afraid if that information is true, when taken with the steroid use, it'll mean a lengthy suspension for Comanche Springs."

"I'll cooperate fully in the investigation. I'll tell the team the bad news later today."

"I don't envy you that job."

◆

That afternoon, Bobby assembled the team in the fieldhouse. The players looked toward him with anguished faces. They already had a good idea of what was coming. Bobby had told them not to put their uniforms on; that there would be no practice. Coach Morris and Coach Bennett stood to the side with regretful, unhappy looks.

The freckle-faced reporter, Ray Stewart, stood at the back of the room. Looking around the room, Bobby saw that McAlpin and Stedman had not come to the meeting. Chambers sat by himself on a bench, elbows on his knees, staring morosely at the ground.

As Bobby started to speak, the butterflies jumped in his stomach more than they had for any of the games.

"I greatly regret what I have to tell you men today. I'm sure you've all heard about the meeting last night and what came out of it. You know there is irrefutable evidence of use of steroids by team members. I don't have to mention the names that are involved; I'm sure you know them already.

"Several hours ago, I reported what has happened to the Inter-scholastic League in Austin. The League has advised me that we have to forfeit our district championship, and that we will probably be suspended from eligibility for district awards for several years."

The players shuffled their feet, and several of them cursed. "Shit!" "Damn!" "What a bunch of crap!" "Chambers, you're an asshole!"

Bobby held up his hands and the noise subsided. "There's no

point blaming what happened on Chambers. Those of you who were at the meeting know I brought the matter up myself. All Chambers did was tell the truth about it. Some of you may think it's unfair for us to forfeit the championship; that we've worked hard and deserve to keep it.

"We have worked hard, but we have no right to hold onto what we won by cheating, and use of steroids is a form of cheating. There are two reasons why steroids are against the rules. First, they can damage your bodily organs and shorten your life. Second, using them gives you an artificial advantage over the guys who aren't using them.

"All season long, I've talked about that burning desire, and how important it is to have it. I've said that if you reach down inside yourself for that desire and find it, you can move mountains. But there's no lasting satisfaction in any victory that comes from cheating. If you win by using steroids, the inner knowledge that you cheated takes all the value out of the victory.

"Men, I believe in high school athletics. I believe high school football builds character in those who play it, and gives the players good values that will last their whole lives. But if you cheat to win, you lose all that. Through cheating, you come to believe that all that counts is winning, no matter how.

"The League decision that we have to forfeit the championship is the only one that could be made under the circumstances. It is a just decision. I know this seems like the end of the world to you, but it isn't. You can grow through this experience. There will be a football team here next year. We may not be eligible to win district, but we will be playing football.

"I invite all of you to put this experience behind you without bitterness. Come out for the team during spring training, and let's start rebuilding, this time in the right way. That's all I have to say. The season is over. Go home, and make the best of things."

◆

That night, at 7:30, the telephone rang. Bobby got up from where he sat on the sofa next to Paula watching television and answered it.

"Am I speaking with Coach Bobby Thompson?" The man on the

other end of the line spoke with a suave, urbane voice; a soft voice with the hardness of nails just under the surface..

"I'm Bobby Thompson."

"Coach Thompson, my name is Patterson Powell. I'm an attorney from Dallas and I represent Mike Proctor. I'd like to drop by and talk to you for a few minutes."

Bobby hesitated. What trick of Proctor's was this? Shouldn't Bobby have his own lawyer before talking to anyone representing Proctor? "What's there to talk about?"

"Mike has fully informed me of what happened at the meeting last night, and the events leading up to it. I want to see if we can arrive at some understanding that will be satisfactory for all involved."

"Is Mike with you?"

"I told Mike it would be best if I talked to you alone."

"I guess it won't hurt to talk."

Paula looked at Bobby quizzically as he gave the attorney directions to get to the house.

"Who the hell was that?" she asked when he had hung up.

"Proctor's attorney from Dallas. He wants to come over and talk."

"Look out, honey!"

While Paula continued to watch the news, Bobby stood at the front window watching the street, still unsure he should have agreed to the meeting. In fifteen minutes, a grey Cadillac turned the corner and slowly approached the house. It turned into Bobby's driveway where the light from the porch lamp illuminated it.

The car shone with polish. It appeared absolutely clean, from the impeccable curve of its roof down to the scoured white sidewalls of the tires. The driver's side door opened, and a man of medium height got out and advanced toward the door of the house. The doorbell rang and Bobby opened the door.

"I'm Patterson Powell," the man said, in the same suave, confident voice he had used on the telephone.

He had iron-grey hair styled close to his scalp and a healthy, tanned complexion that probably came of hours on the golf course. He wore a navy-blue pinstriped suit, starched white shirt with button-down collar, paisley tie, and black shoes that just broke the crease of his trouser legs. His right hand wrapped around the handle of a richly appointed leather briefcase with the initials "P. P." stamped in gold on the side. He smiled warmly at Bobby.

"Come in, Mr. Powell." The lawyer's immaculate appearance made Bobby very conscious of his own faded jeans and the shabbiness of his little rented house.

Bobby held the screen while Powell came inside. He handed Bobby a card. It said he was an attorney with the Dallas law firm of Princely, Powell and Peckwood. Paula had gotten up as Powell entered the room.

"This is my wife, Paula, Mr. Powell," Bobby said. "Do you mind if she sits in on our talk?"

"Not at all, not at all." Powell shook Paula's hand, acknowledging her presence with a gracious, appreciative look.

Bobby turned the television down and led the way into the kitchen, where the three of them sat around the formica-topped table.

Powell cleared his throat. "I've been representing Mike Proctor for a number of years, just as I represented his father before him. I believe I can say without being disloyal to my client that he has acted most unwisely in this matter in several regards. He understands that his actions have been inappropriate, and he wants to set everything straight as soon as possible."

The lawyer's way of putting things made it sound as though Proctor had only been guilty of some minor indiscretion. Bobby leaned forward, resting his elbows on the table.

"What does Mike have in mind?"

Powell smiled politely. "I like a man who comes right to the point. I have advised Mike I really can't see that you have a case against him that would stand up in court, but that, to save trouble, he should offer you a settlement. Just to put this matter behind him, Mike is willing to pay you twenty-five thousand dollars in exchange for a full release of all claims, your agreement not to discuss the matter further with anyone, and your further agreement not to testify regarding your knowledge of the matter concerning Ms. Zamora."

Bobby leaned back in his chair and put his hands behind his head. He shot a chilly smile at Powell.

"That's mighty generous of Mike." Bobby turned toward Paula. "What do you think about it?"

Paula frowned. The high color of her cheeks was a barometer of her anger.

"Pretty damn cheap, if you ask me."

Powell smiled tolerantly. "I told Mike he should be prepared to come up. What figure would you consider adequate?"

"That's not what I mean. I mean it's cheap of Mike to try to buy himself out of this mess."

Powell's eyes narrowed and he spoke with a bite to his voice. "I see your point, Mrs. Thompson, but there must be some reasonable amount that would assuage your sensibilities."

Paula's face darkened. "Don't patronize me, Mr. Powell."

Powell's face turned grim. "Don't be foolish, Mrs. Thompson. Mike is prepared to be generous, within reason."

"He can cram the money up his ass, as far as I'm concerned."

Bobby leaned toward Powell, speaking deliberately. "We don't want Mike's money, Mr. Powell, but there are some things I think he oughta do."

"What are those?"

"First, he should resign from the school board, and agree to stay away from the players. Then, he needs to print an apology in the newspaper for his lies about me. Finally, he needs to agree to stay away from Angie Zamora and to provide for her future. That's the only place his money comes in."

The lawyer frowned, drumming his fingers on the table top. "What you are asking is very unfair. I don't see how I can advise Mike to admit publicly that he lied."

"The point is that he did lie, Mr. Powell, and there are lots of people in this town who believe what he said in spite of everything."

Powell sat stony-faced for several seconds, his face tense with concentration. He looked toward Bobby. "Reluctantly, I am going to recommend to Mike that he meet your demands, if in return you will agree not to disclose what you saw at the motel."

"It came out at the meeting she was with him that night."

"The people don't know for sure there was a sexual relationship."

Bobby nodded. "It wouldn't be good for Angie for that to come out. If Proctor does right by her, and does the other things I've mentioned, I'll agree not to go to the authorities."

Powell put out his hand. "I believe we have a deal, Coach Thompson. I'll discuss it with Mike and call you tomorrow."

Bobby shook the lawyer's warm, confident hand. "The deal for Angie needs to include a trust fund for her college."

"I'm sure that can be arranged."

Powell rose from the table and Bobby ushered him back to the front door. Together, Bobby and Paula watched the rich man's lackey drive away in his correct grey Cadillac.

Bobby turned toward Paula. "Have you ever heard of that law firm?"

"Sure. It's one of those downtown Dallas firms with several floors of marble and fancy woodwork forty stories in the sky."

"Is that the kind of lawyer you want to be?"

She laughed. "I don't want to be like that condescending asshole."

◆

Attorney Powell called Bobby the next evening to confirm that Mike Proctor had agreed to Bobby's terms. Proctor's apology would appear in the Saturday morning edition of the Comanche Springs Courier. Powell said he would mail Bobby a copy of Angie Zamora's trust agreement.

The trust agreement arrived in the Friday mail. It provided ample funds for Angie to live apart from her parents and go to college. On Saturday, Bobby avidly searched through the paper for the apology.

On the front page, the paper had a news story announcing that Mike Proctor had resigned as president of the school board to devote more time to his business interests. The story discreetly did not speculate on any link between Proctor's resignation and the revelations at the school board meeting.

In the sports section of the paper, Ray Stewart had writen an opinion piece questioning whether the Interscholastic League was justified in stripping the Warriors of their title just bcause a few players had experimented with steroids. Stewart editorialized that Bobby had overreacted in reporting these minor violations to the League.

Bobby had nearly concluded that Proctor had welshed on his apology when he noticed a small classified ad near the back of the paper. It said that Mike Proctor apologized for any inconvenience caused to Bobby Thompson by certain charges Proctor had made before he was in full possession of all the facts. Bobby showed the ad to Paula.

"Would you say that was an apology?"

She twisted her lips cynically. "It says it is."

"But it doesn't tell the truth."

"I guess Mike wasn't up to that."

Later in the day, Bobby went to get a haircut. As he approached the barber shop, he saw through the window that Joe Timmons and several other boosters were engaged in a lively discussion with barber Ed Vitek. As Bobby pulled the door open and walked into the room all the group fell silent. A copy of the Courier, open at Ray Stewart's article, lay across the sofa.

Bobby smiled at Timmons. "Afternoon, Joe."

Timmons nodded curtly. "Afternoon." He looked at his watch. "I gotta be going."

Without another word, he walked out, followed by all of the others, leaving Bobby alone with the barber, who cut Bobby's hair in silence, without the usual loquacious chatter.

On his way home from the barber shop, Bobby dropped by Sterling's Hardware, to pick up some parts to fix his lawnmower. Several Warrior fans were browsing through the store. When they saw Bobby, they took their items immediately to the checkout stand and left. Bobby found his parts and took them to the register, where the clerk coldly rang up the sale without his usual greeting.

At home, Bobby complained to Paula. "I feel like a leper. I half expected someone to spit on me."

She snorted scornfully. "What do you expect? These people take their football seriously. It's all they've got without their oil money. You've made them lose something they wanted very badly."

"I did the right thing."

"Not the way they see it."

FOURTEEN

Bobby and Paula stood at the overlook in the roadside park on the road into town from the west, looking down on the town. During the night, a January storm had blown in from the north, dusting West Texas with snow. The movers had left an hour earlier, hauling their household things to Lubbock.

"Do you think the van will have any trouble getting through?" Paula asked.

Bobby shook his head. "I don't think so. The roads are in pretty good shape."

They stood together looking over the snowscape. The black limbs of the trees, stripped of their summer foliage, rose gauntly around the distant buildings. The courthouse clocktower pointed proudly to a leaden sky. The white spire of the First Methodist Church almost blended with the snow-covered roofs around it. In the distance, the yellow-brick pile of the high school dominated the whitened fields beyond the town.

Paula broke the silence. "Looks almost like a New England scene."

"Not enough trees."

"Kinda pretty, though."

"Are you sorry to leave?"

Her eyes flashed fire. "After the bastards fired you?"

"There's some good people down there."

"Yes, there are. I'll miss Wanda and Mel."

"Fullerton wanted me to stay."

"The others overruled him."

"I feel like a sacrificial offering to the town's ego."

"That's a good description."

"They couldn't forgive me for costing them their championship."

"Fuck the assholes."

"My sentiments exactly."

He put his arm around her and pulled her to him. He could feel her warmth through the down-filled jacket she wore. "At least you can go to law school now."

Paula looked at him solicitously. "Do you think you'll like your new job?"

Burly Phillips, Bobby's old boss at Lamesa, had made some phone calls and gotten Bobby on as an assistant backfield coach at Texas Tech.

He grinned at her. "Damn right I'm gonna like it. But I want to go back to high school coaching in a few years."

"By that time, the baby'll be old enough to leave with a sitter while I start my law practice."

"Do you really think it's gonna be a girl?"

"That's what the doctor says."

Bobby looked down at Paula's face. Her green eyes smiled satirically at him. An immense sense of well-being came over him. "If it is a girl, I hope she looks just like you."

"After all the trouble I've been?"

He covered her mouth with a long kiss, and they walked side by side back to the car for the drive to Lubbock.

END

ABOUT THE AUTHOR

Laurance L. Priddy was born in Sweetwater, Texas, in 1941. He grew up in Gainesville, Texas, and Fort Worth, Texas. He graduated from Arlington State College in Arlington, Texas, in 1963, and from the University of Texas School of Law in 1966. After two years in the army, he went into the practice of law in Fort Worth in 1967, where he has practiced ever since. He is presently a shareholder in a small law firm. He lives west of Fort Worth, near Aledo, Texas.

◆